I frown, confused and concerned

about how my actions might have affected him. What the hell does he want me naked for? "But—"

"Do as you're goddamn told!" he hisses, grabbing me roughly by the shoulder. "You've done enough damage for one night; Torenze had better be able to see you behave properly when you're beaten, at least!"

The words hit hard, and I'm suddenly afraid for myself as well as my lover's reputation. "Cash, please—"

He grabs me by the jaw, cutting off further protests. "Not another fucking word from you. You will *only* answer direct questions, and you will *only* do so respectfully, is that clear?"

"Y-yes, master," I mumble.

I hear someone enter the room as Cashiel—as my *master*—lets go of my face.

"Start stripping," my master repeats, and I remove my shirt with shaking hands. I toss it aside, because there's nowhere else to put it. Torenze has joined us, and he's smirking at me, standing proud and pleased at my misery.

"Give me your belt," my master orders, just as I'm undoing it. His voice is quieter now.

I don't want to. I don't want to give him my own belt so he can beat me with it.

Also recommended...

You may also enjoy these other ForbiddenFiction works:

The Charming by J.A. Jaken
The shadow of a past love had blinded Clayton MacAllister until his life was slipping through his fingers. Just as Clay was ready to give up on the idea that he might ever be happy, a charming stranger stepped into his life. Mal was rich, handsome and persuasive; everything Clay thought he couldn't have and didn't deserve. Mal's sadistic desires made Clay uncomfortable, but it seemed like a price he could pay—until he learned the price might be his very soul in chains. (M/M)
http://forbiddenfiction.com/story/jaj-1.000046/

Song of the Lonesome Cowboy by Lynn Kelling
Tucker Reynolds is a rising star in country music. The people from his record label tell him he's destined to be one of the greats—but only if he fits the "good ol' boy" image country fans expect from him. The trouble is, that's not the kind of man's man Tucker really wants to be. Forced into an unsavory relationship with a record executive and frustrated by his regrettably platonic relationship with his best friend and guitarist, Tucker turns to kinky sex with male prostitutes for release. Things hit Tucker's limit when one of Tucker's bandmates, Jess Grayville, begins to suspect what's going on, and puts himself in danger to protect Tucker. Desperate for a way out of his troubles, Tucker realizes only honesty, love, and a true song can save himself and the man who stands by him. (M/M)
http://forbiddenfiction.com/story/LK1-1.000185

Sedition

Demoted
Book Two

Alicia Cameron

ForbiddenFiction
www.forbiddenfiction.com

an imprint of

Fantastic Fiction Publishing
www.fantasticfictionpublishing.com

SEDITION
A Forbidden Fiction book

Fantastic Fiction Publishing
Hayward, California

© Alicia Cameron, 2015

CREDITS
Editor: James L. Wolf and Kel Draves
Cover Design: D.M. Atkins
Cover Art: Natalya Nesterova
Production Editor: Erika L Firanc
Proofreading: JhP323

SKU: AC2-000220-02 FFP
ISBN: 978-1-62234-243-3

Published in the United States of America

DISCLAIMER

This book is a work of fiction which contains explicit erotic content; it is intended for mature readers. Do not read this if it's not legal for you.

All the characters, locations and events herein are fictional. While elements of existing locations or historical characters or events may be used fictitiously, any resemblance to actual people, places or events is coincidental.

This story depicts fictional BDSM; it is not intended to be used as an instruction manual. It contains descriptions of erotic acts that may be immoral, illegal, or unsafe. The characters are not models for the Safe, Sane and Consensual forms embraced by most current practitioners of BDSM. The author takes license with the use of BDSM for dramatic effect. Do not take the events in this story as proof of the plausibility or safety of any particular practice.

This book is written in fond memory of the Sexy Trailer in the Woods and upstate New York in general—without that year, I would never have been miserable enough to torture the boys so much!

Contents

Chapter 1

Companionate

When I bought Sascha, I never expected that I would come to like him. Hell, when I first saw him at the brothel, dirty and beaten nearly beyond repair, my first desire was to get as far away from him as I could so he wouldn't dirty my shoes. He was a burden, a reminder of my failed debut into the world of re-education centers and Demoted slaves, an annoying little thorn in my side who did nothing but challenge me.

Somewhere along the way, I thought the best way to respond to his challenges would be to scare him. At my worst, I tried to threaten him sexually, to make him shy away from me like he had shied away from everyone else who tried to touch him. Except he wasn't scared of that.

I continue to be surprised by how much he responds to me, how perfectly we fit together.

Since I first made a move on him, he's grown increasingly bold. He's hesitant while we work during the day, but at night when we're alone, the barriers drop and his eyes flash up at me. I think of him as a companion of sorts. What sorts, I don't always know, but I enjoy his company and his touch as much as he does mine.

"Cashiel," he whispers in my ear, waking me up. I trust that he's ensured that whatever he's planning for us will have plenty of time to be completed before I head into work for a dull day of financial planning with Dean & Chanu Associates.

"Good morning," I reply, my hands coming up to stroke along the sides of his lithe body. I've got a decade of age on him, but even when I was his age, I was thicker, sturdier. Sascha looks like a strong wind

1

will blow him away, but the years of starvation before I bought him probably contributed to that as much as genetics. He's healthy now, and he's beautiful.

"I thought we could play a little bit before you go to work," he suggests, draping his body over mine and sliding up and down seductively. His hair flops over his eyes, messy from sleep, and he looks more turned on than scared, for once.

"I'd like that," I agree. I can't resist reaching out and running my fingers through his hair gently for a few seconds, watching him arch into my touch. Just when he's relaxed enough that his eyes are starting to close, I grab a fistful and yank him toward me, hard, hearing him whimper a little.

He doesn't fight me as I pull him in for a kiss, and I can feel his cock growing hard against my stomach. He likes to be hurt, just a little, and I enjoy doing it.

I keep him down, holding his head exactly where I want it. It doesn't stop him from taking action in other ways. He squirms and wiggles until he has his ass perfectly positioned above my cock, rubbing against it carefully, getting me hard as well. He enjoys being fucked as much as I enjoy fucking him, and that fact never ceases to amaze me. The research I did years ago, the research that destroyed my life, made it so clear to me that few slaves actually enjoyed being used in that way. It shouldn't have been a surprising result; the Demoted are just like anyone else, just not as successful at passing the test that separates them from free people. They are used as slave labor in almost every industry, but for most of them, life is filled with unwanted sex.

"Cash," Sascha moans, right next to my ear. "Fuck me? I want to be able to feel you all day."

It's all I can do to keep myself from throwing him on my cock right now.

Instead, I reach over and grab a bottle of lube, handing it to him and looking at him expectantly.

He blushes, the coloring spreading quickly over his pale skin, highlighting the scars that were left by his previous abusers. He can beg me to fuck him, but he still gets bashful when I make him do this.

"Go slow," I order. "I want to watch."

The coloring on his face deepens and he nods, quickly reaching behind himself with the lube. I hear the slight intake of breath as he touches himself and he turns away, looking back as if he can see behind himself.

I reach up, gently taking his face in my hand. "Look at me," I command, and his eyes lock onto mine.

He trembles, just slightly, but it makes me want to be more active in this process. I keep one hand on his face, reminding him to whom he belongs. I bring my other up to caress his cock, lazy and careless, like we have all the time in the world. I smile at him, encouraging him as he starts to rock back and forth in my hand. Occasionally, his fingers slip forward, brushing against mine, and I doubt it's accidental.

He waits for me to make the next move, and once I think he's adequately prepared, I speed up the friction on his cock.

"Would you like something bigger than your fingers?" I ask, smiling as the suggestion makes him breathe faster. I like to check, even after all this time, to make sure he still enjoys it.

"Yes, master," he breathes.

I frown. I hate it when he calls me that in bed.

Sascha ducks down, hiding his face against my neck as he giggles. "Sorry, Cash," he mumbles, his tone playful. "I just got so caught up; you felt so good. I didn't think about it."

I smile, my mood quite improved by this confession, not to mention the feeling of his body rubbing against me. Clearly, he's still interested.

"Maybe a little lesson's in order," I suggest, tugging lightly at his hair until he looks at me. "Maybe I should make you scream my name while I fuck you, so you remember."

"Okay," Sascha agrees, eagerly pressing against my cock. He smiles when we fuck, far more than he does any other time.

I shift a little, sliding into him easily. He clutches at my shoulders as I do. He's tight and slick around me, and when I pull out and drive in deeper, he makes a desperate little whining noise.

"Cashiel," he whispers, rocking his hips to take me in deeper. The sound of my name coming off of his lips turns me on more, and I speed up my thrusts.

"You feel so good," Sascha says, pressing back hard as I fill him.

I smile, shaking my head. "I don't want to hear you saying anything but my name," I warn him. "Over and over again, until you remember."

There's a slight look of fear in his eyes, an old habit as he appraises the situation, but it quickly disappears. He says my name again, slower this time, and I reach up and stroke his cock as he rides mine.

We start slow, but quickly build to a fever pitch. He squeezes his legs around my hips, like he's trying to hold on. I meet him thrust for thrust, pleased as he bounces off my cock. He goes quiet, except for the little moans and gasps every time I thrust deeply.

"Keep saying it," I order, grabbing his cock. "Every time I thrust, I want you to say it."

He moans at the order, or at my hand working its way up and down his cock, and he obeys. He repeats my name over and over, at first a quiet mumble, and then louder, building as our excitement builds, and I keep stroking his cock. He starts screaming it, matching my thrusts and strokes with the name, and when he comes close, I start to rake my nails over the sensitive skin on the insides of his thighs. His screams are almost incoherent, but it doesn't matter. He comes just moments later.

I feel his muscles tightening around my cock, the warm stream gracing my stomach. I join him, wrapping my legs around his body and pinning him to me as I come inside of him, thrusting until it hurts to do so anymore. He collapses on top of me and slithers off of my cock. We are both breathing heavily.

For a few moments, we rest together in companionate silence. Eventually, the mess becomes uncomfortable and I remember I still have work to do, whether in the office, or at home, on the reboot of my research project that will hopefully destroy my mother's evil empire. Sascha knows that I'm researching, but he doesn't know about my mother, or her involvement in the matter, or the legal mess that she caused before. I'm comfortable sharing my bed with Sascha, but not the most intimate of secrets. I place a light hand on his side and move him off of me, stroking down his arm one last time before getting out of bed.

During the day, we're master and slave, maybe coworkers when

I allow it. I own him, and my position requires that I maintain the image of a strict slave-owner. Even at home, when we're alone, I worry about maintaining this image, about maintaining a firm hand with my slave. But at night, I do my best to be gentle and caring with him. I always make sure that Sascha wants to do whatever we're doing, and I tell him again and again that he can stop it whenever he wants to. Fortunately, he never wants to. I learn his body inside and out. He's grown to be an expert at giving me head, and I know exactly where to touch and lick and suck and bite to make him lose control. But there's still a barrier, a fine line keeping things almost platonic for the majority of the day. I've always been taught that it's the proper way to handle slaves, and the proper way for slave owners to handle themselves.

My family controls the biggest re-education center system in the world, the two-year training program for newly Demoted slaves. Sascha is a product of the Miller System, the patented program of abuse and degradation that my mother, Kristine Miller, perfected years before I was ever born. In a way, I am too, although there is no training program for slave owners, just years of indoctrination. It's easy to forget with Sascha.

As I get to know him better, I realize he is far too smart to ever have been Demoted, much less treated as less than human. I doubt he failed his Assessment. The test that separates the bright from the Demoted would have been a breeze for him, but there are other ways to be Demoted. Kids with juvenile crimes, those who violate norms or refuse to comply, they can be Demoted too. Sascha is challenging enough and cocky enough that I could see this being the case. I couldn't see him as a true delinquent, but I don't see him as an activist or protester, either. Whatever his reasons, I'm certain it had more to do with his attitude than his intellectual capabilities.

I've lightened up with the cold and calculating orders I gave him when I first bought him, occasionally even deigning to use words like "please" and "thank you." It's strange to address a slave as such, but Sascha feels like more than a slave to me. He responds better to full sentences than grunts and demands. I love having sex with him, and he has a beautiful body, but I don't want to take advantage. He catches me looking at his ass now and again, even when we're working, but

I do little else. I never imagined it, but I have actually grown to enjoy working with him.

There are moments when he seems to forget that he's a slave; when he brings up bright ideas or suggestions. Sometimes he even dares to challenge me. He had been so severely abused before I bought him, and I've added my own share of harshness to the mix. I've beaten him just twice, and both times, it was the disappointment and failure that seemed to crush him more than the pain. I've neglected him, unable to decide how to handle him. Once he started helping me with work, things got better and more interesting. In some ways, I feel like a seductive boss who is having an after-hours affair with his secretary, although I'm not sure who either of us would be cheating on.

The decision to have him call me by my name was spontaneous. I couldn't reconcile the terrified slave I had brought home with the eager young man who I had started fucking, and hearing the word "master" on his lips dampened my excitement. The look on his face when he says my name is enough to bring me off, anyway. Even outside of bed, he seems to appreciate being able to call me by my name. The first time he ever called me "Cash" outside of bed shocked me, and the old habits and decorum made me consider smacking him for his insolence. But a bigger part of me liked it, and every time he says my name, even outside of bed, I can't help but smile and laugh with him. He's smart enough not to utter it in public, and it makes things seem more equitable, no matter how much they are not.

We don't ever talk about him, or me, and that's acceptable. I'd rather not have to make hard decisions about what to tell him. I can't talk about my family without revealing my secrets, nor can I discuss certain parts of my research. My mother tried to destroy my life last time I attempted it; the fewer people who know about that, the safer it is. I can't disclose my full history to a slave, even if he knows I'm conducting research on the re-education centers. I'm working from home more and more, and I find myself having to dismiss Sascha from my office regularly to keep my secrets. It's safer, I tell myself, for him, and for me. I try to make up for it when I com the office, letting Sascha stick around, often muting my side of the com device so I can ask him something or give him an order.

But sometimes I receive a com message and I have to all but throw him out. I snap at him when he doesn't listen or when he interrupts me, but he knows better than to ask. He lets me guard my secret, and I let him guard his, about how he got Demoted, about what happened with the Assessment, about his brother. Sascha is a mystery, but, I suppose, so am I.

Chapter 2
Auction

"I have a work function to attend tonight. You will attend with me."

"Sure," I reply, looking at Cash over his desk. I had just come in to bring him some materials, but I'm eager to see what else he has for me. I try hard to please him during the day, completing his projects to perfection. At night, he pleases me in return. I wake up every day with a sense of dedication, something to do, a reason to live for once. I'd do almost anything for him.

"It's at a slave auction, a very high-class one."

One of the worst things about being Demoted is the uncertainty. I should know better, but the words strike fear into my heart. I swallow, my throat suddenly too dry to speak.

"I'm not selling you," my master informs me. He manages to look both apologetic and annoyed at once. "I need you to attend with me, and I need you to play the part of the perfect slave. That means no backtalk, no doing things without permission, no snide comments or dirty looks. Think you can manage that?"

"Yes, master," I reply instantly. I've come to trust my master quite a lot, but I've had too many bad experiences in the past to not respond to threats.

"I'll be networking with some people in the slave industry. It would seem out of place to not have a slave of my own in attendance," he explains. "This auction is key. You are to stay by my side at all times and speak seriously to no one. You can flirt, answer questions about drinks or food, things like that, but nothing about me, or yourself, or where we live, or anything like that. Play dumb if you have to, but do it tactfully, or get my attention. Can I count on you for that?"

"Of course," I answer instantly. "Is there something I should know about why—"

"That is none of your business." His words are cold and dismissive again.

I hesitate for a moment. "Is it about your research?" I ask carefully.

He considers it for a moment before answering. "I'm officially there for work. For Dean & Chanu. But I am investigating some other interests as well. All you need to do is follow what I've told you. I'd appreciate it if you didn't ask questions.

"Yes, master," I reply. He's not being cruel, but the dismissal hurts.

"Go make yourself look presentable and wear something modest."

I nod, taking my leave and dressing quickly. I help him with his project, risk myself for him, but he still keeps me in the dark. It hurts to be reminded that I'm just a slave who can so easily be cut out of discussions.

As we drive to the auction, I catch my master looking over at me like he's about to say something, but he doesn't. I can't get his odd mood shifts out of my mind, and I can't explain the sudden increase in his usual secrecy.

When we arrive, I dare to look around to see exactly what kind of event this might be. The posh atmosphere and showy lights reek of money. I follow a few steps behind my master, demonstrating the standardized training the formal protocol demands.

"Don't fall behind!" my master hisses, actually pausing and waiting for me to catch up before grabbing me roughly by the back of the neck.

I don't say anything. I'm a slave. If he wants to do something other than act proper, then it's his own goddamned choice.

Cash keeps me close, literally at his side, and while he lets up with the painful pressure at the back of my neck, he keeps his arm around my shoulders. We mingle for a while, my master making appropriate small talk and business conversation with a variety of people, most of whom I have not seen before. I'm surprised by the how many unfamiliar faces I see. I've met so many coworkers at the Peace Day Celebration and the work-related party that my master threw; I didn't realize he was this well-connected. Perhaps my master's business is expanding? He's speaking in vague terms about "acquisitions" and "project" and "discreet," and I give up trying to figure it out because it doesn't seem to concern me. It sounds more like it's a part of his secret research project, but we're supposed to be working together on that. I don't see why he would lie to me about it.

The auction itself is more of an exhibition than a sale, although there are certainly business transactions taking place. There are old-fashioned auctions, silent auctions, and what appear to be private arrangements as well. I'm amazed by the whole process. I've never seen a proper slave auction before, and certainly not one of this caliber.

The slaves are younger than me, and they are clearly of higher quality. Perfectly poised, they smile demurely and hold positions and tolerate inspections as if they love having strange hands all over them. At the request of various members of the crowd, and probably an exorbitant sum of money, two are brought out together and ordered to fuck, which both parties perform with grace and smiles and appropriate levels of moaning and happiness.

I wonder if someone has slipped them some sort of drug.

It's hard to tear my eyes away from the perfectly formed and perfectly behaved bodies in front of me, but I do, if only because I have rarely seen Cash this uncomfortable. Unlike his usual detached coldness, he seems restless, shifting from one side to the other, occasionally even bumping me with his arm or leg as I rest on my knees next to him. He usually avoids fidgeting. He glances at his watch repeatedly, and around at the crowd.

He doesn't bid, which isn't out of place. Plenty of people are watching and enjoying, if one could enjoy this sort of thing. From the looks of it, many of the patrons do, their voyeurism displayed proudly. My master clearly doesn't. The auction finishes, and I think we'll leave, but there's more mingling to be done. My master's face is bitter as he mumbles something of the sort at me.

A slapping sound makes me jump, and a voice booms out too close to my head for comfort.

"Cashiel, my boy! I didn't think I'd see you here!"

The man is older, probably in his fifties or sixties, and the fact that his suit manages to make him look good says a lot about its quality. He claps my master on the back again, not as hard this time, and smiles at him in an overly friendly manner.

"Oliver," Cash replies, placing me behind him. So that's where he wants me now.

"Don't tell me you've actually decided to, how was it that you put it? 'Lower' yourself? Was that it? Or was it degrade?" The older man asks with a twinkle in his eye.

"If I recall correctly, the word I used at the time was 'debase,' but I may have been a bit misguided." My master doesn't blush or fidget, but I can see he's humiliated. It's a fascinating expression on him, reminding me of when his mother visited.

"Youthful ideals?" the other man prompts.

My master nods. "I was younger then, and I had a different view of business. Times change."

"Yes, and that little spat at New Year's didn't have anything to do with it I'm sure!" Oliver laughs as he says it, but it's clear that whichever "spat" he is referring to definitely has *everything* to do with whatever the hell they're talking about. The laugh isn't friendly, either.

"Oliver, you're the only one other than family who was privy to the details of that exchange," my master says quietly, almost pleading. "My family and I have come to an agreement about what I revealed that night. The arrangements we made… we have all moved on. I have a new life, and I prefer to keep it separate from old mistakes."

"I know how to keep skeletons locked up, my boy," Oliver says, a conspiratorial smile on his face. "After all, family can be chosen, and who can help you better than family? Perhaps you can be of help to me. I hear you're looking to expand your company's partnerships."

Hatred. I see it for one second, maybe two, and then it's gone.

Cash clears his face and forces a smile. "I am, actually. Companies like yours are our top recruitment goal. Trying to partner the best with the best. Would you like me to have my team get in touch with one of your representatives?"

"Cash, I'd rather deal with you!" the man says, still smiling. It doesn't reach his eyes anymore. "After all, it's been so long since I've seen you—I was starting to wonder if you were actively trying to avoid seeing me."

"I'd be happy to be your contact point." Cash is the perfect picture of composure. "I'll set up a meeting."

"It's amazing how such a trivial little thing can cause such a change," Oliver muses.

I have no idea what he's talking about, but he's staring at me, so I wonder if I have something to do with it.

"You should bring the boy with you when you visit," Oliver decides. "It's always nice to have one around, even if it's a challenge to find one that you like. But of course, you always did like challenging things."

"I'll check my schedule," my master says. "So nice seeing you again."

I used to use that exact tone when I told my brothel customers that I loved them. They exchange information and a few more pleasantries before we exit. As much as I'm glad to be going home, I have a thousand questions that I can't ask, and I try not to drive myself crazy thinking about too many of them.

The drive home is quiet, and my master is clearly fuming about something. He storms into the house quickly, leaving me trailing behind.

"Make me a drink!" he snaps, before I'm even through the door.

I don't argue. I go to the kitchen as he goes to his office, and I debate for a moment about what to bring him.

"Put alcohol in it!" the order carries loudly through the house. I know better than to question it.

I mix him his drink and carry it into his office where he sits, looking pensive and a little angry. I should go. I should leave and go to bed and avoid any more awkward contact with him.

"Who was that man?" I ask, standing just far enough away that he'll have to move to hit me. Old habits have served me well as a slave.

"Someone you should stay away from," Cash replies, giving me a dark look.

"He seemed to know you pretty well," I hint, wishing he would just tell me.

Instead, he goes silent for a moment before beckoning me over with his finger. Distance was safety, but I can't just disobey an order. He surprises me by pulling out his tablet and handing it to me.

"This is Oliver Torenze's business profile," he says, pointing to the numbers I'm familiar with. "You can see for yourself just how much he's worth, and how much his business is worth. He's the only person who could really destroy me, professionally, and I knew that I had to risk seeing him today. Just like I knew that I had to risk making a deal with him, if I wanted things to look normal. I couldn't let him go without a fight, even if it meant embarrassing myself and revealing all sorts of details I'd rather have forgotten by everyone involved. Someone in my position wouldn't let someone like him get away. He knows that; that's why he pushed it. I need him on my side. For a lot of things."

"That's a lot," I say quietly, looking it over. I'm familiar enough with the finances of my master's business to know that Torenze would be one of the top ten investors, if not one of the top five. I wonder what else my master needs him for.

"If you knew what it cost, you'd still say I was selling out."

"Then tell me!" I blurt out without thinking.

"I'd tell you if you needed to know."

I want to fight him, but he's not angry with me. If anything, he looks sad, maybe even a little scared. I nod my acceptance, and he gives me a grateful look.

I've kept enough of my own secrets to know that sometimes, it's safer to keep them than to let someone in.

I took my brother's place as a Demoted slave when we were younger, and I never let him have any suspicion that I was going to do it.

I first started thinking about my plan during our final year in high school, at the Dine 'n' Shine Café, inconveniently located in the red district an e-rail ride away from school. I had ditched Civic Compliance again, half on principle. I had made it my mission to show only minimal "compliance" to the bullshit propaganda they told us about how the Demoted system works, how it's vital for national safety and public health. The pictures of the fourth world war were supposed to make us buy into it, but they just made me nauseous. I knew they wouldn't fail me for skipping class; kids like me didn't get failed.

My twin brother Abriel, on the other hand, wasn't so fortunate. Our parents had noticed the differences between us early on in life, the way I learned faster, understood better, and was more curious. They had us both tested, and while my results were outstanding, my brother was "below average." Unfortunately, "average" would be the cutoff for the Assessment that is taken at the end of high school, and the cutoff went higher and higher every year, the problem intensified by the desperate effort of parents. Nobody wanted to see their kid get Demoted.

The Dine 'n' Shine wasn't exactly known for its cleanliness or properly functioning robo-clerks, but it was my favorite place to go to escape the watchful eyes of parents and teachers. I was certain that nobody would catch me, and even more certain that they would never have mentioned it if they did. I people watched, grinning at the line of skeevy men who frequented the place and making lewd gestures at them because I knew I could get away with it. I enjoyed the challenge and the taboo, sneaking there least once a week. Most of the patrons came for the "shine," street slang for "getting your dick sucked." I never visited the back part of the café, because underage kids were forbidden, and such a violation could get you taken away, maybe even Demoted.

The only humans who worked at the Dine 'n' Shine were in the back room, on their knees, for hours a day. Demoted humans. The fate that I was trying so hard to keep my brother from suffering.

My pleasant, polite little brother would likely have been Demoted just because he wouldn't do well on the Assessment. And I shouldn't have been Demoted, even though I told my teachers off and skipped class and hung out in a combination fast food joint and whorehouse. I couldn't let it happen, and I couldn't involve him in my plans. Unlike everything else that we shared, this project was just mine. I had to keep him in the dark to keep him safe.

Despite my higher intellect, my hacking skills, and my refusal to do anything but research the Assessment for the last two months of school, I never came up with anything to get him out of it. Abriel told me it was okay if he was Demoted, but it wasn't okay, I couldn't let it happen to him. By the day before the Assessment, I had devised a terrible plan. If I had let Abriel know, he would have gone to any length to stop me, just like I went to every length to keep him safe.

The test started at exactly ten, and we were informed that it would continue until exactly noon. Bathroom breaks, snacks, drinks, leaving the room, and talking were strictly prohibited. Abriel and I went in together; we were seated alphabetically.

I took my test when it was handed to me, smiled at the examiner who frowned in return, and forced myself not to wince as I popped the "blister" I had created on my pinky finger that morning. Clear liquid came out, just a few drops, but it was enough to dissolve the ink from the space where my name and ID code had been pre-printed. I fingered the second blister, waiting for its time to come.

I began by painstakingly writing my brother's name on the top of my sheet. I had practiced for weeks, until I could draw the font perfectly. That taken care of, I got to work on the test. It was harder than I had predicted, because not only did I have to make it good enough to ensure that Abriel wasn't Demoted, I had to make it bad enough that anyone would believe he did it. I wasn't willing to risk having anyone figure out that Abriel didn't complete his Assessment. Altering an Assessment is a huge crime, a Demoted crime, and that was what I was trying to prevent in the first place. I worked hard to make mistakes that would look innocent, and I made sure that Abriel and I were always on the same problem. I figured the statistics in my head for how many to get right and wrong. Math had always been my specialty.

There were about forty minutes left of the Assessment when I finished enough problems to ensure that Abriel could blind guess the last few questions and still not be Demoted. I put phase two of my plan in action.

I started by squirming in my seat. I held my stomach, squirming even more, making sure my chair rocked.

The proctor snapped at me, breaking the silence for all forty of us in the room. "Is there going to be a problem?"

"My stomach hurts," I whined. It really did, thanks to the concoction I mixed up and forced myself to drink earlier.

My stomach churned even more at the thought, and I prepared myself for complete and utter embarrassment. I thought of Dante's *Inferno* as I prepared to make a trumpet of my ass, and it saddened me for a moment that most of my classmates wouldn't even get that reference.

I farted, loud and mortifying and obvious. The simple, juvenile act was too outrageous to be faked. It wasn't classy, it wasn't sophisticated, and it definitely wasn't my top choice, but it was so stupid that it was one of the few things that weren't expressly forbidden during the Assessment. I did it again, resisting the urge to crawl under the table and hide.

The immaturity of the high school students, the sound of someone having gas, and the anxiety in the room combined to bring forth a chorus of laughter. I began giggling as well, covering my mouth with my hands to hide while making sure the rest of the sounds I made were loud and clear.

"Mister Gabbamonte, if you don't stop that right now…."

"I'm sorry, miss," I managed not to laugh as I said it. "I get an upset stomach when I'm this anxious!"

Phase three went into effect when Abriel flipped to a new page in his Assessment. I stepped up my dramatics and tried to fan the "smell" away with my hand, then my test booklet. Everyone was watching me, including Abriel, whose test booklet sat completely empty on a new page.

When the proctor finally had enough and walked over to where I sat, I dropped the test booklet, watching it flutter to the floor under Abriel's chair. I jumped up to get it, my over exaggerated movements knocking his over in the chaos. I grabbed Abriel's test booklet, flipped it facedown, and grabbed the one I had been working on before the proctor snatched it from my hand.

"Give me that! You could get Demoted for so much as *touching* another student's Assessment!" she snapped, glancing at the name. She looked at my brother. "Abriel, this one is yours." I sat, and she picked up the test booklet Abriel had been working on and dropped it on my desk without bothering to look at it. Our Assessments had been switched.

I sat quietly for a few minutes, regaining my composure, then I started working on the problems where Abriel left off. I glanced at some of his answers, and they were bad. Really bad. I had hoped that I could salvage it, to boost the score with the remaining problems or change some answers, but I realized it was futile. I broke the "blister" on my other finger, dissolved the ink spelling out my brother's name and ID, and replaced them carefully with mine.

Billions of dollars of research go into the Assessment, and the security technology gets more sophisticated every year. Eventually, the test designers did away with the technology all together. The simplicity provided a level of protection that continued development never did, but I took it a step further. I found the loophole. Abriel never had any idea that anything was happening.

Chapter 3
Balancing Act

I'm helping my master sort some papers and I must come across one he doesn't want me to see, because he smacks my hand away hard enough to bring tears to my eyes, the red spots where his knuckles impact developing into bruises before the day is over.

He doesn't say anything about it when it happens; he doesn't so much as apologize, or tell me to leave, or anything. He just sits there fuming as I gather up my injured hand and injured pride. We continue business as usual.

That night, he's different again, trailing careful kisses over the dark spots and whispering in my ear how sorry he is that he marked me. He promises that he won't do it again, that he won't lash out and lose his temper when I'm not trying to do anything wrong, and I believe him. I know I shouldn't, but he has no reason to lie to me. I can't leave him, I can't tell him no; he has every right to beat me whether I'm provoking him or not. The fact that he says he'll make an effort is enough to convince me that he's serious. He seems like he's promising it for his own benefit more than mine, and I know that he holds himself to very high standards.

Besides, he makes it very clear that he won't do it again if I'm not *trying* to do anything wrong—clearly, his previous threats and punishments still stand, and I find an odd sort of comfort in that familiarity. Both of us seem to fight to keep things as they are, and I wouldn't change it for anything. I have to pretend to be two people to be content with him, but I'll do it, and so will he.

I go poking and prodding around, a little, but I can't make heads or tails out of what is left in sight. Oliver Torenze worries me; Cashiel

18

makes it sound like they have a history, but I can't figure it out just from glancing surreptitiously through papers and files. When I ask, he just tells me not to be concerned about it.

Still, I pay more attention to Torenze now, especially when we go out. We attend more events with that crowd, now, the crowd we were with at the auction where I first met Torenze. I start to learn the difference between my master's usual business associates and this crowd, and while there is some overlap, there seems to be something different that I can't quite figure out, and I dare not ask. Torenze shows up often, and while my master doesn't seem as thrown as he was that first time, he always seems wary. I feel like Torenze's eyes are on me all the time, appraising me. He's cordial enough, but he makes cutting comments here and there, catty things, trying to bait my master. I can tell he's bothered, especially when Torenze hints that he's interested in me.

I ask him about it one night.

"Sascha, he's just lusting over you," he points out. "Anyone in their right mind would be."

I smile at his joke, and at his hands working across my body. I try to put the brief look of alarm on my master's face out of my mind, pretending I didn't see his eyes widen or feel his body tense before he buried the reaction. He'll get irritable if I push the issue. I remind myself that I'm more fortunate than other slaves, far more fortunate than I've ever been. I'm taken care of, treated well, and I trust him not to hurt me. I should be able to trust him to deal with Torenze, but it's hard to completely stop thinking about something.

It isn't long after that strange party that Cash tells me that we're attending another event, an opening for something important with wealthy, influential people and connections. He hints that this one is more important than the others we've attended, and that I should treat it as such.

It's tiring to pretend to care what's happening at these things anymore; I'm just a slave here, arm candy, a pet to be teased and toyed with, except my master never lets anyone tease or toy with me. Maybe it's more accurate to say that I resent it, because these events are the only place where he really treats me like a slave, anymore. I accept it, though, just like I accept the third personality he seems to adopt at these events. Cashiel seems tense about this particular event, so I do my best to make things go smoothly. He makes some sort of grudging comment of appreciation when he finds an outfit laid out for him. I wonder if the balancing act is difficult for him as well.

I'm surprised when we arrive and I realize the opening is connected to the deal that Cashiel made with Torenze at the slave auction, the first time I met him. I think of how my master hinted that he was important, dangerous even, and I think of the way he watches me. The thought of spending a whole night at an event that he's hosting makes my stomach churn and I press closer to my master, almost touching him. He raises an eyebrow in my direction, but takes my upper arm in his hand, squeezing it just long enough that I know he can tell I'm uncomfortable.

We go through the night as ordinarily as possible, although I can tell that my master remains tense. He doesn't let me away from his side. We blend in; most of the other attendees have slaves on their arms as well, and just as many have chosen conservative attire. The fashion site I was reading the other day clearly advised that half-naked slaves were passé except at the most flamboyant of events, like the Peace Day Celebration, or maybe a bachelor party.

I can't believe I read slave fashion sites.

I wish we could avoid Torenze, but it is his opening, and we are sort of privileged guests. We're going to have to come into contact with him at some point. When we do, I expect more friendliness and less petty competition.

At least, that's what it starts out as. Casual digs about who has the better hov-car, whose house is located in the better district. If they weren't both preposterously wealthy businessmen, I'd say they sounded like high school students bickering; regardless of the wealth and status, that is what they sound like. It escalates to thinly veiled comments on social decorum, reputation, business acumen. I don't understand the majority of the references that Torenze is making, but I can tell that the other people joining in the conversation are getting a good laugh at my master's expense.

Cashiel takes it in stride, too much, as far as I'm concerned, letting the insults roll off his shoulders and trying politely to change the subject to something else. I find myself growing more and more irritated, more irritated than Cash is, even. It's unsettling to realize that I'm actually starting to like this man standing next to me, and it's more unsettling to hear him insulted.

"You haven't done well since you came out from behind your mommy's skirts, have you Cash?" Torenze teases, smiling viciously. It brings a scowl to my master's face.

The other people standing around laugh; although, some seem to find it more entertaining than others. I don't really understand it — my master has nothing to do with his family. Perhaps it's just a joke, poking at his age?

"Some of us have a need to protect our interests with subtlety," my master replies, his jaw set.

I can't understand it. Why isn't he shooting this man down, putting him in his place? He's nothing more than an investment partner for his job, this wouldn't be any big deal.

Torenze almost roars with laughter. "Subtlety?" he repeats. "Cash, you wouldn't know subtlety if it subtly bit you in the ass. Admit it, boy, you like the dramatics! Daring revelations, a pretty slave boy all dressed up in glitter — you want the attention. You forget you're a businessman, not some sort of celebrity."

I make my first slip-up, letting out a snort of disapproval, like one might give to a joke made in poor taste. Cashiel doesn't acknowledge it much, he just pinches my arm, cueing me to shut up. I glance up at him, nervous, but he doesn't seem angry. If anything, he's tolerating me, just like he's tolerating Torenze.

A few of the other free people standing around snicker, and I hear one whisper to another "looks like the slave has the most sense out of all of them."

The other just shakes his head. "Sounds like they have some history," he whispers back. "And a distinct lack of social etiquette."

I feel almost vindicated, despite knowing better than to challenge a free man. Torenze is out of line, and everyone knows it. I should take my master's advice and shut the hell up, but it grates on me to hear this smug little man spout a line of bullshit.

I'm smarter than him and so is my master, but he's acting like he's so far above both of us. He may be the host, but my master is in some ways his benefactor; from what I understand, Torenze's most recent business undertaking would never have been possible without the agreement that Cash and his company made. Yes, Cash was thrilled to have him as a business ally, but Torenze needed him just as much. I can't understand why he would be so eager to harass and demean my master.

Torenze makes his attacks more personal, criticizing my master for his youth, his inexperience, his newness into the business field. It's never so direct as that, but it's the comments, the assumptions, the dismissals of my master as "probably not skilled enough in that area" to understand what he freely discusses with others. It's said with a smile and a wink, as though it should be playful. It's not playful, though, it's malicious, and the rest of the people in the conversation seem to notice it as well, their laughs turning uncomfortable as the conversation grows less pleasant. A few of the people turn and leave, but those who are left are somewhat trapped, not wanting to offend the host, who's launching a cringe-inducing attack on my master.

I manage to stay quiet for the better part of ten minutes, just long enough for the attention that I drew to myself to fade. Then Torenze makes another asinine statement.

"Cashiel, I don't know if you have the business sense to keep going in the direction you're headed," he taunts, giving him a knowing look. "Perhaps you overestimate your connections. Or underestimate your threats."

"Oliver, we don't need to discuss this, now," my master replies, looking away. It infuriates me that he won't stand up to this man.

"Don't you think you should be spending your time making sure your competition doesn't come back to bite you in the ass again, instead of pushing forward so quickly?"

"How would you know?" The words tumble out of my mouth. "Your first attempts failed years ago, and if my master hadn't funded you, your current attempt wouldn't be anywhere *near* completion. You're bluffing, and it's making you look preposterous. If you had half the business sense that my master does, you would have gotten behind this idea years ago when it was still fresh—well before my master was in the business, as you pointed out."

I attacked what I saw as his biggest failure. I know enough about my master's business to assess the situation adequately, and a part of me reveled in the chance to let the bright, capable part of myself out of its cage like I do when Cash and I work together. It felt good, powerful... and incredibly stupid.

Shit.

"Sir," I tag on, as if that will erase everything I just said.

There's silence for a moment, and I think that maybe I didn't really say it, maybe I didn't really just call this man out like I did, and just when I have myself convinced that I'm delusional, I hear my master's voice, low and cold and angry.

"Go wait for me in the coatroom, Sascha."

I want to apologize, to beg, to plead, but instead I just nod, feeling my eyes grow wide as the words, "Yes, master," claw their way out of my throat.

I'm scared that I've fucked things up for him, and he'll be upset, and I've made a mistake that could hurt him, whatever his goals are that he never tells me about. I don't even have time to be afraid that I'm walking around alone and unprotected, and I guess it doesn't matter, because the only eyes on me now are staring at me with shock, offense, and occasional amusement. I walk to the coatroom in a panic, feeling terrible and guilty and wishing he would just come and tell me if everything is going to be okay.

Chapter 4

Humiliation

I don't wait long.

"Start stripping," he orders, scowling.

I frown, confused and concerned about how my actions might have affected him. What the hell does he want me naked for? "But—"

"Do as you're goddamn told!" he hisses, grabbing me roughly by the shoulder. "You've done enough damage for one night; Torenze had better be able to see you behave properly when you're beaten, at least!"

The words hit hard, and I'm suddenly afraid for myself as well as my lover's reputation. "Cash, please—"

He grabs me by the jaw, cutting off further protests. "Not another fucking word from you. You will *only* answer direct questions, and you will *only* do so respectfully, is that clear?"

"Y-yes, master," I mumble.

I hear someone enter the room as Cashiel—as my *master*—lets go of my face.

"Start stripping," my master repeats, and I remove my shirt with shaking hands. I toss it aside, because there's nowhere else to put it. Torenze has joined us, and he's smirking at me, standing proud and pleased at my misery.

"Give me your belt," my master orders, just as I'm undoing it. His voice is quieter now.

I don't want to. I don't want to give him my own belt so he can beat me with it. I don't want someone else to watch this happen. I don't protest, no matter how badly I want to. As I pull the leather through the straps, I glance up at him, begging him with my eyes and trying to bite back tears.

His face stays hard.

I hand it to him and drop my pants, slowly, before realizing that I'll have to take my shoes off to get them off completely. Awkwardly, I bend down, trying to squat to avoid putting my ass any more on display than I already will be. I nearly topple over, clenching my teeth at the goddamn spectacle I'm making.

"He could just leave them on," Torenze comments. "I doubt he needs to move around very much for this part, anyway. It might do him good to have a little restraint."

I feel my skin crawl, and I hurry to disrobe completely. It would somehow be more humiliating to stand here with my pants around my ankles than it will be to be completely naked.

"I ordered him to strip," my master counters. I'm almost grateful.

I'm naked a moment later and I stand, trembling before the man who fucks me and touches me and kisses me every night and a man who is obviously getting off on the prospect of humiliating me. I don't understand how Cashiel can do this to me. The beating is bad enough; he's never allowed anyone to watch before, much less allowed them to enjoy it.

"Sascha, tell Mr. Torenze what happens when you're disrespectful and rude to free people," my master orders.

I feel my stomach churn. He's not just allowing Torenze to enjoy it, he's helping him. I've been deluding myself, thinking I am more than a slave to him. I face the disgusting worm of a man who I blame for my punishment. "I am beaten, sir." It's all the more I can say. I can't bring myself to utter another word, because all I want to do is berate him for his cruelty, and my master as well, and god knows that would end up worse.

"But you haven't learned your lesson, have you boy?" Torenze teases, actually grinning at me. "Has your master been too soft on you? Let you pretend to be some sort of fancy pet instead of an over-priced sex doll?"

I feel my face start to burn. "My master has corrected me appropriately, sir. I just messed up."

"Go stand against the wall," my master orders. I follow his commands like a puppet. "Lean forward. Legs spread."

I brace my hands against the wall. I'm surprised he doesn't have me bend over, putting my ass on display more prominently, but he has always given me something to support myself with in the past. Maybe he's worried that I'll fall over when he hits me, which is probably true. I'm glad; standing means it will hurt a little less, as my skin isn't stretched too tightly over my ass.

"How many lashes do you usually get, boy?" Torenze asks, the self-satisfied smile coming through in his tone. "Is it a lot? Enough to make your pretty little ass sore for days, maybe make you shed some tears? I bet you cry easily."

I hate him. I hate him more than I hate being beaten. "That's up to my master, sir." I don't care to tell him that I usually don't get many. Then he might ask for more.

"Ah, like to keep him guessing," Torenze must be addressing my master now. "Great way to keep him in line. These types, they'll take advantage of you if they know too much about what's going to happen to them."

"Stand back," is all my master says in response.

I tense, waiting for the first impact. I don't wait long, although I'm stunned that he's hitting me across my back and shoulders. He's never hit me there before. It hurts.

But as much as it hurts, I'm instantly aware of how much he's holding back, and I'm shocked. He moves quickly and efficiently, lashing me from the tops of my shoulders, down my back, across my ass, and then down my legs. I can't keep count and I can't keep track. I certainly can't keep from crying and whimpering. But he's not hitting nearly as hard as he usually does, and he hasn't hit me in the same place twice. It's almost like he's trying not to hurt me, but that doesn't make sense. If he didn't want to hurt me, he shouldn't be beating me in the first place, and he certainly shouldn't be doing it in front of Torenze.

He's covered my backside with pain and probably bruises and I've leaned forward so I can rest my head against the wall and cry. I know it doesn't hurt as much as it could, but it still hurts, and the reminder of what I am and how little I mean stings worse than the belt.

"He's scarred up," Torenze comments, as if I'm not there. I wish it was true. "Must have been a bad boy."

"My slave's previous masters wasted far too much energy on him," my master explains, not elaborating further.

I bite my lip to keep from protesting, to keep from crying out. Is that really all I am to him, a waste of energy? Is it not even worth his time to beat me; is that what he's saying? I can't help but sob, curling my arms tighter around my face and trying to press myself into the wall.

"Well, with a smart mouth like that, no wonder!" Torenze exclaims. "I bet he could be taken down a notch with a good thorough whipping, though. Maybe on a regular basis, keep that ass nice and sore."

"He requires only a minimum level of pain and correction to be brought under control," my master comments. "Marking him and damaging him that badly was a complete waste of energy and counterproductive to teaching him anything. Look at him now, Oliver, imagine how hysterical he'd be if I were to use a whip on him. He'd be unable to process anything. They need balance."

My head spins. Is that all this is about, then? He's not treating me well, he's conserving energy? Being more productive? Bringing me under control? I've never tried to convince myself that he really cares about me, but I thought he at least saw me as a person. I thought he had some respect for me.

I want to hate him, but I can't, not just yet. It's too fast, too awful, and he's given me a reprieve, hasn't he?

"Turn around, Sascha."

I obey instantly, considering his words. *Processing*. Not thinking, not what humans do. Just processing. Like a machine, or maybe an animal.

"Put your head and your hands back against the wall and don't move them."

I do so, and I'm suddenly struck by the realization that he's going to hit the front of me as well. Not just my legs, this time; he's told me to hold my head back because he's going to hit my chest. It's all I can do not to fall to the floor and beg him not to do it, but that didn't work out so well last time, and this fucking man is watching us. It's not so much that it would be inappropriate that stops me, it's the fact that Torenze would enjoy it. I won't give him that satisfaction, not if I can help it.

I don't beg, but I yelp as the leather snaps across my chest, lighting a fire between my shoulders and across my sternum. I've been hit there before, with fists or on accident, but I've never intentionally been beaten there. It's more intimate, somehow, and the fact that my master would be looking into my eyes if he was focused on anything at all makes it that much worse. Somehow, I feel violated. The lashes move lower, and I can't help but squirm as the belt snaps across my nipples, searing me with pain.

"Look at him move, he must like it! You've got yourself a pain slut, don't you?"

My master stops, and I'm not sure whether to be grateful or angry. If anything, it gives me a minute to compose myself. I like pain, but not this kind, and not like this. Torenze clearly has no idea what it looks like when someone enjoys pain, not someone other than himself.

"Do you enjoy this, Sascha?" my master asks. He doesn't really sound curious though, he sounds like he's reciting lines from a play.

"No, master," I grind out, wanting nothing more than to cup my hands over my chest and cry for hours. "I do *not* enjoy this and I'm sorry I misbehaved." In a different situation, I might enjoy something similar, but all I feel now is horror and mortification and burning pain.

"I'll continue, then," he says, almost a whisper.

The belt is louder as it snaps across my chest a few more times.

He continues, thankfully avoiding my stomach and crotch, and picks up the momentum again at my thighs, and then down my legs. I can tell he's barely putting any force behind his swing, using the belt with practiced ease to avoid wrapping it around my legs, but it still hurts, every part of me hurts. He's hit me probably a hundred times, all together, and all I want is for it to end.

"You may apologize to Mr. Torenze."

I lurch forward, eyes blurry with tears, and drop to my knees. I don't want to apologize to this bastard. I want to scream at him for making my life miserable. I want to see him destroyed for taking pleasure in my misery. I want his business to fail, his family to die, his health to suffer, because he has just facilitated my destruction.

"I'm so sorry, sir," I force out. "I... I was rude, and disrespectful, and I shouldn't have spoken out of turn." I don't mean any of it. I'm too busy hating him, because I still can't bring myself to hate my master, and if I let myself take responsibility for my actions tonight, I'll curl into a ball and Cashiel will have to drag me out of here. "I apologize, sir," I repeat, meaning it no less this time.

Torenze frowns down at me, and I wonder for a moment if he might kick me. I wonder for a moment if my master might let him.

"Cashiel, is that the best he can do?" he sneers. "I've seen the new slaves at the re-education centers do better than this, maybe he could use a few more lashes?"

I panic, dropping lower to the ground and reconsidering my motivations. I can humble myself in front of him if only for self-preservation. "Please, sir, I really am sorry, I just didn't want to impose, didn't want you to have to waste time on me! I didn't understand, sir, how offensive my words were, and how much they were inappropriate, and now that I've been punished, I get it, I do, I promise! Please, please, sir, excuse my master, and don't let this cloud your judgment of him, and know that I really am remorseful, please sir, I swear!"

I hope I sound sincere now, because I am, in that false way that terror and pain can make you believe anything you say. Or anything someone else says.

"He's not too used to having to speak after being punished," my master says. "I don't want to hear it. Tell him what usually happens after you're beaten, Sascha."

I glance up at him, wondering why and how he can be so cruel as to make me say this. He provided an excuse, and if Torenze doesn't buy it, I'd rather have the extra lashes that he suggested. But my master's face is rigid and he looks away from me, refusing to meet my eyes. I don't understand; he's never hesitated to take charge and glare at me before. I feel like he's abandoning me, my only anchor casting me aside so callously. I turn my gaze back to Torenze, sickened by his smile.

"My master usually gags me, sir," I tell him. I can feel my face flushing with shame, like I'm a naughty child. The corners of Torenze's mouth curl up into a smile, a perverse look of satisfaction that makes me thankful for the tears that are blurring my vision. I just want this to be over.

"Continue," my master orders, the word as tight and clipped as possible.

"I wear the gag all day, sir, and sometimes the following day, so I can remember to hold my tongue." I don't like thinking about the gag, and I don't want to experience it again. Even more, I don't want to talk about it. I wish he'd just do it, so this could all stop, so I wouldn't have to be complicit in my own torture anymore.

"I'd wash your mouth out with soap," Torenze replies, almost a challenge.

"That is highly impractical and not nearly as effective," my master comments, sounding irritated at the suggestion. "It's hard on him not to be able to speak."

"What should we gag him with?" Torenze asks, too eager. He looks around the room, and I can just hear his evil mind thinking of all the things he could shove in my mouth; all the things he could use to keep it there.

"I will *not* walk around with a gagged slave," my master replies, haughty and dismissive. "I trust that he will not speak another word at this event, and he will be promptly gagged when we return home as a reminder."

"I can think of something else that might remind him of his place," Torenze suggests, his tone lewd and lustful. "After all, that was a pretty lenient punishment. Slaves like this are good for one thing, and that's certainly not giving unwanted business advice to free people."

There is silence, and for a moment, I'm terrified that he's going to let him do it. Use me, fuck me, put me in my place. I guess it makes sense, it would drive the point home, and while my master has promised not to lend me out, this would be different, this would be punishment, this would be done to hurt and humiliate me even more than I've already been hurt and humiliated. I don't know if I can handle it, and if I wasn't on my knees already, I'd be dropping to them. I know better than to speak, so I settle for trembling instead.

"Get dressed, Sascha." My master's words are cold.

I scramble to get up and dress myself, biting hard on my lower lip to keep from crying out as the fabric slides across my bruised, burning skin.

"As I've posited before, it's not the severity of the punishment that matters, it's the fit," my master explains. "Obviously he's been severely beaten and worse in the past. Obviously it did nothing. Careful timing, humiliation, predictability — that's how to train them. I am not a savage, Oliver, and neither are you. It's entirely uncouth to drag a slave around gagged and beaten like a common brothel whore; surely you don't display your personal slaves like that?"

I glance up, pleased to see Torenze's face turning nearly as red as mine.

"Of course not," Torenze mutters. "I just... I guess you're right."

"Then we shall return to the party." My master smiles at the man, but it's an empty smile.

Torenze leaves, leaving me alone with my master for a minute. He turns to me, and I open my mouth to speak.

"Not a fucking word, Sascha," he hisses, his jaw set.

I nod, grateful that he is too proud to be seen with a gagged slave. Not that I don't deserve it. I'll stay silent to try to repay him, to try to show him how grateful I am. I'll stay silent because I do deserve it; I deserve to be gagged for speaking out of turn, and I deserve far worse for ever letting myself think that I was anything but a slave. He turns away from me in disgust, and it's all I can do not to start sobbing again, but I've promised to be silent. I follow him into the party in disgrace, trying not to show how much pain I'm in. The other guests might notice me, or they might not. Right now, the only thing that is real is the shattering of my false contentment.

Chapter 5

Secrets

I can't tell whether to be furious at Sascha or worried that Torenze is going cause trouble for me. I try to remind myself that Sascha didn't know, that he had no idea how much risk he was exposing both of us to, but it makes me feel no better. We leave the party early; not too early that it is noticeable or in poor taste, but I want out of there as quickly as possible after Sascha's outburst. I come home and retreat immediately into my office, intent on making sure there are no loose ends or dangerous lines of communication left open. I slam the door, letting Sascha go treat his wounds or whatever he wants. I'm too angry to deal with him.

But he knocks on my door, anyway. I walk across the room, throwing open the door open.

"What?" I demand, feeling guilty when he cowers away.

"D-did you want the gag?" he asks. "Master?" he adds at the end, his voice small.

"Go to bed, Sascha. Take an ice pack if you need it." I slam the door. I can't comfort him, but I don't want to speak to him either. He could have destroyed everything, endangered both of us, but there was no way for him to know that.

I beat and humiliated him because I'm too paranoid to let him in on my secret.

When I finally go to bed, he's not there. It's the first time in weeks, and it's unnerving. I don't sleep well and I'm surprised to wake up to breakfast the next morning. He brings it to me silently. I don't know how to bring up what happened, but I hope he's not too upset. It's strange that I even care. After all, he's a slave, he should have been punished. I just can't help regret what happened after things were going so well.

I try to thank him, but he turns and leaves before I can say anything else. He's silent the whole time, just as he is while he works all day. He works harder than usual, perhaps to make up for his mistake, but he doesn't speak to me. Even when I tell him I'm going into the office for a while, he just nods. When I go into our bedroom to change, I realize that he's taken his clothes and toiletries and everything that has accumulated since we started sleeping together. I stay late at the office, messaging him to let him know I won't be home for dinner.

I remind him to eat, because I worry about him.

He's in his bed when I come home, pretending to sleep. I stand in his doorway, not knowing what to do. I could handle a pouty slave; I have no idea how to handle an injured lover.

"Sascha, are you all right?" I ask. I realize too late that I sound more irritated than concerned.

"Yes, master," he answers, stiff and cold.

I don't know what to do or say. I stand there for a few minutes, taking note of the bruises that are visible even in the dim light from the hallway. I did that to him, and he doesn't even know why.

I try to let him take space the next day and he does so silently. I look at him sometimes and wish things could go back to the way they were. I don't know if he's scared, or angry, or something else. It bothers me that I have no idea how to fix it.

My mother has always had a knack for knowing when I'm struggling, and she always manages to exacerbate it. She coms while I'm avoiding Sascha. I'd ignore her, but I've experienced the repercussions of avoiding her contact. I don't need a private investigator following me around again, nor do I want to discover another tracking device on my com unit. She's made it clear over the years that answering her is a priority.

"Oliver Torenze is partnering with Dean & Chanu? Quite convenient," she starts, her voice taking on the thick, syrupy tone it used to when she caught me doing something wrong as a child.

"He has a successful business. We manage finances and investments for successful businesses."

"One of my associates saw you at that slave auction," she reminds me, her voice taking on an accusatory tone. "And I heard you and your little pet were honored guests at Torenze's opening?"

"Plenty of people saw me," I reply, cold. "I was there on business. Which was why I did business there."

"That better be all you were there for."

I let the line go silent, unwilling to respond. I can lie to her, but it won't matter. She thinks she knows what I'm doing already. She's right, of course, which makes it that much harder to hide.

"Cashiel, I've done the best I can to protect you from business dealings like this. Torenze, the people in the slave industry — you want to stick with the legitimate businesses."

"Like yours?" I mutter.

"The Miller System isn't just the most effective training system in the world, it is one of the most financially stable," my mother reminds me. If she were anyone else, I'd say she was really calling to give me advice.

"I'm just following the business interest," I say, trying not to sound so meek.

"Do they know?" my mother asks. "Do they know about your history? I mean, except for Oliver. Do any of your other 'business interests' know that you tried to destroy them in the past? That you'd do it again if you could get away with it?"

I fume, because she's always ahead of me. When I first conducted research into the Demoted system and the re-education centers, the research had been conducted under the guise of continuing my family's business. I had plotted the grand reveal for months, but I let my news slip at a holiday party. She discovered my results before I ever had a chance to take them public. The results that could have torn down her empire were buried under layers of legal and administrative security, and she has monitored me closely ever since. She's onto the reboot of the project; she has been for a while. The only advantage I have is that she has no proof, and I have Sascha to thank for that. He hid it from her last time without even knowing what he was hiding. I've told him about my current research, but nothing about the past, or my mother. Whether I continue to enjoy that benefit of his help in future seems unlikely at the moment.

"I'm sure the partners at my company are well aware of the existence of the Miller System," I snap. "And nobody but Oliver knows anything about me. It will stay that way. That was what you wanted, wasn't it?"

"You've always been the most ungrateful child!" she yells through the phone, making me cringe despite the distance between us. "One day I won't be there to help you. You'd better keep your nose clean!"

She disconnects before I have a chance to reply, leaving me thinking about my options and hers. She's tried to interrupt my progress, but she has nothing on me, thanks to Sascha. I doubt Oliver would turn on me, but then again, he was at my mother's call for years. I have only trusted one other person with my research, and even then, my insistence on keeping secrets got in the way. I didn't tell him about Oliver's connection to the original research, or his history with my mother. What happened at Oliver's party was Sascha's fault, but it was mine as well.

I don't want to lose him over my own paranoia.

After dinner, I follow Sascha into the kitchen, watching him wash dishes and pretend I'm not there.

"You took your things out of my bedroom," I comment, trying not to sound angry. I just want him to talk to me.

"Yes, master." He doesn't look at me.

"You didn't need to do that," I say, frustrated. "It's fine, though."

"Yes, master."

He keeps washing dishes. I wonder if he's waiting for me to forgive him or invite him back. I try making the first move. I come closer, standing hip-to-hip with him, and I place my hand on the small of his back. I lean close, whispering, "You are welcome to come back, if you'd like."

I feel him tense, but he tenses so often. When I hear him say "Okay," I start rubbing his back slowly. I know he likes this; he always relaxes when I do it.

"I know you were upset," I whisper, letting my lips brush against ear. "But that doesn't have to have anything to do with it. Things were good like they were before. I can make you feel good again."

Sascha carefully sets down the dish he is washing and I start to regain hope that we can fix this.

"If that's your wish, master, I'll obey."

His tone is detached, defeated, and I jerk away in horror. He turns to look at me, and I don't bother trying to conceal the look on my face. I'm shocked that I've made him think I would do that to him.

"Jesus Christ, Sascha!" I snap, retreating away from him. "That wasn't what I meant!"

He looks at me with hatred in his eyes, something he has never done, not even when I first bought him. I've betrayed him, and he's not going to let me forget it. Where I used to see lust and longing in his eyes, now I just see fear and disgust.

"I didn't mean…" I start, stepping farther away. But what did I mean? I wanted him to forget it, to go back to being the pleasing little pet he was before the party. "Forget it."

I storm out, sickened with myself. I try to be angry with him, because I've given him everything, but I can't. I kept him in the dark, it backfired. I should never have gotten involved in the first place, but I can't bring myself to sell him.

Over the next few days, I make a point of leaving before he awakes, staying late at the office and avoiding Sascha at dinner time. He works hard and keeps the house in perfect order. He acts like the perfect slave, but I don't want the perfect slave. I want Sascha, the Sascha who was starting to come out of his shell, the Sascha who used to melt under my hands. I watch him at home, when I think he's not looking, but all I see on his face is hatred and wariness. I ruined it; it is my responsibility to fix it.

After careful planning, I come home from work at a reasonable hour and gather my materials as meticulously as I would for a business meeting. In a way, it is a business meeting, just with a different sort of partner. Sascha's in his room where he's been avoiding me lately. I knock on his door.

He takes a few seconds longer than I expect. When he answers, his voice is polite and detached.

"Yes, master?" he calls through the door.

He doesn't even bother to get up to answer it, which annoys me. "I'm coming in," I tell him. He doesn't respond.

When I enter, he's looking down, trying to hide the glare. He must not realize that the rest of his body is all but telling me to go to hell. But at least he still feels something for me.

"Lose the attitude," I order. It's harsh, but I know I risk losing my temper if he gives me attitude. I throw my tablet at him, feeling guilty as he flinches away.

"Read this," I order. "I'll answer any questions you have."

He takes a minute, maybe being scared, maybe being defiant, but he finally begins to read through the page I've left open on my tablet. I would have flashed the information over to his as usual, but the information on the screen is so highly and heavily secured that it is only *ever* visible from my tablet. I watch him becoming interested in it as he reads.

The documents tell my whole story, as I told it to the federal and international investigators so many years ago. Sascha seems annoyed as he starts to read it, but he looks up at me with interest as he quickly puts the pieces together.

"This was you?" he asks, shocked.

I nod.

He stares at me for a moment, then looks back to the tablet with renewed interest, studying it intensely. "But, it says your name is Donovan Miller?"

"My first name was Donovan," I explain, shrugging. "After my father. I've gone by my middle name since before I can remember. And my last name *was* Miller. Keep reading. I was disinherited, stripped of my name, and forbidden from discussing 'trade secrets' — basically, anything about the re-education centers."

Sascha looks up at me, eyes wide.

"She's your mother?" he asks, shocked. "Kristine Miller is your mother? That woman who came over here... she is the head of the Miller System?"

"Yes," I reply. "I was supposed to follow in the family business. I knew it inside and out, all the methods, all the rationale, all the short-comings."

"This is your big secret, then," he says slowly, putting everything together. "I asked about her when you told me about your research. Well, when you told me about half of your research."

I nod. It is my secret. The one I refused to tell him about, time and again. The one I beat him for. Admitting what I've done shouldn't be this difficult, but as Sascha puts together how often I've lied to him, the hurt is evident on his face.

"Your research more than suggests that harsh treatment results in subpar slaves," he reminds me. "So why did you treat me like that? Sometimes, you'd just ignore me, but other times… it was like being back there. In one of the re-education centers."

"In my family, slaves were business products, not pets, and they knew their place. A slave like you would have been broken, but I've never wanted to break you. I chose to ignore you instead, and perhaps that was crueler. The charges of intellectual property theft and treason taught me that speaking up too soon can be a liability. I thought I was keeping you safe."

"Safe from what?" Sascha demands. "Obviously not you or your mother."

I accept his accusations. They are true, even though they are not the biggest concerns we have as we move forward. "It's bigger than that. Even my initial results could have torn down not only my family's business, but most re-education center empires in the world. It's a multi-trillion-dollar enterprise. The everyday functioning of society depends on it, and it depends on keeping it the same."

"If you found something better, why wouldn't your mother have wanted to use it?" Sascha asks.

Sascha is bright, but he is young, like I was when I first started researching the topic. He still things can be fixed cooperatively. "My mother saw exactly one way to get results — her way. She knew exactly how to cause the most intense and terrible pain while still keeping a slave conscious. She knew exactly how many days one could starve before suffering physical ailments. And she made *certain* that every one of her trainers and guards knew as well and followed her protocols. Her re-education centers rose to prominence due to her blood-thirstiness and exacting standards; once she expanded, her methods caught on here and in dozens of other countries. Her system worked. Adopting a new one would mean admitting that she was wrong, admitting that she had steered entire nations in the wrong direction."

Sascha's eyes go wide. I can see him begin to understand the implications of all this.

"I didn't just attack her system; I attacked the entire way of thinking," I explain. "And I never took into account the big players — money, finance, legal influence. I was naïve enough to think I was doing a good thing."

"Since the first people were Demoted a few hundred years ago, the re-education centers have always focused on control," Sascha recalls, thinking aloud. "The Miller System made some improvements; it got rid of most of the physically disabling technologies, but made discipline and systematic terror even more important. You aren't just going to destroy your mother's system, you're trying to turn everything upside down. All the laws, all the policies, all the recommendations — every part of our society that deals with the Demoted would have to be reconsidered. And in the mean time, everyone would realize they had failed for so long... someone would have to be held responsible."

He's starting to see it, now. The cold, hard truth that I discovered from the inside of a locked cell. "My results could have changed the state of the world, but I never considered how much I would be hated for revealing them. The second I let word slip at the company holiday party, I found myself arrested and locked away and accused of being a threat to national security, of all goddamn things."

Sascha looks stunned.

"Didn't you know?" I reply, a bitter smile on my face. "Trying to overthrow the Demoted system is a matter of national security. And my family has considerable sway with law enforcement. Donations, partnerships — law enforcement and re-education center developers are in bed together. A lot of medical research, too, but I didn't find that out until later."

"How did you get out of the charges?" he asks.

"My mother arranged for me to get out of jail once she felt I had learned my lesson," I admit. Everything she gave, she could have so easily taken away again. "In exchange for my silence, I was set up with a bank account large enough to support me for a lifetime, and a lucrative position with Dean & Chanu. I disappeared, and I wasn't supposed to come back. A cordial parting of ways, if you could call it that."

Sascha gives me a hopeful look. "But you didn't stay away?"

I shake my head. "I was planning to try again from the moment I was released from jail. It sounds rather nice — not the Miller System anymore, but the Michaud System. I'm in a position now where I can start over, if I have enough support and insider information, but I also need to find the exact right people. And I need extensive funds to do so. Funding the project entirely on my own makes the results look less legitimate. I need backers, industry stakeholders who lend credibility."

"Oliver Torenze?" Sascha asks. I nod. He deserves to know.

It's been almost twenty years, but I still remember visiting the re-education centers with Oliver Torenze. He was a close family friend, active in the business, and he had taken me to many work-related events, priming me, even as a teenager, for my future in the family business.

He also supervised the week when my mother sent me there as punishment.

"What the hell did I do?" I snapped, glaring at him indignantly as he ordered two of the guards to hold me while another beat me. "I've done everything you told me to since you brought me here!"

My requests were met with silence, then another sharp slapping noise as the leather made contact with my skin. I tried not to cry out, not to add to the wails of the Demoted who surrounded me.

"You're still fighting," Oliver commented, a slight smile on his face. I couldn't tell if he was proud or disappointed. "Another dozen."

He never held the strap himself, but he ordered it to be used, and he watched while it was. He held back the food I wasn't allowed and he ordered the restraints that forced me into painful positions on the cold concrete floor that reeked of blood and bodily fluids, even through the stench of disinfectant. While I cried and screamed, he supervised and smiled. The guards were the ones who hit me, but he was the one who leaned in and whispered threats in my ear when I was so sleep deprived that I was hallucinating.

Oliver was acting on my mother's orders, but he embraced my torture happily. He had been told to make an impression on me and he did.

I realized that there were no lengths he wouldn't go to in order to succeed.

Chapter 6

Partnership

It makes sense all of a sudden. The insistence on decorum, the mingling at slaveholder events. Me. I had tried to justify it by telling myself that my master was keeping up appearances, that he was working on his current research project, but that was never enough. It never explained why he was so harsh, why he demanded so much of me, or why he was so uncomfortable around certain people.

"I take it Torenze is more than just a wealthy business man?" I ask.

"Yes," Cash explains. "He was once my mother's closest business associate and family friend. He trained me, I used to confide in him; he was my inside connection in the business. He was there when I slipped and exposed my plans. After everything happened, I didn't think I'd see him again, but my mother fired him. Word is that he wanted more control than she was allowing him, so she cut him loose. When he started his own business, the acquisition of his business was one of my new company's top goals."

"But you want him on your side for more than official business. Why is he so cruel to you? He's constantly cutting you down, threatening you—" I think of all the hints at Cash's family. "He threatens to expose you! Why would you want him working with you?"

Cash smiles. "Torenze was to be my other half at one point; I was going to handle advertising and research and development, he was going to handle the practical side. He enjoyed that sort of thing. He was my mentor, for a while, it's so hard to believe that now. But then I stumbled upon this other research—you know, when I first started it, I thought it would be welcomed, applauded. It was only after the fact that I realized how ignorant that was. As it stands, the Demoted system isn't about efficiency or success. It's about brutality."

I nod. I've always known that. "Torenze was your mentor... is that why you want him to be part of your project?"

Cash laughs. "I'd rather have him dead," he says, quite bluntly. "When I was fourteen, my mother arranged for me to spend a week in a re-education center. I brought home poor grades in my history class, and she decided that would be the best way to motivate me. Oliver was the one in charge of supervising me during this very creative punishment. He made sure I wasn't too badly damaged, but he helped to get the point across."

I stare at him in shock. "You can't do that," I say, even though he's just told me that you can.

"When your name is in the training manuals of all the re-education centers, you can," he points out. "My mother didn't give the orders for me to get damaged badly or raped or anything of that sort, but she let them starve and beat and terrify me. Oliver was with me most of the time, supervising. The whole experience made it very clear that I didn't want to end up there. In a way, it started my interest in the subject."

I consider the kind of parent who could do this to their child, and it sickens me. It also explains why my master is the way he is. The ends justify the means, always, no matter how horrible the means really are. "How can you stand the thought of working with him again?"

Cash smiles. "I'm disgusted by him personally, by how much he enjoys torturing people, but he's everything I need. Besides, he's the only person I know who hates my mother more than I do. After she let him go, he made it clear, both personally and professionally, that he was going to stand in her way, just like he perceived her standing in his. He's well-connected, personable, interested in competing with my mother, and I trust him in business. He won't question me too much, not until it's too late for him to realize what he's invested in. He's my ticket to re-establishing myself in the slave training world."

"You can't just start from scratch?" I ask, considering the option. There are new faces in research all the time; surely, he could just pretend everything was new.

"I have to, but I need legitimacy of some sort," my master explains. "I had some as Kristine Miller's progeny; I have none as a wealthy financial advisor. Besides, it would consume almost all of my savings — there is an end to them, you know. I need business partners, the right kind, both for funding and for the image of my project. Keeping up my front not only as a business leader, but also as a slaveholder, is key to getting what I want. I can't afford to look like I oppose the system; that's asking for treason and rejection again. That's why it's so important that I impress, well, men like Oliver Torenze. Having him support my current project is perfect because he's established in the field. I've been stripped of everything I used to be. He hasn't."

"You just changed your name," I mumble. "It's not like you inhabited a new body."

Cash smirks at me. "No, but when I was younger, I was mostly working behind the scenes. Few people knew me in person, and if they did, they just knew me as my mother's son. I didn't make much of an impression back then, and what's another attractive twenty-something? They're everywhere, like bottled water, or slaves. Plenty of time has passed. You didn't recognize me, although I'm sure you saw the story on the news. Presented with a new name and history, I may as well have inhabited a new body for all anyone else is concerned. I've had to reinvent myself. Everything I've done since my first project got exposed has been part of that. I need to fit the part I'm playing."

"That's why you were so harsh," I realize. "Keeping up appearances. You've rarely punished me for anything in private. That's why you... the other night..."

"I know." His voice is soft, and if I try really hard, I can detect a trace of regret in it. "I humiliated you the other night, Sascha. You know, I hope, why I did it?"

"Because I was disrespectful," I answer instantly, without thinking. Slave training goes deep, and it comes out at the strangest times.

"Don't think *or* answer like a slave," he orders, staring expectantly. It occurs to me that he's not demanding obedience; he's demanding that I work to my potential, that I think critically as he's always known I could do.

I think a little harder. "Because Torenze demanded it, or could have," I realize. "Based on your history, he expected you to whip the skin off my back, break my jaw, something of that level."

My master nods. "I humiliated you so I could avoid the pressure to hurt you badly. I would have warned you beforehand, but I wanted it to seem genuine, and you're a terrible liar. Also, I was furious at you, and at myself. You couldn't have known the problems you could have caused, because I didn't tell you. I would do differently now, but the other night, I was rather vindicated to see you afraid. I suppose that was cruel, but you've got to understand the risks inherent in such an outburst."

I nod. It's strange to realize that he hurt me like that to avoid hurting me worse in other ways. I can't decide which I would have preferred, given the choice, but I wasn't given a choice anyway. "That's why you didn't follow up with the gag when we got home."

"What, did you think I forgot?" My master rolls his eyes. "It was unnecessary. No one was watching, and you knew well enough that you had done wrong. I think you knew that from the moment the words left your mouth."

I don't want to ask the next question, but I can't help myself. He's sitting here, talking about the horrible treatment that slaves are subjected to, and yet he's done some of the same to me. "Then what about the other times?"

He studies me for a moment before answering. "You needed to be reminded of your place, Sascha. I had told you politely and it wasn't getting through. I felt something more severe might get through in its place."

I glare at him. He doesn't deserve a response to that.

"You couldn't be reasoned with, couldn't understand because you were too busy trying to act like a slave and too full of fear," my master continues. "I told Bobby once that you were smart enough to know better, and it's true. If I didn't think you could hold your tongue, I would never have expected you to."

It's like a burning salve on an open wound. It takes some of the sting off, but replaces it with a different kind of pain. If he thought I was just a stupid animal, his treatment made sense, he could be excused. He's telling me that he knew otherwise, but he hurt me, anyway, repeatedly. "Maybe if you had told me about you plans, I would have been more agreeable. *Master.*"

"I was wrong." My master looks away as he says it, glancing out the window into the darkness outside. "I was wrong to keep it from you as long as I did. Even when I realized that working with you was easier and more pleasant than working against you, I still didn't think that something of that level should be shared with a slave. I let that color my decisions, and I don't think it was wise."

"You told me about your research, but not about your family," I remind him, unsure of whether to be grateful to be let in now or angry that I've been kept in the dark for so long. "Your mother came over here and put her hands on me, and you still didn't tell me. I covered for you while she was here, after you tormented me for days, and you *still* didn't tell me."

"I know," he admits. "Old habits die hard. You keep fucking the same things up, putting me at risk, and it infuriates me. It makes me want to hurt you; not talk to you, but I think I've tried that enough times. It's not working any better than your behavior is."

"You're kind of repeating the same thing that got you into trouble years ago," I point out, realizing only after the words leave my mouth how offensive they are.

My master smiles at me. "Yes, and the flaws we have ourselves are often the most annoying in others. It is uncanny how much you remind me of myself at your age, and I promise that doesn't make me any more likely to go easy on you. It was hard to separate the two at first. Hell, it was hard enough to keep from smacking the attitude off your face on a daily basis."

I grin, almost in spite of myself. I really am that bad of a liar. "You have the training and expertise to punish or torture me in a thousand ways, and the only thing you've done is smack me around a little and beat me with a belt?"

"There was the cleaning thing, too," he reminds me.

Ah, yes, that time he made me cry every day by working me to death. "That was creative."

He shrugs. "Pretty standard, actually. Breaks a person down. Of course, I didn't expect you to call me out on exactly what it was that I was doing to you, calling me inefficient and wasteful and spiteful."

I shrug. I saw right through it, at the time. I hadn't been telling him those things to make him stop, I was telling him those things to push him to hurt me, to break out of the cycle. I suppose it worked, just in a different way than I was expecting.

"You were bright enough to figure it out, and you called me on the exact thing I had called my family on years before. You and I think alike, too alike, and I'd rather not see my flaws reflected."

"I wish I had been punished with a lucrative job and a loaded bank account," I retort, daring to be offensive. I want to push him again, to see if he'll turn on me again. He's letting me in, but is it just a part of a bigger plan?

"I shouldn't have been so cruel. But again, old habits."

I nod. He's not apologizing, but he's not making excuses either. I feel the same way about how I treated him. "So, what now? Why tell me now; what does it change?"

"I can't stand hurting you when you don't have all the information," he shrugs. "Now, I keep you up to date on what I'm doing. Everything. You deserve that much. You can help me more now that you know everything. You know why I'm so careful, and you know what the stakes are. The full stakes. You can help me play the part in public. No more secrets, no more lies. I want to work with you on this. I might not have intended to buy you, but now that I've seen a hint of what you're capable of, I need you."

It sounds like he's offering me the opportunity to be equals, but I know better. I know that anyone who thinks slavery is okay and who can justify beating another person repeatedly doesn't want to be equals.

"What if I say no?" I challenge.

He frowns. "That is, of course, your decision. But I will say that I'll start looking for another slave. The slaves I worked with before, the ones I purchased for research... they were considered tainted, corrupted by my interference. They were put down."

"They were murdered?" I ask, not wanting to believe it.

"Euthanized," Cash replies, his face blank. "You can't murder a slave."

No, not equals. I look at him in horror. The occasional abuse was bad enough; how can he sit here and casually threaten to have me killed in the interest of his research?

"I'd try to keep you safe, Sascha," he promises. "I like you; I think you have a lot of potential. But this is a dangerous business. You need to be aware of the risks."

"You didn't give me a choice to be involved!" I snap.

"No, I didn't," he agrees.

I don't understand how he can be so calm and reserved. He's just told me these terrible secrets; what's more, he's told me they could lead to my death. I'm interested in the research, but is it worth the price?

"Can I think about it?" I ask, studying his face. It's so much to process; I want the chance to think this through, to consider my options. But his priorities are his research, not me.

"Yes," he agrees. "I'll show you more, let you see all of what I do. Then you can make your decision."

I nod, accepting that. "What about Torenze?"

Cash shrugs. "I hope his fascination with you will fade with time. We need him on our side, Sascha, but I'll do what I can to keep him away from you. I want him to partner with us, but in the meantime, you have to stop engaging with him. He'll come up with something far worse for you than what happened the other night, and it might not be for punishment. It might just be for his own sick enjoyment."

I just stare at him. If he's willing to work with this monster, what will happen to me if I don't agree to work with him?

"I told you once that you'd think I was selling out," Cash reminds me. There is no trace of regret on his face.

I do, but I don't say anything. Until now, I thought my biggest danger was getting beaten or slapped, or sold to a brothel. Now that I realize exactly what my master is capable of, I'm not sure if those things are so bad. And yet, I'm still interested in the research.

Chapter 7
Going Forward

"What do we do now?" I ask, still trying to digest all the information. There's so much, I want a day or so to just think about it all, to make all the connections. It's what I've always excelled at, but I can't do it with him staring at me.

"We start again," Cash suggests, looking tentatively hopeful. "No more secrets. No more treating you like a dumb slave. And hopefully, once you stop being angry at me, we can be better than we were before. I enjoy your company, Sascha. There are very few people who I say that about. You're smart enough to work with me, to challenge me, and now you know pretty much everything about me. There's no one else who has that privilege. I want you to be a bigger part of my life, but more importantly, I want you to be a bigger part of my work. I've been limiting both of us."

I nod. I feel his pressure: his desire to make me his researcher, his hacker, his spy, whatever he wants from me. It's intriguing, but risky. "Can I see more of it?" I ask, nervous. I'm expecting him to demand some sort of loyalty oath or something before letting me go any further.

"Yes," he agrees. He takes a step closer to where I'm sitting on the bed with his tablet, and then pauses. "May I sit?"

I nod, moving over to give him some room.

Suddenly, he's in bed with me, comfortable next to me, like he belongs here. I try not to be too distracted as he pulls up plans and outlines for his research, explaining the testing process to me in great detail as well as the barriers that he's facing. Some information he can't access because it's too heavily guarded; I can get through the barriers in a matter of days. Other information he can't access because it's simply not on any network. For those, he needs a spy, someone to listen at events, make sure the right people are interested and willing to pursue the same goals as he has. He's staging a huge movement, drawing investors, owners of re-education center franchises, researchers, and more. He couldn't ask me to do this much before; I would have found out his secrets, who his mother is and who he was. He seems pleased when I tell him how easily I can get through at least the technological barriers. He's even more pleased when I grow more interested, asking him questions about how it will play out, the details, the tests that will be used.

"This is why you should never have been a slave, Sascha," he mentions casually. "A waste of potential. You're capable of changing things."

I smile. I'm learning that slaves can change things, too, if they're lucky. "What would you have done if you hadn't found me?"

He shrugs. "Spent years working on this, struggling, waiting. Gotten exposed, probably. With your help, from what you've told me, this could be live in just a few months. Without it... I was thinking four, five years, maybe. Five years of risk."

"How is it any less risky to do it more quickly?" I ask.

"Less chance of being found out," he replies, smiling a little. "Once the data is out, it can't be erased. Not from public record, not from people's minds. They stopped me before that happened last time; this time, it can't happen again. You're a part of that."

He pauses, looking a little nervous. "I mean, if you want to be."

I still haven't answered. I still haven't decided yet. Would I trade safety to satisfy my curiosity, like he has? I've done it before, but never on this scale.

"Can I try, just to see, without committing?" I ask, bracing for him to say no.

"Of course," he replies. "I want you in on this. I need you. But I won't force you."

I smile at him. It's so much more than I expected. I've thought he was cruel on so many occasions, but what's more accurate is that I wasn't his top priority. From that perspective, I had a big part in earning the punishments he doled out; it's not as though he beat me for no reason. He's been rather lenient, given the scale of things. "I hope I didn't mess anything up for you."

"Don't worry about that. I'll consider it settled if you'll do the same."

As is typical, he doesn't apologize, nor does he demand that I do so. Things are uncertain, but at least I know what's going on. I lean against his side, missing his touch, and I'm surprised when he puts his arm around me. He's never touched me like this while we worked, but then, we've never been in bed revealing our deepest secrets. I think of my own secrets, Abriel, but I can't tell a man who would casually "euthanize" a batch of slaves that I helped my brother evade the Demoted system. I don't trust that his generosity will extend past his own interests.

He must notice my discomfort, because he gives me an uncertain look. "Is this all right?"

I'm startled, but not offended or anything. As much as I thought my crush on him was gone after the party and the subsequent humiliation, I do like the way he feels against me. In between all of the stealth and goals and planning, I remain attracted to him.

"You don't have to say yes," he informs me before I can even formulate an answer, his tone suddenly serious again. "You can say whatever you want."

I consider it. "You said you'd sell me if I didn't want to research with you..."

My master shakes his head. "This is different. This is personal. I don't want you to feel like you have to. The other night, you agreed, you said you'd do it if I wanted you to... I never want that. I hope you have enough respect to tell me whether you want to have sex with me?"

"I guess I do," I answer, trying not to sound too decisive. Playing hard to get. I do want to, but I think I should be less willing. I want it to be harder for him.

He glares at me. "Sascha, I'm pretty sure I've told you before that you can stop when you'd like, and you didn't hesitate to turn me down the other night, even when we were on bad terms. I'd appreciate a clear answer."

"Yes," I mumble, feeling ridiculous. "Happy?"

He takes his tablet from my hands, leans over me, and places it on the nightstand. I lean out of his way, and once the tablet's gone, he shifts, pinning me there. I try not to get turned on. I fail.

"Are you angry at me for wanting to fuck you?" he asks. "Because, last I checked, you enjoyed it when I fucked you, and I know for a fact that I enjoy it, so I cannot think of a reason why we wouldn't do it."

Because it's too fast. Because I want to punish him. Because, an hour ago, I had swore never to have sex with him again. But I didn't know then what I know now, and he hadn't approached me with some offer to be partners on something. Because I want to prove that I'm not just some sex-crazed slut who's addicted to cock, even though I know *he* doesn't think that. Instead of answering, I contemplate the minimum time that I should put between hating my master and wanting to fuck him.

"Would it help if I buttered you up and gave you head?" he asks, finally.

Of course it would. He's fucking amazing at giving head. And that would be him servicing me, right? I try to convince myself that that's the reason I'm growing more excited, not the weight of his body above mine. "Maybe," I mumble, trying to smile at him. There's not even a word for what I'm feeling right now. Something between horny and spiteful and grateful and curious. Try finding that on a feelings chart.

"Still won't give me a straight answer, will you?" he mutters, tugging my pants down anyway.

I don't grace that with a response, but I have no desire to stop him from undressing me. Actually, I lift up my hips to help. He obviously wants to go down on me, and I can't say I want to turn him down. In fact, as he takes my cock into his mouth, I definitely don't want to turn him down, and the ridiculously breathy sigh that escapes my lips confirms that.

I don't know why it's so mind-blowing every time he gives me head; he does it fairly often, far more often than I return the favor. Maybe it's because it's something I never expected. The men I've been with in the past have almost always wanted me to service them, not the other way around, but with Cash, it's like it's his way to still be in control. He might be on his knees with a mouth full of cock, but he knows as well as I do that he's the one pulling all the strings. I don't even think to challenge him.

Not like I have a chance to as his hands work their way around me, teasing out the areas that need additional stimulation, brushing past my ass almost innocently. God, that feels wonderful. I forget everything that happened between us, focusing on the sensations, on the way he makes me feel. I relax back down on the bed, letting him work me over, letting him bring me almost to climax before stopping.

He comes up slowly, lifting me back farther on the bed as he does and trapping me with his arms and legs as he hovers over me, predatory and sexy. He grips my jaw firmly and turns my head to face him, catching my eyes.

"The truth, Sascha, do you want to fuck?" he asks. His voice is completely serious, calm and controlled, as always. "I do want to be inside of you again, but I wouldn't force you, and I don't want to coerce you. Hell, even if you just want me to suck your dick and then leave, I won't push you. I always want you to want this."

Well, if I wasn't hot for him a minute ago, I am now, hot enough that I can let my pointless rage go and admit to both of us how I'm feeling. "Yes, Cash, I want you to fuck me. I want you to fuck me every night until I scream, even when I'm angry at you, unless I explicitly tell you that I don't. But even when I'm angry at you, I'm still attracted to you. I still want you to fuck me."

He smiles.

Asshole.

Then he gets some lube, which makes me feel a little better. Okay, a lot better. Okay, a *whole* lot better. I'm trying to forget his stupid smirky smile and focus on the slippery finger he's introduced, but he insists on talking.

"You know, I didn't quite mean that I needed *that* much confirmation," he teases, taking advantage of the fact that all I want to do is fuck and squirm and moan my pleasures for the next hour or so. "But I appreciate it. I enjoy that you like this."

I make some sort of pathetic whimpering noise of joy as he makes quick work of getting me ready, his fingers relentless and practiced as they stretch me out. He grips me by the hips and shoves me further onto the bed, pausing for a moment. I'm drawn out of my blissful trance by the frown on his face as his hands linger on one of the more visible bruises left from the other day.

He doesn't say anything, but he sees that I've noticed him. He smiles at me and drives himself into me, making me forget anything else is happening as I'm caught once again in passionate bliss.

He doesn't take his time, and I appreciate it. He's completely inside of me in seconds, thrusting hard and forceful as he holds me in place by my hips. It's such a familiar feeling, something that I've grown so used to and so happy with over the past few weeks. I missed fucking him, as much as I didn't want to admit it, I missed being close to him in general.

It's not long before I feel myself aching to come, to find the release that I've rarely bothered to seek out on my own in the past few days. He's too careful, though, too gentle, and I want that little edge of pain that will put me over the edge. I squirm underneath him.

"Cash," I whimper, putting my hand up to clutch at his arm. His arms are so sexy. He's so sexy. God, I wish I could just get off already! "Please?"

"What do you want?" he asks, leaning down to whisper the question in my ear.

He knows damn well what I want. "Cash, don't make me beg?" We've talked about it before, and I don't like to beg for it.

"Sascha, what do you want me to do to hurt you?" he clarifies. "I don't want you to beg. You don't like it and it does nothing for me in this context, either."

Oh. I forget that he does this sometimes, actually asks what I want him to do, or how he should hurt me. It's strange, but he can be considerate when he wants to be. I can't bring myself to tell him that it doesn't really matter what he does, that any old pain will do, regardless of who or what causes it. Hell, I could probably get off from a fucking bee sting right now.

"Teeth," I mumble, feeling my face burn as I say it. It does actually turn me on to be bitten, it always has, but the few times Cashiel has done it it's blown my mind.

He nods, looking serious as usual. "Where?"

I want to scream "wherever the fuck you want!" but I figure that won't end well. "My chest," I whisper, feeling embarrassed again.

"My shoulders." All over, is what I really mean, but I don't say that. I have some shame left.

That shame disappears as I feel his teeth grazing my neck, my collarbone, my chest. It's wonderful, and he bites me in time with his thrusts, each one a little harder. He pauses the biting, which draws a grunt of frustration, but then he grabs me by the hair and pulls me close for a kiss. To say I'm caught off-guard is an understatement. I yelp and writhe underneath of him, startled by the sudden closeness. We rarely kiss, but when we do, it's enough to bring me to my knees, except I'm lying on my back.

I'm still melting from the kiss when he goes back to biting me, harder this time, enough that I don't know whether to pull away from the pain or lean closer as he brings me closer to orgasm. He doesn't give me the choice, though, he pins me down with his body as he bites harder, trapping me with the pain, driving into me roughly. I cling to his arms as I come, the pressure of his body on mine sending me over the edge. I cry out as he continues to fuck me, harder now that he's more excited, and I'm relieved when he stops biting so hard and contents himself with pressing his lips against my skin. It's not long after that he comes as well, capturing me with that penetrative gaze that he has.

After a few moments he pulls out, and I wince when I feel the sting in my ass and in all the places he's bitten me. I know there will be bruises, but they hold good memories. Still, his hand traces over them.

"A lot of training goes into making someone so dependent on pain," he comments.

I shrug. "It was a gift."

My master looks at me, doubtful.

I sigh. I did set this up for an explanation. "My trainer was fond of me. She knew I'd be in for a lot of pain, given my attitude and all, and she saw what she described as 'potential' in the way I reacted to pain. She helped me to use it for sex, like an enhancement, rather than just feel the hurt of it."

"And now you can't come without it," my master muses. "Hell of a gift."

"She didn't expect her training to work so well." No, actually, she had been horrified when she realized I basically *couldn't* come without some sort of pain. More horrified than I was, to be honest. I had learned quickly enough that sex and pain were closely correlated for a slave, and I accepted it. "It made life less unpleasant."

"I suppose." My master is quiet for a moment. We lie together for a while. He strokes his hands across my skin, feeling the scars that decorate my body like bad graffiti. He stops at the bruises again.

"Do they still hurt?"

I shake my head. He must know that they don't, given the amount of expertise he has, but I suspect he just likes hearing it from my lips. "No, sir. You're remarkably capable of hurting me without causing any lasting damage."

"You're not the only one who's been trained," he says softly. "It was ingrained into me from the time I was old enough to understand. Slave training. Torture. Punishments. My mother ran our home as strictly and efficiently as she did her re-education centers. I only hope I'm not so dependent on it."

"Do you enjoy hurting me?" I ask. It's an odd question, but I want to know. I want to know if he gets off on my pain like Torenze did.

"No," he answers, confirming what I've thought all along. "And if I thought something else would get through to you, I would do that instead."

"Others have done worse," I point out. I think I'm trying to make him feel better, but from the way he stiffens up, I think I accomplished the opposite.

"I'm sorry," he says, his face actually showing regret for once. "You don't deserve this kind of treatment."

"Thank you." I can't excuse him, because it's not excusable, and I can't forgive him, because how is it my place to forgive my master for doing something that he is well within his rights to do? So I say thank you, because I want to acknowledge it somehow, and this is all I've got.

"Whether it happens again or not is up to you, Sascha," he reminds me. "I have to keep up appearances, and if you slip up in public again, I will beat you or humiliate you or both. But I'll do my best to make sure you aren't put in a situation like that again. Please, be careful. You know the situation now, know what's at stake, and I know you're smart enough to keep your mouth shut. If you need a break, or if you want out all together, tell me. I'll do what I can."

I nod, because I believe him. I might not be completely invested in this project, but I'm willing to give it a try. "I'll be more careful."

"I hope so," he says, looking sad. "I don't want it to happen again."

I nod, resting my head against his shoulder. For once, he doesn't seem to mind, and for a moment, I wonder if this is really what human interaction can feel like. It feels good.

Chapter 8

Merger

It's amazing how quickly things go back to the way they had been.

Except it's different; we're both on the same page. The incident with Torenze and the confessions from Cash have thoroughly disillusioned me in a number of ways, but I think it's better. I know what I'm facing, so there's less to fear. I can evaluate things logically instead of doing whatever scares me the least.

I'm still not sure if I want to be Cash's partner in this venture, but I appreciate that he's letting me try, and I enjoy the sex we're having again, as regularly as before.

That first night was a little underhanded on Cash's part. I was vulnerable, and he was demanding, but I did want to have sex with him, The underhanded nature of it didn't even start to hit me until I was drifting off to sleep in my bed, my master beside me, and by then, it didn't seem to matter. He didn't ask me to come back to his bedroom, but he didn't leave mine, either. I suppose it was a compromise. My master deals in business mergers, and everything that we discussed that night seemed like part of our own private merger. A part wonders if he really will sell me if I decline his offer. I wonder if he'd go beyond that, if he'd have me "put down" like an animal, but I doubt it. He's never hesitated to threaten me before. I could see him selling me, locking me away, but if he was really concerned about security, he would have eliminated me already. As I find out more about his plans and research and goals, I become more invested.

Cash's project has some humanitarian gains: the training process has grown more violent throughout the years, more destructive, and that's an area where real progress can be made. It ignites the tiny spark of hope that I think every slave has, that maybe things won't be this bad forever. And even if they are, at least I get to join the research that seeks to prove otherwise. I feel like I'm doing something worthwhile for once, really worthwhile, more than just helping my master. I'm careful with how close we get, and I'm careful with the sex. If I let myself think that he cares about me more than just a business and casual sex partner, he can hurt me again, humiliate me, devastate me. I can't let that happen again. I move my things back into his bedroom, because I spend so many nights there. We fall into patterns, traditions, jokes, habits. On busy mornings, I brush my teeth while he combs his hair, but I do my best to keep distance between us, even if it's a false distance. Sometimes I sleep in my room, alone, whether it's for a midday nap or all night. A few times, I even turn him down for sex, just because I can, and just because I like the feeling of it.

The first time he looks startled, gives me this goddamned sad puppy dog look, but he doesn't fight me. The second time he just accepts it, and that's almost more disturbing. The third time, when he comes home from work and finds me in my bedroom and asks if I want to join him, I shrug, looking at my tablet to hide the desire I'm feeling for him.

"I think I'm okay in here for the night," I mumble, wishing I could at least sound firm and assertive about it.

He looks at me for a moment, a little confused, and then he walks in, depositing himself on the bed next to me.

I wait, a little nervous, wondering what he's going to do. To rape me after all this time would be counterproductive at best, and the thought is ridiculous enough to calm me down a little bit.

"Sascha, are you playing hard to get, or do you really not want to come to bed with me tonight?" he asks, sounding frustrated.

"I'm just not in the mood," I reply, lying, because he's kind of hot sitting here at my mercy. It sounds weird to admit that I'm testing him because I can and because I want to prove it to myself that I'm right.

Cash sighs. "Is it something I've done to upset you?" he asks, frowning.

I'm amused that he would think that I'd keep sex from him as a weapon, although it's a good one to have in my arsenal. "No. I'm just not feeling it." That's a little closer to the truth.

He's quiet for a minute, puzzling over this revelation. To be fair, I'm usually aching for sex, it must be a surprise to think that I'm suddenly not interested.

"Okay," he says, looking no less puzzled. "Would you tell me if it was something that I did?"

I need a moment to think about this one, because such a scenario has never crossed my mind. I am still his slave, I shouldn't be manipulating him. I wouldn't have any right to do that, even if I do have the right to refuse him sex. Even if he's *given* me the right to refuse him sex. It's an important distinction to keep in mind.

"I'd rather you tell me than try to sabotage things," he says, the words coming out as more of an order than a preference. "It still stands that you can say no whenever you'd like, but if you're doing it to get back at me for something, you need to tell me what I've done that's made you act this way. I'm doing my best to keep you informed; I'd appreciate it if you give me the same courtesy."

He's not trying to be demeaning or shaming, but I do feel ashamed. I'm treating this as a game, a test to see if he can pass without knowing the rules, and he's seriously concerned about my happiness. "It's nothing you did," I mutter. I go for a lie, because I can't bring myself to tell him the truth, that I don't completely trust him, that I'm testing him. "I'm just not feeling that well tonight. My stomach's kind of upset, but I didn't want to bother you with it."

"Oh," he says, suddenly looking relieved, but also worried. "Well, can I get you anything? I don't want you to be in pain."

I smile, feeling even more guilty about the white lie. "I'll be fine," I promise him. "I just... I kind of want to just let it pass, you know?" What I really want to let pass is my bizarre insistence on pushing him.

"Of course," he replies, moving to stand up.

I grab his hand, smiling as I feel the warmth in my own. "Cash?" I ask, drawing his eyes to mine again. "Would you really want me to tell you if you've done something that makes me uncomfortable?"

"Yes," he answers instantly. "Sascha, you're not just a dumb slave that I keep around for cooking and cleaning. You're not even just a wonderful bed partner, although, trust me, you are that. You might end up being my partner in research, or even in crime, and it's vital that we both be as honest as possible about how things are going. I made a mistake in not telling you about it sooner, and I don't intend to make that mistake again. It was stupid and risky for both of us. However, I can't have you keeping things from me, either. I'm willing to trust you with a lot, Sascha; I hope that the courtesy gets extended both ways."

I squeeze his hand. "I'll tell you if you do something that bothers me," I promise. I'm not lying to him; he hasn't done anything to upset me at all. I'm upset by being a slave. I'm testing him because a slave should expect his master to demand sex, not because he has ever demanded it from me.

He believes me, which doesn't make me feel any better. He doesn't push the issue.

"Get some rest," he says softly, walking to the door. "I hope you feel better in the morning."

It's moments like this that make me start to trust him. He is still cold and hard as ice sometimes, and if I interrupt him, he's quick to snap or correct me. I work to be less sensitive to it, especially after observing him on a video call with one of his associates. He cuts the person down with as much viciousness as he does me, but the business associate doesn't cower and hide, he corrects himself, corrects Cash where he has misconceptions, and moves on. I think back to the times when Cash and I have engaged similarly, and I realize he does respond better to a fight than to sheer submission. He's looking for someone to meet him at his level.

I try to, while still being respectful enough as a slave. It's a fine line, but I start to understand the boundaries quickly, and it becomes clear that he won't hurt me for disagreeing with him, or even for arguing with him. He gets particularly demeaning when he's tired, and one day, I dare to remind him that he's the one who asked for my help, not the other way around. I tell him further that his treatment isn't making me any more likely to get things done well. He bristles, but he doesn't retaliate, and he approaches me next time with a bit more respect in his tone. We both need to be reined in at times.

We work best when we're slightly at odds, each one challenging the other and pushing toward perfection. Worries of pushing too far and ending up sold start to slip from my mind, and the familiar fun of rivalry comes back to me. I was coerced onto the debate team as a student, and despite being antisocial and outperforming everyone else, it was nice to have someone to play the game with. It's still is. Even when I lose the debates, I am pleased to butt heads with someone on an academic level. Sometimes I can even forget, just for a minute or two, that I'm a slave, and he has every right to beat me or sell me or kill me as he does to respond politely to my questions. As much as I spend my time and effort testing and feeling Cash out, sometimes in hurtful little ways, just to see what he'll do, he seems to be putting up as much effort as possible treating me decently. He is as quick as ever to correct or criticize me, but he can take what he gives out, and he's never as dismissive as he used to be. I appreciate it, just like I appreciate the way that he is starting to thaw a little bit. He needs a business partner; I need to feel human again.

We're watching the vidscreen one day, a rare occurrence, since both of us usually prefer to read or browse information on our tablets. But one of us flicks it on, and the other comes along and joins, and for a second, I start to fantasize about what it would be like if we were something different, if we were just friends watching the news together. I never really had many friends, but I think that's what they do, and I think I'd enjoy something like that.

A special comes on the vidscreen about Assessment season, dramatizing all of the associated stories that pop up every year. As usual, there are riots in two or three radical towns, a few reports of a suspected cheating scandal, numerous debates on current politics and next year's prospective officials and what their views are on it. Should the Assessment score cutoff be raised higher, to create more stringent standards, or lowered, since population control is so successful? Can re-education center budgets be cut to free up more funding for college education?

So many free people, fighting about the lives of people that they don't even give the benefit of personhood. It's been four years since I was part of that free people group. I hate being reminded of it, and I get up, all of the happy fantasies I was entertaining just a moment ago effectively spoiled.

I storm into the bedroom that Cash and I share on most nights, flopping into his bed and curling into a ball. A part of me wants to cry, but I've promised myself that I am over this already. I berate myself for feeling so miserable when everything is going well. I try not to think of myself as a stupid, ungrateful slave, but that's what I am. So I lie in bad, curled up like a bug, and feeling about as small.

For once, the sound of my master approaching and the sensation of his weight depressing the bed next to me don't inspire arousal or trepidation, just a dull acceptance. I feel like all the effort I put into caring has gone to waste, and I may as well have just attracted him from the start by spreading my legs and opening my mouth for him to fuck. Nothing else I've done matters, because I'm a slave, and nothing that slaves do matter. I made one meaningful decision regarding my own freedom, and while it may have saved my brother, it has destroyed me.

"Four years, right?" Cash says softly. He's sitting close, but he doesn't touch me, which I appreciate. "Hell of an anniversary."

I don't answer. I can't. I just lie here.

"Sascha, you know you're different," Cash says, and it takes me a moment to process the sentence as something kind, a compliment, an affirmative statement. I know him well enough to trust that he's not just saying nice words; if he's saying it, he means it, and he wants me to know it.

I still doubt it. I huff, still unable to speak, unwilling to put that much effort into it. Why bother arguing or even looking at him?

Effort be damned; Cash grabs me firmly by the arm and wrenches me around, forcing me to lie on my back while he sits above me, his eyebrow raised in amusement.

"Regardless of whether you're free or Demoted, you are extremely bright and capable," Cash says firmly. He doesn't order me to believe it, because he doesn't need to. "You learn amazingly fast. You've mastered my business paperwork better in the past six months than I have in years, and you can be good with people when you want to be. You know all of these things, and you know there is still plenty left for you to do."

A part of me immediately agrees, because that's what I've been conditioned to do, but another part of me rebels, scowling at him. "You just want me to agree to help me with your research."

"I do, but I know you're interested in it, too," he reminds me. I hate that he's right. "Don't be so hard on yourself for something that happened years ago. You're not dead; you have years left to rectify things."

"You don't even know what I did, how can you say that? I made the worst decision of my life."

Cash rolls his eyes. "You're talking to someone who got wrapped up in treason accusations and nearly destroyed years of research. I don't think you had time to make a decision of that magnitude by the time you were up for the Assessment."

I manage a weak smile, because Cash is trying. His dry jokes have become familiar by now, if his willingness to talk isn't. I consider telling him my secret, the one I've held close in spite of everything else. Could it hurt anything? It could, and I realize it the moment I open my mouth. "I took bets with some people that I could pass the Assessment high," I mumble, the shame of lying hopefully covered up by the fact that doing such a thing would be worthy of shame in and of itself. "I thought I was so smart, it didn't matter what I did, I'd still do well. I didn't even finish my Assessment."

Cash smiles at me, his grip on my arm loosening as if he only realizes now that I'm not going to struggle against him. "So all the scare-tactics that they used to try to scare you straight in school didn't work?"

I smile, nearly having forgotten the stupid videos they made us watch of people using drugs or not studying or driving carelessly or any other social vice that they could think of to scare us with. "I kind of used them as an instruction manual," I lie some more, laughing at how ridiculous it is.

"You would," Cash smirks, leaning over to kiss me. It's oddly tender, and I tremble, startled by the fact that he would bother to go out of his way to try to cheer me up like this. "Nothing's ever challenging enough for you on its own, is it?"

Aside from all the lies leading up to it, the statement is true. Sure, I mostly wanted to stupidly, nobly save my brother, but a good ten or fifteen percent was the challenge, seeing if I could do it. I've always wanted to win, to beat the game, to prove myself superior to everyone else. Hell, I even deluded myself through a few weeks of training by viewing it as a challenge, and through everything, the challenges are what keep me going. "I don't like being bored," I admit.

"I do hope I'm providing you with enough challenges now," Cash teases, pulling me on top of him and running his hands over my body lazily. "After all, you do tend to start trouble when you're bored."

I blush. It's such a fucking paternal statement for him to make, only highlighting our differences in power and status and age. He must notice my response, because he smiles at me.

"I'd probably do the same thing," he admits. "I'm never content to just do what I'm supposed to, I've always wanted to change things, to leave my mark, to prove something. I don't think that you're automatically excluded from that because you've been Demoted, Sascha."

I'm silent, considering it. Isn't that the purpose of the Demoted system? Excluding people?

"When you were growing up, what did you want to accomplish?" he asks, curious. "Was there something you wanted to see, something you wanted to do? What did you think you'd be doing for the rest of your life?"

"I don't know," I admit. I've always been rather reactionary. I never bothered to plan, because I knew I would be successful at whatever I tried, and nothing really interested me enough that it stood out over other things. "I just knew that I liked to learn about things, and I thought I'd go on to college, and learn more, and maybe do research or something. Kind of behind the scenes stuff. Academic."

"Then what is stopping you?" Cash points out. "You've been Demoted. So what? Their system doesn't include you, *fine*; it doesn't apply to you, either. Do what interests you in your spare time, and don't worry about funding research or taking a job to put food on the table or any of that. If there's something you need, let me know and I'll get it for you. It's something that most free people don't have at their disposal."

I nod, seeing the logic behind his words. An opportunity to be happy. I'd be a fool to turn it down. I've never wanted fame or recognition. If someone had told me five years ago that I'd be able to spend all day eating gourmet food and having access to anything I wanted, I would have been ecstatic.

But if someone told me that I would be challenged every day, that

I could help to change, if not actually destroy, the system that tore my brother and me apart, that went on to destroy my life? I would have jumped at the challenge. The Assessment ruled my life as a child; as an adult, my status as being Demoted filled that void.

"I want to help you," I say suddenly, placing my hands over his to stop him from distracting me. "I want to work with you, all of it, like you offered. I don't care if it's dangerous, and I don't care if it's hard. I need this."

He smiles and nods, and when I finally let go of his hands, he resumes touching me. "Thank you," he says, smiling at me. "We'll move this to the next level together."

I grab his hands again, shoving them out of the way so I can access him better, kiss him on my terms. He's surprised, but he seems to enjoy it. I'm not joining his research project because he wants me to, and I'm not going to fuck him because he wants me to. I want to.

Chapter 9
Stealth

Cash and I become closer as a few more weeks pass, and we both become more invested in his research. I'm content; what's more, I'm interested in what he's doing. What we're doing, now that I've agreed to be a part of it. The more I learn about it, the more interested and fascinated I am. It's thoroughly grounded in existing research, psychological theory and science. I devour the background information he gives me as quickly as I can, and I pester him about it, when I'm not helping, or when I'm not taking care of paperwork from his day job. It seems like we're so close to being ready; gathering our funding sources, partnering with the right people. I want to see it happen, I want the results already.

He's been down this road before, though, and he's determined not to start until he knows he will finish successfully. He tells me to just wait "a little longer" or "a few more weeks," and it's not satisfying. I want it *now*, as much as I once wanted the Assessment results *now*, and I throw myself into research on the Demoted even more than Cash does. I've been able to read and learn as much as I wanted to since Cash bought me; it's just never held as much appeal as it does now that I have a reason behind it. He encourages me, engages me in discussions, shares my excitement. I forget to be afraid of anything, too eager to see this succeed.

Of course, despite our academic debates behind closed doors, I am still expected to play slave at social functions, whether at my master's legitimate business or at his other business. The work for Dean & Chanu is easier, because I usually don't need to care about it. Cash is polite and cordial, I play the pretty, dumb slave, and all is well.

The words that are spoken mean less than nothing to me, now that I know it is little more than a front. I can relax; sometimes even flirt with coworkers who seem interested in me, because it makes Cash seem more normal. He fits in this way, and I'm happy to help him.

He makes progress toward our research as well, making com calls to strangers, sending messages, even setting up meetings with people in strange places. He lets me in on the details, confiding every illicit act, risky alliance, and shady arrangement. There are no more barriers between us, at least, not on his end. In response, I start to offer him little pieces of my life as well; bits of my history, stories about my childhood, about me and Abriel, things I've always hoped. It's not so terribly painful to consider memories and hopes anymore, because I have new ones. We become more connected, more powerful as a team. He takes me out with him everywhere now, and I make him look like a reputable slaveholder. It's easy to hold my tongue and play nice; now that I know what the stakes are, and what our goal is, it's not a simple test of my obedience. It's smarter to stay quiet and observant than it is to run my mouth, no matter how much I want to.

The project-related social functions are an exciting challenge, because I am completely informed about what is happening now. I understand the subtle hints and turns of phrase between Cash and others as they discuss "the project" in hushed tones, because only some of the people attending really know what they are working on. In general, it seems that everyone in attendance has some sort of underground dealings or secret businesses, but nobody knows who is working on what.

At first, no one but Cash knows the true purpose of his research; even some of his potential backers, like Torenze, think that he is conducting business on more legitimate things. He lets word slip out carefully, through informal channels, that his research is on the re-education centers, and on slaves. He preps me before we go, letting me know that I am to be his ears. After casually mentioning his research interests to a group of people, he glances around, making a show of finding a bathroom.

"Would you mind keeping an eye on my boy?" he asks. "The bathrooms here are so crowded. I'd hate to take up extra space. He'll entertain you, if you want."

They smile amenably, waiting until he's out of earshot to begin discussing him. They pet and play with me as they do, nothing awful, just a hand on my head, or my ass, something like that. Sometimes I even kneel at their feet, innocuous as a house pet, and they speak freely in front of me just the same.

"He's got some interesting ideas," one man comments. "But it's too risky. Messing with the Demoted system is a sure way to get the law after you."

"I don't think it necessarily has to be illegal," another woman comments. I make my way over to her, nuzzling against her legs to be sure I hear her. "There are plenty of good improvements. Besides, the Demoted system is getting past the point of usefulness. Kids today are so obsessed with the Assessment, they do nothing else. It's unhealthy."

"What's unhealthy is fighting that system," another comments, looking at me. "Aren't you worried about your master?"

I smile up, feigning innocence. "Sometimes he can take a long time in the bathroom, ma'am," I reply, smiling at her like I have no idea what she's even asking. "That's probably why he didn't want me to come with him."

They laugh at my expense, and I laugh along with them. They think I'm too clueless to realize the joke is on me; the best part is, the joke is on them all along.

When he returns, he asks what snacks I'd like, and I tell him, rifling off my preferences like a spoiled, flighty slave. "Crackers sound good, but grapes might upset my stomach. A soda would be nice, but not until later. I definitely don't want any pie."

While the other guests smirk at my inane preferences, Cash is listening carefully. We've coded each guest to a particular food; those I'm "craving" correspond to guests who are amenable to the project, and who are privately invited to join with promises of grand financial returns and publicity. The others are the ones who are given the impression that the project is failing, allowing them to withdraw gracefully and forget the project ever existed. They are always surprised when Cash asks them to join, because they can't figure out how he knows. I nibble on my crackers and pretend not to be aware of anything.

Torenze remains our top recruit, and by far the hardest to pin down. The man is slimy and evasive, never committing to one ideal or another, and half the time it is difficult to tell whether he's lying or telling a complete line of bullshit to everyone.

He hints, time and time again, that he'd like to borrow me, inviting Cash over for dinner, asking what he likes to do to me, hinting that he should be allowed to take me into the bathroom for a "sample" of my abilities. It makes me increasingly uncomfortable, and Cash is clearly growing irritated with him as well. At first, the attempts are turned down playfully, insisting that Cash is too fond of me, or that I am not trained well enough, or that Cash just generally doesn't like to share. Finally, the last time that Torenze hints at it, Cash turns him down, right to his face, even grows a little angry with him. As much as it pleases me to see him turned down, and as much as I'm glad not to be shared with him, I can't help but think of the repercussions.

I'm even more worried when Cash tells me that we're desperately in need of his support for the project, and that we'll be attending another event with him the following week.

The week flies by, since I'm actively trying not to think about it, and before I know it, I'm being dressed up and dragged to the event that I absolutely do not want to attend. I know Torenze will be there, as well as some other key players, and I'm worried about all of them. Hell, I'm worried about the ones who aren't involved, because it is as important to keep them out of things as it is to get Torenze into it. I assess the guests, taking note of who is here and who isn't, who is representing which industry and business interest. I know that most of the people here aren't aware of Cash's project. They just see him here as an investor, representing his day job, pretending to be an up-and-coming young businessman. Torenze knows, though, he knows too much, and he's furious at Cash for his earlier refusal to share me. I can tell from the moment he refuses to greet us when we pass by.

We settle in, and I hear Torenze make an off comment about my master to someone, someone who shouldn't know. It's a thinly veiled hint about the scandal that my master caused years ago. Torenze glances at us as he does it, and the challenge is evident in his eyes. I poke insistently at Cash's arm until he attends to it, looking irritated and puzzled by the betrayal his former mentor is threatening.

"Oliver, nobody wants to hear old stories like that," he tries, the lie coming off as awkward from such a confident man. "Why don't you—"

"Well, Cashiel, I could always tell them about more recent research instead?" Torenze suggests, his tone far more benign than his intentions.

I feel my blood pressure rise. I don't know what the fallout of this would be for Cash or for me, and I don't want to find out. I clutch anxiously at Cash's arm, because, as a slave, that's really my only option.

"You know there are a lot of… privacy issues inherent in that," Cash mumbles, tense.

I hate seeing him this vulnerable, so completely at the mercy of someone else. I hate feeling that way myself; somehow it is worse to see my master acting that way. At least I've had practice.

Cash shoots him a desperate look. "I'd appreciate it if the business proposals I've shared with you stay between us, for now."

"Hmm, sharing, what a concept," Torenze points out. He's not pushing any further, but the threat is there, and it is clear. He's retaliating against my master's refusal to share me. Threatening to destroy a business, destroy a man's life, all because a pretty little sex slave isn't up for grabs. I'd feel like Helen of Troy, except I really don't think I'm *that* special. It's the principle of the matter; any slave could take my place for Torenze.

I can't take the conflict, and I decide that recklessness is the best solution. With a little bit of a tug, I break away from Cash's grip, ignoring the furious glare he gives me. I don't care if he rips me away and beats me again; I'd prefer that to watching our project summarily destroyed by this man I hate. It seems that the only weapon I have against Torenze is myself, my body, and I'm willing to put it on the line to shut him up.

Cash is far too proper to fight with me in public. He lets me go, and when he does, I go to Torenze, dropping to my knees at his feet. It's showy, but it works. It's what I'm trained for, and when I'm fully clothed and adequately motivated, I can play the part of pretty sex toy very well.

I don't speak, because I know that Torenze prefers overly formal slaves, and formal training dictates that I'm quiet until I'm spoken to. It also dictates that I don't flinch or bat away the hand that comes down in my hair, petting me appraisingly, as if I'm a show dog. I don't care about the humiliation; I care about my master and our project.

"Well, this is certainly a more interesting topic," Torenze declares. "Such soft hair."

"Yes, sir," I whisper, glancing up at him in the most seductive way possible.

"Is the rest of you this soft?" he teases, coming back to catch me by the nape of my neck, holding me there. It's oddly uncomfortable; it doesn't really hurt, but it's so controlling and done so carelessly that it makes me want to squirm away from it. I know better.

"I have many soft parts, sir," I answer, smiling seductively. The only soft thing right now is my cock; everything else is tense and struggling not to pull away. But I can't embarrass myself and my master that way. I chose this, now I have to follow through.

"He is quite captivating," one of the women conversing points out, oblivious to the power play. Good. It's working. "Wherever did you find such a slave?"

Cash flushes deeply. While he doesn't seem to resent talking about me anymore, he doesn't enjoy it, and he especially doesn't enjoy answering questions about where he got me, because it's completely below him. "It was an off-market," he manages, obscuring the details. "Out of business, now, they weren't really the most reputable. Sometimes, you find gems where you least expect them."

I blush as well, not-so-secretly pleased to hear my master call me something so nice.

"They treated him rather roughly from what you've told me, Cash," Torenze teases, the wink in his eye far more malicious than playful. He's also hinting that he's more familiar than he really is with me or with my master. He knows I'm scarred up because he watched me being beaten, not because we're friends. But nobody watching has any idea about that.

"Not everyone knows how to treat a quality product," Cash dismisses, and I am pleased by his words again. Even though he calls me a product, even though Torenze is pulling a little harder than necessary at my hair and fingering my lips, I'm pleased to hear that my master disapproves of how I was treated.

"Mind if I look him over?" the woman asks, innocently interrupting Torenze's plot with her own curiosity.

"Of course not," Cash answers, smiling more widely than he probably needs to. He's pretending to be cordial, but really, he's as thrilled to get me away from Torenze as I am to get away from him. "Sascha, go to her."

I rise gracefully, assisted unnecessarily by Torenze's hands pulling at my hair, and I walk over to the woman. She smiles at me, motioning for me to stay standing, and she reaches out to squeeze my upper arm, intimate, appraising. It's a little uncomfortable to be evaluated like this, but she's not hurting me. I try to keep my face blank.

"Well, he's as skinny under the clothes as he looks," she teases, and unlike Torenze, it's in good humor. "These young boys sure can keep the weight off, can't they?"

"Sascha is healthy," Cash replies, a little bristly. The woman hadn't meant offense, but my master is tense, and he snaps when he's tense.

I glance at the woman, assessing her to be a lot more relaxed than Torenze. I make my next move carefully, both to distract, and lighten the tension that my master caused. "I get a lot of exercise, ma'am," I say, shy, like I don't notice the innuendo. I smile when I say it.

The people standing around burst into laughter, like they might at a child who unwittingly made a sex joke, and I glance back at my master, pretending to be confused. He doesn't look entirely pleased, but then, he's not one to make a show of himself. I smile, and he returns it, letting me know that we are on the right path.

"Turn around for me, dear," the woman suggests, turning me gently. "Let's have a look at you."

I turn for her, and for the others standing around, and I make sure to smile at Torenze when I pass him, even though I hate the very sight of him. I've orchestrated a situation where he can't really discuss Cash's research any further; it would be entirely out of place, now that there is something else interesting to discuss and look at and even touch. I tolerate the eyes and hands on me, relieved that they are mostly friendly. Torenze pushes it too far, his hand lingering on my ass and squeezing too hard, making me want to squirm away. I whimper, instead, like he's hurting me. While I hate to break protocol, I don't want to give him the impression that this is acceptable, and few people fault a slave for being hurt.

"Someone sure appreciates you, boy," another man says, calling Torenze out on his inappropriate public behavior. "Better run back to your master before someone gets too friendly!"

I give the man an appreciative smile, although it doesn't even come close to how appreciative I really feel. I make a show of scampering back to my master, dropping to my knees and hiding behind his legs, giggling like I'm some sort of trite little boy. Torenze can't fight it, especially when everyone else thinks I am so charming. Even Cash plays along, petting me like he has to reassure me before pulling me to my feet and wrapping his arm around my waist. I cuddle into him, only partly because of show, and I breathe a sigh of relief as the conversation turns to reputable auction houses and memorable slaves that each person has owned in the past.

The rest of the event is tense; Torenze doesn't try anything, but the look on his face says that he wants to, and it's all I can do to shake off the feeling of his grabby fingers. He catches us as we leave, putting an arm around my master and me at the same time, trapping me between them.

"I do hope you'll take me up on my invitation soon, Cash," Torenze hints, his voice threatening. "It would be a pity if I decided you weren't still good partner material."

"I'll look at my schedule," my master mumbles, hurrying out and practically ripping me away from him.

The hov-car ride is quiet at first, and it's me who breaks the silence. I can't handle the tension or the uncertainty.

"Cash... are you going to..." I can't even finish asking, and the irritated glare he shoots my way doesn't help at all.

"No, Sascha, I am not going to give you to that man!" he snaps at me, like he hasn't done it before.

"What about your mother?" I ask. "Isn't she a bigger threat? You said she's pressuring you. Don't we need Torenze to get her to back off?"

"I'll keep you safe from both of them," Cash insists. "You're my responsibility. I'll figure something out, and it will not involve putting you in more danger!"

"All right," I agree, going silent after that. I won't argue about it. I feel a little more comfortable with the reassurance, but I wish we could have discussed it. Torenze scares and repulses me, but the opportunity to further the project might be worth it.

We get home, and we've barely been sitting down for five minutes when the door rings. I sigh, irritated at the interruption. Cash and I have just finished evading this last drama, and now some asshole probably wants to sell us stocks or timeshares or religious views, none of which I am even remotely interested in, not like it's really my decision to make.

Reminding myself to keep my snarky attitude under control, I open the door, and I feel my world implode at the sight of the person in front of me.

"Sascha."

He stands there, looking different than before, but still so much the same. Still exactly how I remember him, over four years later. My heart races.

"Abriel?"

Chapter 10

Visitor

I hear voices in my foyer, and I frown. Sascha isn't much for conversing with strangers, and I'm not expecting anyone. I make my way out quickly, surprised to see Sascha ducking away from someone I don't recognize. The other man looks confused and hurt, and he's looking at Sascha like he knows him.

"Sascha, who is it?" I demand. He stares back and forth between me and this other man, looking completely lost. I haven't seen him this unsettled in a while, and I wonder who this man could possibly be to upset him so.

Finally, he speaks.

"This... this is Abriel."

For half a second, I am confused, wrinkling my brow as I try to place the name. Suddenly, it hits me.

"Your brother?"

Sascha nods, and the room goes silent. His twin does look like him; not identical, but they clearly resemble one another. Of course, the biggest difference is the look of complete shock on Sascha's face.

Abriel is the first to speak. "Mr. Michaud, please, let me introduce myself. My name is Abriel Gabbamonte, I apologize for being so forward, but your slave, see, he's my brother. I've been searching for him for years, and —"

"Where and how did you find this information?" I ask. I'm instantly suspicious of him, and I try to pretend it's not because I know he's going to take Sascha away from me. I try to pretend that I'm just checking my own security, covering bases.

"A lot of sources, sir," Abriel replies vaguely. "I've searched for

Sascha since he was Demoted, followed him through his re-education center and everything. I lost him for a while, but it was important to me, and I made the right connections. Finding your address was quite difficult, but if you look hard enough, you can find anything, and I just kept looking."

I have plenty of security systems in place, and the man doesn't seem to be very efficient, but then, my security system was designed to ward off sophisticated attacks, not diligence and persistence. I'm still suspicious. What if one of my competitors has somehow involved him?

"What are your intentions?"

"I just wanted to see him. To talk to him," Abriel confesses. "And, um, I might have a sort of… business proposal?"

He wants to buy Sascha. It's so obvious, I don't know why he just doesn't come out and say it, but perhaps he and Sascha share the same guardedness. They both share the utter inability to hide their feelings; Abriel reads like an open book. He is delighted to find his brother. Sascha just looks scared, probably because he doubts I'll release him. I should be excited for them both. Abriel is here to take Sascha home. Sascha will be safe with his brother; he won't be the object of Oliver's attentions, and he won't be a pawn for my mother to toy with. All the worries I've had about his safety can be solved by simply letting him go.

"Mr. Gabbamonte, please, come in." I lead Abriel to the living room, with Sascha tagging behind. "If you would please wait here, I will return in just a moment. Sascha, a word."

Sascha obeys, following me into my office. I lean back against my desk, thinking back to the very first day I found him and brought him in here. It was so long ago; it seemed so insignificant in my life. Now, I can barely imagine my life without him.

"Cash…" he starts, confused and scared.

I can't keep him here. He's my property, my slave, my partner in research, but he's also grown dear to me. I told him before that I'd sell him if he didn't participate in my research, but I didn't really think there was anywhere for him to go. I thought he was safer with me. He seemed content just earlier today, but that's only because he had no other option. I couldn't live with myself if I sold him to someone who would harm him, but he'll be safe with his brother. If he stays with me, he's at risk of being used in my plays for power, and that will always come between us. I need his help, but I value knowing he's safe far more. The best thing I can do for him is let him go.

"It's all right, Sascha," I say, pretending to be calm. I can't let him see how much this hurts me. "I know you want to go with him. He's your family. It's only right. You deserve it after all I've put you through."

He nods, confirming my words.

"You can take your things," I tell him, still calm and detached. "While your brother and I are discussing the purchase price, you can pack them up. You can take the tablet I gave you—"

"Cash—"

"—just make sure to flash over anything I might need from you," I continue, ignoring his interruption. I can't bear to discuss anything more than logistics with him. "There are suitcases in the hall closet. Take the brown ones, I like the red ones when I travel. And don't worry about leaving anything, I can have it donated or—"

"Cash, please—"

"Sascha, just go."

I force the words to come out cold and callous. He needs to go, and I need to make him. Admitting my feelings for him will only make it harder for both of us. When he stands there motionless instead, I turn it up. "I still own you, and I won't hesitate to slap you if you don't get moving. Don't make me do that in front of your brother."

It's an empty threat and we both know it, but it gets him moving. He nods and walks away, the hurt visible on his face for only a split second before he looks away from me. It's all happened so fast, but I have to do it. It's better for him. He won't be at risk from being involved in my project, he won't be passed around to men like Oliver Torenze. He can live out his life comfortably with his brother. Maybe I'll even find a way to slip some money into Abriel's credit account when he's not paying attention, make sure they're all taken care of.

I hear Sascha getting the suitcases as I ordered, and I return to the living room, plastering a cordial smile on my face and inviting Abriel into my office. I'm tempted to just give Sascha to him, but he opens with an offer that probably represents his life savings, then asks how much I want for Sascha. There is no price for him, but I don't want to seem disrespectful. I suggest a price nearly double what I paid for him, and Abriel looks at me in shock.

"That's... not much," Abriel says, looking at me suspiciously.

It's a drop in the bucket for me, but for him to realize it's low suggests something wrong.

I force a smile. "He's had some rather rough treatment in the past," I explain. "I got him at a bargain, and I don't want to make a profit off of him. He's been a loyal slave, a hard worker. I hate to let him go."

"That's all you paid for him?" Abriel asks, shocked.

"It's been a while," I try to backtrack. "I don't quite recall the figures. And he's done a lot of work for me in the meantime. Really, he should be with you."

Abriel smiles, pleased that he's making out good on the deal. I hear the ding from my tablet, indicating that Sascha has flashed some data over, and I wonder if I'll ever hear that particular sound again. I'm sure he'll move on, enjoy his family, and forget about me.

I draw up some transfer papers and hand them to Abriel to sign. We finish and shake hands as Sascha returns, overstuffed suitcases in hand.

"That settles it," I say, like this is just another business transaction. "Sascha belongs to you now. It was a pleasure to do business with you."

"Same to you," Abriel agrees. "Come on Sascha, let's go. If we make good time, we should be able to get through the city before rush hour."

Sascha hasn't said a word. He glances between me and Abriel, who looks utterly thrilled. He looks confused, but I'm sure he'll be fine. He just needs to let me go.

"Thank you, sir," he finally says. He looks crushed, but I want him to leave. I want to do something, to tell him goodbye, to kiss him one last time, to grab him and refuse to let him go. But I can't. When he doesn't make a move, I assume it's the right decision.

I nod. "I wish you the best, Sascha."

I stand there and watch as Abriel pulls him out the door, full of excitement. I think Sascha should feel that way, too, but he has always been reserved. He looks back at me, and I can't stand the look of rejection on his face, so I close the door and lock it tightly behind me. The house seems too big now that I'm alone.

It seems no smaller in the next few days. I glance at Sascha's room, see the clothes he's left scattered about. Some remain in my room as well, and I can't bring myself to take them out. It's stupid, moping over a slave, but he had become so much more to me. I struggle to complete the massive workload I have now that he's gone; not only am I left with all of the work from my day job and the research, but everything I do reminds me of Sascha.

I think about contacting him, but I don't. It's better to have a clean break. He wouldn't want some clingy master harassing him. I light up when I hear the sound of my tablet announcing a message from him again, but it's only work information he hadn't finished before he left. Nothing else accompanies it, not so much as a casual greeting. He must have moved on already. If he could do so that quickly, it must have been for the best. I try to convince myself that he's happy, happier than he ever was with me.

Oliver calls me a few days after I sell Sascha, only confirming my belief that I did the right thing.

"Cash, my boy, are you ever going to let me play with your pretty pet?" he asks, not even bothering to say hello, first. "You don't want word getting around the professional circle that you're greedy, now, do you?"

"I would," I tell him, too despondent to even gloat. "But I sold him."

"What?" Oliver demands. The annoyance is clear in his voice. I've offended him.

"His brother hunted him down and made me an excellent offer," I force myself to lie. "I can buy myself a real pretty one, now. Not all scarred up, not so damn mouthy. I'm thinking of getting a fresh one, one of the premiere ones from the re-education centers."

"Well, isn't that convenient," my former mentor pouts. "Planning on keeping the new one all to yourself, too?"

"He was just another slave, Oliver," I force myself to say, trying to believe it. "You go through new ones every few months. And of course I'll let you borrow the new one—just as soon as I acquire one."

"I could find a good one for you," he offers. "I have a few more connections left than you do. Or have you reconnected with more than just me?"

Will I be stuck partnering with him now, instead of Sascha? I reject the thought. "I've re-established a few connections," I reveal. "And I've made a lot of new ones. The playing field has changed in the last decade. I like the new blood."

"Always trying to show up your mommy, aren't you?" Oliver taunts.

"She's not my mother anymore," I snap. Oliver always has the ability to make me feel like a wayward child. "Besides, you're not working with her anymore, either. You got a little too close to what she was working with, and you were gone, too, just not as bad as I was. Kristine Miller's reign of the re-education centers needs to come to an end."

"While I agree with that, can't you find some other wealthy person to fund you?" Oliver asks. "What do I bring? I washed my hands of the re-education centers when I washed my hands of your mother. I'm doing well with my medical research."

"You're connected, and you're not afraid of her," I admit. Oliver was one of the few people who had never been too afraid of my mother. "You've made it quite clear that you want to see her fail, and your current projects aren't doing that. Work with me, and you can be part of the new re-education system that destroys her."

"Ah, yes," Oliver says, cool and evasive. "Your little research project. You really think it will work, this time. But why do you think I'd be so eager to join?"

"Because we have the same goals," I admit. I hate being on the same side as this monster. "We both win with this. I get my research funding; when it goes through, you get first dibs at restructuring the medical research. You've said it yourself; that's where the money lies, and that's where your interests lie."

"*If* it goes through, Cashi," he reminds me. "Which is a big if. I liked the deal better when there was something to sweeten it."

I'm glad I let Sascha go. The things Oliver would do to him... "You can get whores by the dozen," I remind him. "Sascha was nothing special."

"If that was true, I think you would have found time to let me sample him before letting his brother rescue him," Oliver reminds me. He's clearly onto my game, and he's not happy about it. "I have no interest in doing business with someone who wastes his time coddling slaves instead of focusing on what's important. One thing about your mother, she always had her priorities in order. You could have learned that lesson from her."

"Oliver, I saw a good sales opportunity and I took it," I insist, knowing I'm lying as much as he does. "I'll make it up to you when we partner."

"If it was just about money, I'd partner with your mother again," Oliver says casually, as if it's not a threat.

"You'd do that just to spite me?" I ask, in disbelief. "You hate her."

"Well, I wouldn't partner with her, but she'd pay dearly for what I know about your project," Oliver comments. "I don't appreciate having to beg for what I want. I've tolerated your reluctance long enough because I was fond of you once, and I still believe you have great ideas. But cross me again and I'll make the week you spent in the re-education center as a boy look like a trip to a theme park."

I shudder, recalling the torture he supervised at my mother's orders. He viciously exploited everything I was afraid of back then, and he's doing his best to do it again. But I'm not afraid of him anymore; I want to use him. I need him on my side. "I will be the best partner for you. We have the same goals. Now that the slave is out of the way, I can focus on business. You will have my complete loyalty."

"I'll think about it," Oliver tells me. "Let me know if you do get someone special."

He hangs up, leaving me even more frustrated. The feeling only increases when my mother coms me the following day, and I have no doubts that the two are connected. Oliver and my mother aren't on good terms, but they move in the same business and social circles, as do I. I wish I had moved out of town years ago, but the best slave industry connections are here.

"I hear you sold your slave," my mother starts off. "If you're in the market for a new one, I'm sure one my centers could arrange something. Your birthday's coming up; well, your old one is. Did we make the new one the same?"

"You didn't com me to offer to buy me a birthday present," I snap. Those sorts of motherly gestures stopped when she disowned and disinherited me. "What do you want?"

"I wanted to remind you of our agreement," she states, her tone going from taunting to cold. At least this is honest. "I hear you're networking in my circles."

"And I hear you're getting old and irrelevant," I retort. I've been careful. Nothing I've done in public has been forbidden by any of our agreements. Everything has been hidden, except from me, Sascha, and Oliver.

"I'd stay away from Oliver Torenze if I was you," she cautions. "He'll turn on you, same as he did on me."

"Funny," I reply. "I could have given him the same advice regarding you."

"Just stick to your little financial game, Cashiel," she warns. "I will not have my name associated with scandal again!"

"We don't share a name anymore, remember?" I snap at her.

"Just watch out, or you and your little whore will be in for a surprise."

"My little whore is irrelevant," I retort. "Remember? I sold him."

"There will be more slaves, Cashiel," she warns. "There always is, with you. And their actions reflect on you. It would be quite a pity if someone had to come investigate the mansion I paid for, wouldn't it? A formal investigation, not just a social visit. Could you imagine a team of trained investigators, searching your home, searching whichever new slave you have by then? What sorts of secrets do you think we could dig up if we obtained a full, legal warrant to everything you've ever cared about?"

I seethe, wondering if I will ever get out from under her thumb. She's already intruded on my house, terrified my slave, poked and pried and prodded into my life. If it hadn't been for Sascha, she would have found out far more than she ever needed to, enough to get me into legal trouble again. I don't know why I don't just hang up on her, but defying her so blatantly has never worked out well. "If you're done talking about the hypothetical future, I have work to do."

"Then, by all means, get to it."

She hangs up on me, and I spend the rest of the night double- and triple-checking the security of everything I'm working on. I know it's tight, utterly inaccessible from anywhere other than this house. I just hope it's enough. Sascha is far safer with his brother.

Chapter 11

Found

When Abriel pulls me out the door, I'm too stunned to do much of anything else but follow him. I don't know if I'd ever take my eyes off of Cash, except he shuts the door as we exit, and I hear it lock behind us, locking away that part of my life. Somehow, the bags make it into the trunk of Abriel's hov-car, and once my hands are free, he captures me in a hug, the likes of which I haven't felt since the day of the Assessment. I panic a bit at first, but I relax quickly, letting him hug me and tell me how worried he was and all that sort of reunion shit. Finally, he lets me go, and I make it into the seat of the hov-car, and we're driving.

"So, uh, it's been a long time."

Abriel has never been much of a conversationalist; that much hasn't changed.

"Yeah." I used to guide all the conversations, but I *have* changed. I haven't guided anything but a cock into my ass in years, and it's not like riding a bicycle. I don't remember how, and I certainly don't want to figure it out again with my brother. I stare at the part in his hair instead, wishing it was more even. He never parted it evenly, and it always annoyed me.

"You have no idea how much I've gone through to find you," Abriel says, proud and satisfied with himself. Maybe his world isn't blown like mine is. "I never stopped looking, not from the moment they announced the Assessment results. God, Sascha, it's so good to see you!"

"Thanks," I manage. "It's good to see you, too."

"Did he, uh, did he treat you all right? That rich guy?"

He has a name! I snap inside my head, but I don't say it. Abriel doesn't deserve to be snapped at. He's doing something most people don't even try to do for their Demoted family members. "He was very good to me," I manage. "He cared about me in his own way."

"Yeah, he said as much," Abriel agrees. "You're jumpy, though— did he hurt you?"

How do I even answer this? Of course he did, but no, not really. Not like the others. "No," I settle with the answer he wants to hear. "But things were rough before him."

"Yeah. I heard about the brothel you were at." Abriel makes a face. "Sounds awful, although that was where I got that guy's name from, so I guess they're good for something."

I just nod. I don't want my brother to know what happened to me, not all of it. I know Cash wouldn't have told him much, either. I've been protecting Abriel all my life; I need to keep protecting him from this. Let him guess what he wants, he doesn't need to know all the details. We can move on with our lives normally now, no need to dwell on the sad things that make up my past.

"You've got a bunch of stuff," Abriel observes. "Must be nice, having a rich master and all."

"Yeah," I say, because I nodded to the last question. "Money wasn't a problem."

Abriel laughs. "Well, it's not as free flowing at home, but we do all right."

There. A change of subject. Good. "You and Maggie?" The girl my brother had dated all through high school had been sweet and hopelessly in love with him. I think if she could have sacrificed herself to save him from the Assessment, she would, but that would never have worked out. It had to be me; I had to trade myself for him.

Abriel shakes his head. "No, uh, Maggie and I… we stopped seeing eye to eye, if you know what I mean."

"Oh." I guess it makes sense. People move on, grow up. Just because they were together all through high school doesn't mean that they still would be. It's weird to think of Abriel with anyone else, though.

"I'm married," Abriel announces, grinning. "Her name's Lisa. We have a daughter, Bella. She's going to be four in a few months."

Holy shit. Holy shit. I'm an uncle? I think about the timeline. "Whoa, you got some chick knocked up when you were barely out of high school, then?"

Abriel turns red, keeping his eyes focused on the road. "Bella wasn't planned, no. But Lisa and I got married and did things the right way. Her family is pretty conservative, and so is she. Listen, Sascha, don't let her hear you say things like 'knocked up,' she'll take it the wrong way."

I think that if she was so conservative, maybe she shouldn't have fucked my little brother and made a baby with him, but I choose not to say this out loud. Five years ago, I would have said it in a heartbeat, but slavery has changed me at least enough that I can bite my tongue *sometimes.*

"She's a great person," Abriel insists, a little too forcefully. "And I'm working with her family's business. I'm really part of their family now."

That strikes me as strange. "What about mom and dad?" Something that died inside of me years ago lights up at the idea of seeing them again. The disappointment that I know they would have written across their faces at my decision would be worth it to see them and explain my plan and reunite with them and Abriel, like old times.

"They're fine," Abriel says, dismissively.

His tone tips me off. I start to panic, wondering if something has happened to them, shit, they're not that old, and they were in good health, but things happen. "Abriel, what happened? Are they okay?"

"Sascha, they're *fine*," he snaps.

I draw back out of habit, barely resisting the urge to cower away. The other half of me wants to give Abriel a smack for snapping at me, or maybe tease him about being touchy. Instincts tell me to protect myself, but this is my goddamned brother! We used to have tickle wars and play pranks on each other. I can't flinch away from him! What's really true is that I can't reconcile the two lives I've had.

"Sorry," he mutters, fixating on the road. "It's kind of a sore subject. Nothing to be concerned with. Look, Sascha, I'm just closer with Lisa's family now, okay? They've helped me out a lot and with Bella and all... I just don't talk to mom and dad that much now, okay? Let it go."

"Yeah, all right." I resist the urge to say "yes, sir," or maybe even "yes, master." When did my little brother get so serious and closed-off? He used to be so friendly, so transparent—has he really grown up so much?

He clears his throat, ending the conversation, and rather awkwardly moving it to something else. "So, uh, anyway, what were you doing? For that rich guy. You seemed pretty comfortable there."

I really was. More comfortable than I can think about without tearing up, at the moment. "Nothing special," I lie. "Just helping him out with work, you know, filing, fetching things, cleaning up around the house. Oh, and I learned to cook."

Abriel laughs. "Well, you always did like to eat," he attempts to joke.

It goes quiet for a minute.

"So, uh, a brothel?"

I wish it had stayed quiet. "Yeah."

"What, did he buy you as some kind of sex slave or something?" Abriel's face shows his disgust. I guess I might have felt the same way if our roles were reversed. I wonder if he's disgusted with me or with Cash.

"No, he, uh, he just bought me for work," I say. It's partially true. "He wasn't really interested in that." How do I tell him that I *wanted* the sex we had? Would that disgust him, too?

Abriel nods. "That's good. Glad to hear."

The rest of the ride, thankfully, is silent. I feel myself drifting off as we drive, the view starting to darken as day turns into night, and I wonder briefly how far we have to go before we get to his house. *My new home,* I realize, still startled. But I can't shake the feeling that I've left my home behind.

I'm jerked awake as we make a sudden turn off the highway and onto a smaller street. Ah, suburbs. I glance questioningly at Abriel, wondering if this is really it. It's so close to where Cash and I lived— maybe a few hundred miles. For so long, my brother and I have been this close and had no idea. It's so far from where we both grew up.

"Hey, Sascha, remember how I said Lisa and her family are pretty conservative?"

Abriel must have noticed I was awake. He's always been observant like that, paying attention to people in the same way I pay attention to information. "Yeah?"

"Well, uh…" Abriel shifts, uncomfortable, as he pulls into a driveway leading up to the most average house I've ever laid eyes on. "Just… watch yourself around her, you know? She's not so keen on the idea of having a slave that's not traditional."

A slave? Traditional? Fuck, I thought I was his goddamned brother, making Lisa my sister-in-law. "Um, sure, whatever you say, man. Sounds fine." He's probably just overreacting. Either that, or I am. He can't mean for me to be a fucking slave for real.

He gets out of the car, prompting me to follow him, and opens the trunk. "Grab your bags," he mumbles. "I'll show you your new home."

I carry my bags, glad to have something to do with my hands. He probably wants his hands free to unlock the door and stuff. I follow Abriel inside silently, trying not to think of myself as a slave following his master. But then, would that be the better way to think of it?

I brush the thought aside as a woman comes to the door to greet us, pulling Abriel in for a surprisingly possessive kiss. I stand there awkwardly as the woman seems to put on a show for me, unless she makes out with my brother every night when he gets home. I resist the urge to shudder at the thought. Call me a prude, but watching my brother play tonsil hockey with his wife every day is not something I'd enjoy.

"So, you found the slave?" she says, finally sparing a glance at me. Her eyes scan me once, up and down, like a barcode. A blink, and she's disregarded me.

"Yeah," Abriel says, a sex-drunk smile on his face. "Lisa, this is Sascha, my brother."

"Well, we can't very well have him sleep in the doorway, now can we?" She asks, and I wonder if that's not exactly what she'd like to do with me. "Show him to his room, Abe, and if you hurry, you'll have time to tell Bella goodnight. She didn't realize you'd be gone this long, you know. She gets upset."

"Sure thing," Abriel smiles at her. "C'mon, Sascha."

"Uh, nice to meet you," I fumble, startled when I'm not even given a second glance. I follow behind Abriel as he leads me to a small, stark room.

"The bathroom's just down the hall," Abriel tells me, as if I couldn't have figured it out. "I'll show you around more tomorrow, but it's getting pretty late and we're probably going to be going to bed. There's a whole night time routine. Bella doesn't sleep well if there's noise."

"Sure thing," I mumble, realizing I'm effectively being put to bed. I guess this was a disruption, though, maybe that's why Lisa was so put out.

"Abe?" I ask, trying to keep myself from laughing. "I thought you hated that nickname."

"Don't make a big deal out of it, Sascha," he mutters. "Lisa thinks it's cute."

I figure she must be damn good in bed, because I know my brother *hated* that nickname. "All right, loverboy," I give in, trying to tease him a little. "And Abriel, thank you so much. I can't imagine the work you must have put into finding me."

"Yeah," Abriel shrugs. "Goodnight, Sascha. I'll see you tomorrow."

I'm left alone, in the small, strange room. It's weird, I can hear them down the hall, Abriel and Lisa, and they don't sound happy. Not the best time for me to have dropped in, but I'm sure they'll get over it. Married couples bicker, right?

I start to unpack my few belongings, marveling at how impressed Abriel was by what I brought with me. At best, I have maybe a third of the clothes that Cashiel bought me, but it's clear they won't all fit in the tiny closet or the tiny dresser provided. I sigh as I rearrange some of them in one of the suitcases, figuring I can just stack it on top of the dresser for a while. Until… well, I don't know until what, because I have no idea what is planned for me. The old sense of fear and vulnerability threatens to take hold, as I realize that my life is again in someone else's hands. But it's all right, because it's Abriel. I think.

I always thought I would be safe if I was with my brother, but I have never felt more like a slave.

Chapter 12

Home

I wake up the next morning with the sun in my eyes. The bedroom that Cash and I share, or I guess, *shared* is more accurate now, that had a beautiful view, but it also had a beautiful set of blinds and curtains. No such luck, here. I glance at my watch, surprised by how late it is. I didn't sleep well last night, too full of confusion and unanswered questions and paranoid thoughts.

The fact that it has been weeks since I've slept alone didn't help.

I lie in bed until the call of nature forces me up, and I stumble to the bathroom. Returning to my new bedroom, I get dressed and comb my hair, delaying the inevitable. Finally, I head toward the kitchen where I can hear Lisa and a small child speaking. Bella. My niece. It's still amazing to think that I'm an uncle; Abriel is a dad. Weren't we just kids? Being parents and uncles is something adults do. How is my brother doing this already? He's only twenty-two, the same as I am; he should be partying and looking at graduate schools. Isn't that what life is supposed to be for free people?

I enter the room quietly, wishing Abriel was with me as I sit at the table. A little girl sits across from me, coloring neatly on a page full of block letters and numbers. Three goddamned years old, and already preparing for the Assessment. I remember Abriel and I doing the same activities at her age, except Abriel colored more neatly and quietly than I did, and I was more interested in writing the letters on my own and finding out why they had been given stupid names like "double u" when it was clearly a "double v."

"Hi there," I manage, hoping today will go better than last night. I get to meet the next generation of my family, and that thought alone brightens my mood. "You must be Bella."

The girl looks up at me, her expression cold and dismissive. It's frighteningly similar to the one I saw on her mother's face last night. "Slave," she announces, as if it answers everything.

Maybe it does.

Lisa walks in, her lips pressed tightly together. She places a hand on Bella's shoulder. "You may call him 'Slave Sascha,' darling." Her eyes are on me as she says it, almost challenging.

No, not "Uncle Sascha" or anything.

"Slaves sit on the floor," Bella announces, calmly picking up another crayon. "Like at Grampa's house."

"Daddy has different rules for our house, Bella," Lisa corrects her mildly. "We've talked about different rules, haven't we?"

"Yes, mommy," Bella answers obediently before holding out her paper. "Look, mommy, I colored the 'B' blue, because that's what blue starts with, and that's what my name starts with!"

"Good girl," Lisa smiles, petting her head.

"Good. Girl. Green!" Bella announces. "I'm gonna color the 'G' green! I bet I know more than Slave Sascha about letters."

It seems my niece is quite a little bitch. "Wait till you get to 'Z,'" I mutter.

Lisa glares at me. "I suppose *you* are hungry?"

"Yeah, we kind of missed dinner last night," I shrug, figuring Abriel just forgot or something. He always did tend to be the type to get caught up in things. Both of us did, really, and yesterday was definitely pretty exciting. I can see how we forgot dinner. "We should have stopped for something on the way home last night."

"My husband missed dinner because he went to pick *you* up the moment he received the message letting him know where you were," Lisa informs me. "I've told him plenty of times that if he can't make time to eat a healthy dinner with his own family, he certainly doesn't need to waste money eating from some restaurant."

"Oh…" I say, unsure of how to respond. It's one thing that slaves are starved, but when did it become okay to do this to a free person? How is my brother putting up with this? "I, uh… I guess I missed breakfast, too?"

Lisa frowns. "Well, Abriel insisted I keep something for you, but in the future, if you can't bother to make it up for breakfast, you can wait until lunch."

She disappears behind a wall, and I try to hide the shock on my face. Either she's a rotten bitch, or I've inconvenienced her beyond belief with the simple act of existing.

She returns quickly with a bowl of oatmeal and a plate with scrambled eggs and toast. It's obvious they've been sitting out getting cold, but I figure it's wiser not to complain. I hate oatmeal, but I don't want to risk offending her and being sentenced to starve.

I force myself to eat, rising quickly to clear the dishes away when I've finished. "I can cook, you know, if you want some help around here."

"I am perfectly able to take care of this house by myself," Lisa snaps. "Who do you think has been taking care of Bella and her father for the past four years? I don't need some charity case slave trying to poison us."

"Right," I agree. "Just thought I could be helpful."

"Well, thinking obviously isn't your strong suit, is it?"

I don't bother to respond. If she wants to treat me like shit, fine, but I'm not going to participate in it.

"Don't think you can just sit around and do nothing," she warns, despite the fact that she just snapped at me for offering help. "Your brother might accept that, but I most certainly won't. There are plenty of things that could be cleaned around here, and some laundry to be done. I suppose you can be useful; it will free up more time for me to get Bella ready to start school."

"Okay," I shrug, hoping that if I just seem helpful enough, I can thaw out her frosty meanness. Maybe she resents me for taking Abriel away from her, hell, maybe she resents our whole family for getting her knocked up. I'm no therapist, and I'm certainly no mind reader. But I can tell she doesn't like me.

"And I expect you to address me properly, boy," she tags on. "Just because my husband lets you get away with acting like a free man, don't expect the same from me."

Or, maybe she just doesn't like slaves.

So that's how it's going to be. "Yes, mistress," I reply, hoping that the glare isn't obvious, and that my tone isn't as haughty as I think it is.

I spend the day doing pointless tasks, the likes of which Cashiel would have turned his nose up at. I still clean for him, or at least, I did, but since he and I started working more closely together on things that matter, he no longer cares if things are spotless. A quick cleaning every other week or so took care of most of it, and he even helped sometimes. Lisa has me washing laundry, cleaning the toilets, dusting, and even weeding the stupid flower garden outside. Aside from the laundry, everything else seems clean enough already, but I don't complain. It's easy enough work, and I certainly don't hurry to do it. If anything, it helps time to pass until Abriel gets home from work. I can only hope he'll straighten this out.

Dinner is equally awkward. Abriel places himself next to me, and most of the meal is consumed with silence, or with the mindless chatter of the little girl, who talks over everyone in order to boast about her latest accomplishment (drawing an anatomically correct bunny), and goal (to learn how to make people fly so *she* could fly see her grandparents even though she isn't old enough to drive a car). Abriel attempts to say a few sentences to Lisa, and is cut off by his daughter. He doesn't even dare to directly address me. Looking in my direction is enough to make Lisa glare and Bella whine. I was pretty self-absorbed at that age, like all kids, but I'm pretty sure I lacked her absolute disregard for others. Our parents never would have tolerated that, much less encouraged it. Hell, at that age, all I wanted to do was make sure Abriel had the sharpest crayons, the biggest piece of cake, the fork with the handle with stars on it that he liked, even though he couldn't really draw a star yet. Where did my little brother go?

I retreat to my room after dinner, lying on my back and staring at the ceiling. I suppose I could do something on my tablet, but I don't want to. What I want to do is cry.

Abriel comes in without knocking.

"Hey, Sascha," he sits next to me on the bed. "You doing okay?"

"Yeah," I lie. "It's just a big change. I'm sure I'll get used to it."

"I'm sure," he agrees. "Lisa tells me you were a lot of help around the house today, thanks for that. I wish I could stay home more, but Bella's pretty attached to her mommy, and I guess… I don't know. I'm sure Lisa's better able to get her prepared. We decided it would be better for her to stay home instead of hiring a nanny."

I doubt that Bella would be such a budding little monster if Abriel spent more time with her. He was the friendliest kid ever. Why doesn't he think that he would do a good job with her?

I wonder if Abriel knows about the Assessment, knows what I did back then. He's got to have some clue. I don't ask, though, because that's just not something I can talk about, and I have an even bigger problem I want to address anyway.

"Abriel, what am I doing here?" I ask, unable to contain it. "I mean, is there anything you want me to do, or…?"

Abriel gives me a funny look. "Sascha, I bought you so you weren't being treated like shit. Or… you know, raped or whatever horrible things they do to slaves. I don't need a slave — hell, the only reason I could even afford you is I've been saving up ever since the Assessment to rescue you when I could. Just, I don't know, hang out. Help Lisa around the house. That sort of thing. There's nothing else you need, is there?"

No, nothing else. Not a purpose in life, a reason to exist, a reason to get out of bed every day. Not someone who actually cares about me sometimes. I can't put this all into words, especially without sounding completely and totally ungrateful. "No. I'm set."

"Good." Abriel is still smiling as he walks out the door. He has no idea.

The next few days pass similarly. I occupy the role of mindless drone, Lisa glares at me and talks to me like I'm missing the better part of my frontal lobe, Abriel is clueless, and even little Bella looks down at me.

She catches me walking by one day, on my way to finish up some more pointless work that I've been given.

"Slave Sascha!" the little demon demands, a haughty look on her face. "You will come and join my tea party!"

My heart softens a little bit, because I think that maybe she's going to try to befriend me. To be fair, I haven't seen her play with any other kids, or even heard of a play date outside of pre-preschool, and I think that maybe her evil bitch mother just hasn't socialized her properly.

"All right," I crouch down on one of the little toy chairs, careful not to put too much weight on it.

"No!" she throws a plastic fork at me. "Slaves sit on the floor! This is *my* tea party and *my* rules are like at Grampa's house!"

I roll my eyes and drop to the floor, starting to cross my legs before her glare prompts me to my knees.

"Good Slave Sascha," she smiles at me, and her eyes are as cold and dark as her mother's.

I suffer through a half hour of her "play," which mostly involves me pouring all the imaginary tea for the dolls, and fetching play cakes for them, and shining their shoes. What the hell? Since when did three-year-olds play like this?

I've had about all I can take when I finally get up, about to return to the work I'm supposed to be doing.

"Slave Sascha, where are you going?" she demands.

"I've got work to do, kid," I mutter. Cleaning toilets would be preferable to this.

"You stay here!" she demands, stomping her little foot. "Or I'll tell mommy and she'll be very angry and she'll punish you!"

She's got me. She's got me by my sterilized balls.

"Oh, and my name isn't 'kid,' it's 'Miss Bella,'" she announces, turning her nose up. "You'd better bemember it."

Bemember. I'm being fucking held hostage by a toddler who can't even pronounce the fucking word "remember."

Turns out that I would much rather take a bloody whipping than play "tea party" with an arrogant three-year-old for two hours, because that's how long it lasts. I haven't seen her this interested in anything else for two hours, but she seems absolutely delighted at making me make the shoes "shinier" and screeching at me for letting Queen Polly Dolly's imaginary tea get cold. At least her cutting remarks and childish threats are enough to guarantee that I don't accidentally walk by her playroom again.

I'm miserable by the end of the week, but house is spotless, thanks to the list of chores that Lisa gives me every day once Abriel leaves. I wonder if he knows, or if he cares. I don't tell him, because it would just sound like I'm complaining, and he doesn't ask. I pretend that he just thinks I'm spending the day at home with his family, having a good time. Lisa is at least a little more cordial to me when he's home, maybe she's lying to him about everything.

We talk sometimes. Yesterday he even took me out for a walk —

yes, it felt *just* like that, like I was a pet being taken out for a walk, but it was still nice to talk to him outside of the house. I can't bring things about Lisa up with him, and he clearly doesn't want to hear about my life as a slave, and we're left with little to talk about. Sometimes he'll tell stories from his first year in college, before Bella, but he's vague about it. From what I can tell, he just drank a lot and looked for me. He doesn't mention our parents at all, except to repeat that they're in good health when I ask him directly. He keeps things pretty generic, talking about work, or his hopes for Bella, or stories from back when we were kids. I enjoy that part the most, in a bittersweet sort of way. I don't refer to him directly, especially not when we're in mixed company. I don't refer to any of them directly, except Lisa, when Abriel is gone, and then I call her "mistress" like she's ordered me to. I hate her, and it isn't wearing off.

But I am at least following her orders, doing what she asks, and I'm quickly out of work to do. She's taken Bella to pre-preschool or some sort of enrichment class—she has at least one every day—so I take the time to flop down on my twin-sized bed, pulling out my tablet for the first time. If nothing else, I have books to read on here, news to catch up on. Lisa has made it very clear that I am forbidden to access anything from their underdeveloped library. The tablet reminds me of Cash, which hits a bitter note, but I remind myself that I'm here now, in my new home, with my family. This has to be better, right? This was what I wanted, always.

Intellectual stimulation is wonderful, and my tablet is full of it. I'm engrossed in what I'm doing, so much so that I don't hear Lisa come into my room.

She snatches the tablet from my hands. "Where did you get this?" she demands.

I sigh. "My old master gave it to me." At her glare, I fight against rolling my eyes and add on, "Mistress."

"What does a stupid slave need a tablet for?" she snaps. "Reading some sort of low-brow trash, I'm sure."

Actually, I was finishing up reading the research that Cash had flashed over to me a few days before he sold me, some complicated psychological theories of slavery and freedom and training. The other screen will show a few business proposals that I had been studying.

"My master gave it to me," I repeat, wishing I had never taken it out during the day.

Lisa rolls her eyes. "Well, it's obvious that *you* don't need such a nice piece of technology. Perhaps I'll see if Bella's ready for a tablet by now; she should have the coordination."

I seethe, but I know better than to correct her. I'll talk to Abriel about it later; it will do me no good to fight with this woman. "Can I at least clear some things off it, then, *mistress*?"

She glares at me. "Don't get smart with me, Sascha, just because your brother spoils you doesn't mean I will."

Spoils me? Hell, he lets her treat me like a fucking prisoner! "Mistress, I just wanted to take off anything that might be inappropriate for Bella," I manage, unable to stop sneering at her.

"Disgusting," she snaps. "The things you must have put on here— let me guess, you were looking at *pornography*?"

Pornography. She says it like it's unheard of, like it's the most corrupt and dirty thing she's ever imagined. "Among other things," I snap, wishing I could send her to the brothel for just one day to see what corrupt and dirty really means. "Things your pretty little face has probably never seen. Lots of gay stuff. Anal. Just men fucking men fucking other men. Maybe even some animals. Kinky like you wouldn't even know how to imagine."

She slaps me.

I'm stunned more than hurt, but it hurts, too, the fucking bitch hits hard. I sit there and glare at her, and she grabs me by the jaw, forcing me to look at her.

"If you *ever* speak to me like that again, I'll see to it that you're whipped," she threatens. "My husband might be too sentimental to sell you, but there are far worse things than being sold. Stay in your place, slave, or I'll find a way to make sure you do."

I don't answer, and she fortunately doesn't require me to as she turns to leave, taking my tablet with her. She pauses in the doorway. "Don't bother coming out for dinner. I'll tell my husband that you're feeling ill."

Right. Because she's going to starve me, too. Fucking bitch. I don't respond as she slams my door, but I shudder when I hear it lock. I'm a prisoner where I'm supposed to be home.

Chapter 13

Boundaries and Plans

It's the next morning before the bitch lets me out, after Abriel has left for work, and I have to piss badly enough that I'm actually honest when I say, "Thank you, mistress."

I'm on edge all day, I can tell that she's waiting for me to fuck up. All I want to do is talk to my brother and get this figured out. What else can I do?

I'm afraid of her. I don't want to be. I want to believe that my brother will keep me safe, but he isn't, and I don't know if he will. I have learned to identify threats as a slave, and she clearly is one, and I hate it. I feel my whole body tense up at just hearing her walk through the house.

She can't hide me away forever. The first thing Abriel does when he comes home from work the next day is demand to see me. Lisa leaves to take Bella for her modern dance class, so I'm relieved to have the chance to talk freely with him.

"Sascha, is everything all right? You look, I don't know, nervous or something. That stomach flu still bothering you?" The look on his face indicates that he has no idea at all what's wrong, and I want to slap him for being so thick and trusting his evil bitch wife.

"Abriel, I wasn't sick, she locked me in my room and wouldn't let me out," I snap, suddenly offended. I intend to shock him, to snap him out of the daze she has him in.

"What happened?"

What happened? What happened is *not* what I am expecting to hear. "Does it matter?" I yell, enraged. "I talked back to her and she hit me and then she locked me in my room!"

Abriel goes pale. "Shit, Sascha, I'm sorry."

He should be sorry. He should be more than sorry. Sorry would be acceptable if she yelled at me or ignored me all day. He should be horrified, like I have been, and he should be trying to find a fucking solution to this.

"What did you say to her?" he asks.

"Nothing much, she just took my fucking tablet—by the way, my tablet? She took it to give to Bella and I asked if I could take the inappropriate things off, and she suggested I was looking at porn, and I was pissed off at her so I described the kind of porn that might have been on it and she slapped me!"

Abriel goes quiet for a minute and I wait, hoping he's got a plan for how to deal with this. It's not like I'm expecting him to leave his wife over one little altercation, but I want to hear some sort of plan from him, some sort of reassurance that he'll at least *attempt* to keep me safe in the future.

"Sascha, you really shouldn't be saying those kinds of things to her," he says, feebly.

My jaw drops.

"Look, I know you've had some pretty tough times, but that doesn't mean you should be talking about things like that." He can't even look at me as he says it. It's like he's reciting lines from a play he doesn't even particularly like. "Lisa's not from a world like that, and Bella shouldn't be—"

"Bella was nowhere around!" I snap. "And your *wife* didn't even bother to let me take anything off the tablet, and there are plenty of things on there that a child shouldn't see, which is aside from the fact that it's my goddamned tablet in the first place!"

"She does need one," Abriel changed the subject. "I mean, at least when she goes to school. All the other kids will have one, and we want her to stay competitive."

I can't believe I'm hearing this. I'm silent, in shock.

"I mean, really, Sascha, what do *you* use it for?" Abriel asks. "The money I spent on you could have bought her a tablet—do you think that maybe you could let it go?"

Let it go. Let go the source of stimulation in my life, something that my master had given me, something I enjoyed. I wish I had left it with Cash. "Sure," I say, numb.

"Thanks, big brother," he smiles at me, and for a second, he's Bri-Bri again, my little brother asking me for an extra cookie at snack time.

But he's not. He's my master now, and he has a wife, and she's mean to me. And it's being glossed over.

"Abriel, you don't know what it's like here when you're not home," I mumble, feeling like a small child confessing that mommy beats him. "It's Lisa, she's —"

"I know." Abriel goes quiet for a moment. "I know. She's told me how she wants things to be tighter, more disciplined, for there to be... clearer boundaries, as she puts it."

I stare at him silently, waiting.

"I'll talk to her about it, Sascha," he promises, trying to smile.

"Talk to her, hell, Abriel, she fucking hit me! She locked me up and starved me!" I snap, the sting of betrayal far more painful than any slap from his rotten wife. "She's threatened to do worse — to have me whipped, to sell me!"

"I won't let her sell you, Sascha."

It's what he doesn't say that frightens me. Of the things I listed, that's the only one that he contested? I look down, trying my best not to burst into tears on the spot. I may have changed over the years, but Abriel changed more. I don't recognize him anymore. Where is the boy who never hurt anyone, who did the right thing pretty much all the time, while I was off being a teenage rebel? How could things have changed so quickly?

"Sascha, are you okay?"

I nod, even though I'm far from okay. As a slave, I've learned to identify threats, and all my instincts are screaming at me, telling me that my brother is a threat. My general reluctance to believe it makes it no less true.

"I'll talk to her. It'll take some adjusting for everyone, but I really think this can work out. There can be some compromises from everyone," Abriel smiles as he says it. I wonder if he believes it. "I'm so glad you're safe."

I nod again, even though I'm not safe here. "Can I at least have the tablet back so I can clear it off for Bella?" I ask, a last-ditch effort.

"There's just too much adult stuff on there, and a lot of it is password-protected and everything, but I'd hate to be responsible if she gets into it. She's my family, right? I've got to protect her."

"Of course," Abriel says, smiling again like nothing is wrong. "I'll go get it now. Don't mention it to Lisa — just give it back to me tomorrow night, okay?"

I force a smile. It's not just me who has to lie to her, it's him. The difference is he could leave if he wanted to. "Sure thing."

I lie in bed that night and pity myself. But I only give myself this luxury for a few minutes, because I have other plans. A power-hungry suburban housewife isn't going to be my final demise. I plan my moves carefully, like I've done for years, and if my safety wasn't at stake, I would enjoy myself. With my tablet back in my hands for a few hours, I can put the next step of my plan into place, and I do so quickly, breaking into my brother's network with almost no effort. He never was very good at security, and it seems Lisa isn't much better. But it's Abriel's data I'm interested in.

I work my way in, arranging and rearranging, sending messages and receiving them, making purchases and allowances and finally, when it's all over, I clear off any trace that I was ever there. Someone good would have known, someone like Cashiel, but this isn't his network, it's Abriel's, and he has no inclination toward protecting his own privacy. Lisa probably just assumes that a slave would be too stupid to attempt something like this, just like she didn't even bother to look through any of the information on my tablet.

I arrange for a train ticket two days out, as well as a slave allowance that indicates that I am travelling on "business" for my master. For Abriel. As far as anyone knows, I'm on a legitimate trip, so if my SID gets searched when it's noticed that I don't have a wristband, I'll be covered. The confirmation messages will go to an address I've set up with automated responses that will verify my travel. Abriel will know nothing of it until he discovers that I'm missing, and by then, I should already be on my way. Reporting me as missing would be a challenge, and even if he does, or if Lisa does, the confirmed message would make it look more like an error than what it is, a runaway attempt. I'm buying myself time and distance, and I'm banking on the hope that Abriel won't be overly aggressive in hunting me down.

The waiting is painful, and I swear Lisa is suspicious of me. Either that, or she's pissed that my brother talked to her, because she's started locking me in my room all day and forgetting to let me out for lunch. Fine. I make sure to eat a lot at breakfast and dinner, when Abriel is there to protect me, and I use the time alone to review my plans. Let her clean her own toilets and weed her own flower garden.

Finally, it's the day I'm supposed to leave. As much as I wanted to leave days ago, I know that today, Abriel is at work and Lisa is taking Bella to back-to-back enrichment classes, followed by a play, where Abriel will meet them. I will have a good eight hours to myself, in which I can make my escape.

"In your room, slave," Lisa mutters, as she's getting Bella ready.

I comply, hating her as she locks the door behind me. "Mistress, what if I need to use the bathroom?" I complain, making sure to sound pathetic. I don't need to try very hard. I'm starting to whimper when I speak to her anyway, years of training doing their job to enhance the fear.

"Shut up about it," she orders. "You just went, and since you'll be missing dinner tonight, you should be fine until morning. If my husband asks, you had a sandwich and a lovely night alone doing whatever it is that useless slaves do."

"Yes, mistress," I mumble, trying to sound contrite. She has no idea what a valuable piece of information she's just given me. Nobody will miss me until morning.

I hear the sound of my brother and his family walking out, and the security alarm activating as they close the door. When I hear the hov-car start and drive away, it's my cue. I move quickly, pulling the key out from under my mattress. Stealing it wasn't difficult. Lisa obviously didn't think it would occur to me to steal it in the middle of dinner last night, and it clearly never occurred to her that her underwear drawer would be the most obvious place to keep it, even though she's made me put away her laundry before. There is an upside to being treated like a stupid slave. I unlock the door to my bedroom, let myself out, and then lock the door again from the outside. I even return the key to where I found it.

Next, I go to my tablet and work my way into the security system again. It was simple the other night, it's a breeze today. I set it to disarm temporarily and rearm in ten minutes. Long enough for me to clear out any trace of my actions. I clear off the history of the tablet, first, wiping it down to just the most basic operating structure. No trace of me or Cash, no trace that it had ever been owned before, because of course, Cash installed some self-destructing software on it. I am sad that I have to leave it behind, but it would be another clue of my departure, and it would be a red flag for a slave to travel with something so expensive. I place it back in the drawer where I found it, and I give the house one last, bitter look.

My heart still races as I open the door, because if this was some movie I was watching, there would be tense music and then the alarm would sound, and I'd be caught.

I step out and begin to walk, slow and confident, as though I'm doing what I'm supposed to. This is the hardest part. I want to hide, to run as fast as I can, but anything like that would make me look suspicious. I have to keep looking like I'm doing what I'm supposed to be doing. Hiding in plain sight.

It takes me two hours to get to the train station. I hate small towns. Even where Abriel and I grew up, the train station was only a fifteen minute walk. Abriel and Lisa live so far from it that it's almost not an option; it probably wouldn't be an option for either of them. But I get there early, and I stroll up to the ticket counter confidently, giving the attendant my SID number and reference number, which I've written on a piece of paper as if I need help remembering it. Act stupid, look convincing. Just a good slave, on business for his master. Not plotting anything.

"Traveling alone, eh boy?" the attendant asks.

I think he's just trying to make conversation; he looks bored, but the threat of being caught makes my throat catch. "Yes, sir?" I answer, wishing it didn't sound like so much of a question. "I'm not in trouble, am I sir? My master said I would be okay?" I hope my act works.

It does.

"It's fine, it's fine, no law against it," the attendant rolls his eyes. "Just be careful though, all right? A slave can get hurt out by himself."

"Yes, sir," I mumble, the blush on my face fitting in with the act.

I take a seat and wait for the train. My mind is filled with visions of armed officers carting me away, or Lisa storming in and beating me and dragging me home. I panic when strangers look at me, expecting them to know, somehow, but they don't. They just give me a generic smile, like you give to people, even slaves, and they continue walking. It's only in my head that I have a neon sign alerting everyone to my runaway status.

My trip is equally uneventful. My stomach is sick and my heart is racing at the fact that I've just run away in broad daylight, but nothing happens. Why would it? Runaways are almost unheard of. Slaves don't have anywhere to run to. Most slaves, anyway. By the time the train reaches my destination, I know that Abriel and his family will have already arrived at home, but still, they won't be looking for me for hours, not until morning. Abriel might want to talk to me, but Lisa will make sure that he's prevented from doing so, like she's been doing since he brought me home. Odd that I can count on her for that.

The walk when I get off the train is worse, the fear that I will be stopped and questioned or apprehended at any moment eating away at me. In the daytime, I was more confident, now that it's dark, I'm irrationally worried. I'm terrified I will get lost, despite having looked at the maps a hundred times. The cold weather doesn't help, and the fact that I'm not well-dressed for it makes me wonder how I think I can pull this off. The train ride was long, and it's now the middle of the night, or maybe the middle of the morning. I can't tell. All I know is it is not the time to be out.

None of that matters, though, because I make it, finally. I'm standing on the steps of my final destination.

I knock on the door.

Nothing.

I hadn't expected this. I feel the tears welling, falling down my face as I knock again, more frantic this time, feeling everything collapse around me. Nobody will come, and I'll stand here in the dark forever, and maybe the neighbors will hear, despite how far away they are, and some authorities will come for me, and all of this will be for nothing. I can't escape the despair, just like I can't stop pounding on the door.

And then the door opens, and I start to sob in relief.

"Sascha?"

I stumble over the step in the doorway and fall into Cash's arms. I don't know what happens from here, but I feel safe the moment I see his face.

"Sascha, what the hell?" he asks, pushing me away and holding me at arm's length.

I keep sobbing. "I couldn't do it! I couldn't sit there and let her hurt me and let him treat me like a slave, because he's my fucking brother, not my master, *you're* my master, and she took everything and even the kid was a bitch!" I realize I'm not making any sense, but I don't care. "Everything was supposed to be okay, but it was awful, and I couldn't live there, couldn't live with myself, and I had to get away, and this is the only place to go! I didn't want to go!"

"Come inside, then," Cash replies, having to physically move me out of the way to shut the door.

I want to cling to him, but I don't. He's never liked me being clingy, so I stand there sobbing instead. I've managed to stay strong at Abriel's, but now that I'm here, I can break down.

"I take it your brother's house didn't work out?" he says, finally.

I shake my head, unable to form words. A moment ago, I was babbling; now, it's like all the air has disappeared out of the room. Speaking is too hard. Haven't I done enough?

"So, did he send you back here, or are you a runaway?" his voice has that logical, detached vibe to it, and while I usually find that comforting, right now it's terrifying, threatening. I am a runaway, and if he sounds so cold about it, does it mean he disapproves?

Did I make the wrong decision?

He studies me. "Runaway, I'm guessing?"

Thank god he's answered his own question. I nod, feeling stupid and miserable. I still can't make words happen, but I can nod, and I can see the irritation and anger that crosses his face when I do.

"For fuck's sake, Sascha."

"Don't send me back, Cash, please, please don't send me back!" By all means, it's what he should do. Harboring a runaway slave is a pretty serious offense, and a slave who runs away from his own well-intentioned family must be the worst thing ever.

"We'll talk more about it in the morning, Sascha," he says, frowning at me. "My god, how did you even get here?"

"I took the train," I spill my plan to him, the words tumbling out in no particular order. "I snuck out and walked to the train station in Vermuse from my brother's house and I hacked Abriel's data and I knew they'd be gone for a long time so they wouldn't miss me, and I took the train and I walked from the train station here and it's raining out and I didn't realize it would be so late and—"

He puts a finger to my lips, silencing me.

"That explains how disheveled and scared you are," he says softly. "You must be exhausted."

"I just wanted to come home," I whimper.

Cash shakes his head. "I thought you *had* gone home."

I don't say anything, I just look at him, and he looks back at me with the most compassion I've ever seen from him, which is saying a lot.

"Go take a shower," he says, his voice carrying an order. "You should probably get some sleep after that. I'll take care of what I can, just relax. It'll be all right."

"Thank you, master," I mumble before tearing myself away and following his orders. For once, having orders to follow is comforting. I don't want to make any more decisions.

I'm numb and drained by the time I reach the shower, crying in relief as the familiar smell of his soap washes over me, chasing away the awful smell of train and sweat and rainwater. I finally start to feel warm as the hot water drains out, and I collapse in his bed without a thought, wrapping myself up in his blankets and his smell.

Chapter 14

Belonging

By the time I go to check on Sascha he's fast asleep, curled up in my blankets like he hasn't slept in weeks. I watch him for a moment. I'm glad he's back for purely selfish reasons. I missed him, and I want him back in my house, in my life. It was just the other day that I was glad he was gone, but that was when I thought he was safer with his brother than with me. I'm not entirely sure what happened while he was gone, but he hasn't looked so terrified in months. I fight the urge to check him for injuries. That can wait. He can sleep now.

I spend the morning investigating Abriel and his wife. They are boring, mediocre, just like everyone else in their tiny town. They shouldn't be a problem for anyone, but just in case, I see what I can find. Unpaid bills, illegal information downloads. I find out what I can, and I store it away in my head for later.

I'm not surprised when my doorbell rings in the middle of the day. I'm harboring a runaway slave, but it's not police. I have systems in place that would alert me if this address was reported to anyone official. I don't hear them, but I do hear Sascha moving around, most probably woken by the doorbell. I pretend like I don't hear him creeping around the house.

I take my time opening the door, and when I do, I find an angry-looking woman standing there. "May I help you?" I ask, keeping my face blank.

"Are you Cashiel Michaud?"

I glare at her. This must be Sascha's sister-in-law. Lisa. A young mother who dared to terrify my slave. "You're at my home; you should know who you're talking to." I inform her coldly. "Who are you?"

She puts her hand on her hip, shooting me a glare that might be intimidating if she was in any way relevant. "Look, if you have my slave, you'd better give him back, and you'd better give him back right now before I have the authorities called."

If Sascha can hear, he must be terrified. I have never wanted to harm another free person so much in my life. "That's funny, because last I checked, this was private property, which means you are trespassing, and you've still neglected to give me your name."

"My name is Lisa Dover-Gabbamonte, and you have my slave!"

I stare at her for a full minute, silent, until she starts to fidget. Sascha is mine. "Miss Dover-Gabbamonte," I start, my tone icy. "Why on *earth* would I have a slave of yours? I don't even know you."

Lisa makes an exasperated sound. "There was a boy purchased about a week ago. I'm sure he'd come here! Where is he? Are you hiding him?"

"Miss Dover-Gabbamonte, I have never seen you before in my life. I have *never* done business with you, so if you please, I'd appreciate it if you took yourself off my property."

"My *husband*, Abriel, he bought the boy from you! Surely, you must remember?"

"What business I conduct with others is of no concern at the moment," I answer, my voice cold and dangerous. If this woman was a slave, she'd be groveling. I wouldn't appreciate it from a slave, but I would love to see her break. "If your husband has lost his slave and wishes to speak with that slave's previous master, I suggest he do so in person instead of sending a representative."

"I'm his wife and—"

"I do not do business with representatives. *If* your husband has had business with me in the past and would like to speak further about it, he will need to come in person. Do I make myself clear, Miss Dover-Gabbamonte?" I start to close the door, just a little, because if she barges in my house, I will be going to jail on assault charges tonight.

"I'll report you for harboring a runaway!" Lisa threatens, whining like a spoiled child. It makes me no more likely to help her.

"I'll report you for trespassing, stalking, and being a general pain in my ass," I retort, keeping the emotion out of my voice. "Trust me,

your petty little complaints are nowhere near as influential as my connections. You are nothing. Get off my property."

She makes a move to walk through the doorway, and I slam it
before she gets the chance. She stands there, cursing loudly, revealing
her low breeding. A few seconds later, she finally gives up, stomping
away and revving the engine of her hov-car as she speeds off.

I breathe a sigh of relief. "You can come out, Sascha."

He steps out from behind the wall where he was hiding, looking
scared, still trying to hide in plain view. He looks uncertain, and I hate
that someone has done this to him. How could I have sent him there?
He stops a few feet away from me, freezing in the middle of the room,
looking at me warily.

"So that's what you were running away from." I take a step toward him, reaching out to pull him close to me, and he flinches. I'll kill
whoever did this to him.

I shake my head as I come closer, grabbing him firmly but still
gently by the shoulder. He cowers, but I ignore it, pulling him close
and wrapping my arms around him.

"Did you think I chased her off so I could smack you around?" I
ask rhetorically. "Come on. We'll order food and you can tell me what
the hell happened that's got you so upset."

Sascha offers to make something, but he didn't come back here
to cook for me, and I don't want to wait for him to finish cooking to
figure out what we're up against. I roll my eyes at him and place an
order with our favorite Indian restaurant. We sit at the table, and I
even get him a drink, something I rarely bother to do. He sits there,
scared and silent, waiting for me to make the next move

"So, enough suspense, tell me what happened." I keep it calm and
low-key; if I ask him something more emotional, he'll just shatter. I
need him logical for now.

He tells me, and he includes the emotional parts as well. He talks
about how scared he was, how lonely, how his brother has changed.
He tells me that he felt like he had left home instead of going there,
and I regret pushing him. He starts crying when he talks about his
niece, who thinks of him as "slave Sascha," instead of "uncle." It's
heartbreaking. He spent so long miserable as a slave, only to have his
family hurt him far more.

When he tells me about the ways that Lisa hurt him, slapping him, starving him, locking him away and denying him the most basic things like the bathroom, I become tense, angry. I try to hide it, because I don't want to scare him, but I'm furious. She had no right. When our food comes, he devours it like he's starving. From what he's told me, he might be starving. It puts me off my food, which is fine, because he finishes his and is still looking hungry. I push it to him without a word.

Finally, he gets to the end of his story, telling me the details of the escape plan, forging his brother's permission, taking the train, the walk through the rain in the middle of the night. And then, he stops. He sits there, drained, still looking uncertain. I don't even know how to fix this.

I start with the simplest solution I can think of. "Do you need to see a doctor?" I ask, quiet.

He looks offended, but he mumbles his answer. "I'm fine. She didn't hit me that hard. She just slapped me. I've had worse. Hell, *you* have done worse."

I nod. I have, but Sascha is mine. That woman had no right to put a hand on him.

"What are you planning to do?" I ask.

He starts shaking. "I don't know, sir. Would... would you take me back?"

What a ridiculous question. I've kept him throughout so many other things, how on earth does he think I wouldn't take him back, now? I got rid of Lisa this morning; that should be proof enough. "What do you think, Sascha?"

All of a sudden, it's like he disintegrates. He crumples to the floor and crawls to my feet, clutching at my legs and sobbing like I just delivered the worst news in the world to him. I'm shocked; my question was meant to be rhetorical.

He begs desperately, still clinging to me. "Please, master, please take me back. I promise, I'll be good, I won't mess up anymore, I'll do anything you want, please—"

"Sascha, get up!" I order, grabbing him roughly by the hair and dragging him to his feet. Once he's standing, I grip him firmly by the shoulders. "Do you really think I let you in here and stayed up all night making arrangements and let you sleep here and sent that awful woman away because I *don't* want you back?"

It takes a moment, but he finally seems to understand that I'm not going to abandon him.

"I want to stay with you," he says, calmer now, but still so vulnerable. "It's all I wanted ever since I first saw you."

I try to play cool, but I smile. It's so rare for him to make a confession like that, no matter how much I've always known it.

"I'm sorry, sir," he mumbles, hesitating and shifting a little closer to me, his hands coming up to feel my forearms. "I should never have left."

I pull him close, needing to feel him near me. "You had to," I reassure him. "You had to find out, and you never thought it would be this way. Hell, I practically forced you out, and I never thought it would be this way, or I would never have let you go. You're mine, Sascha, and nobody messes with what's mine."

Suddenly, he buries his head in my neck and starts kissing me, like he's desperate for skin contact. I hold him tighter, feeling his tears on the collar of my shirt.

"Why didn't you com me?" I ask. "Or email me, even. You had your tablet. You did all sorts of other shit with it, why didn't you just get in touch with me?"

He tenses, and he keeps his face pressed into my neck as he speaks. "Because... you might have said no. What if you didn't want me back?"

"So you thought you'd just show up at my doorstep and I couldn't turn you down?"

"I had to leave," he whispers, kissing my neck again. He's practically glued himself to me.

"Will he come for you?" I ask, gently prying his lips from my neck. "Your brother, will he come?"

He thinks about it for a while before answering. "Yes," he answers. "Before, he would have come because he was worried. Now, I think he'll feel obligated to."

"I'll be prepared," I promise him. I hold him back for a few more seconds, proving to myself that he's really here, and then I pull him close and kiss him hard, reclaiming his mouth as my own.

He tries to kiss back, to have some semblance of control, but I won't hear of it. The moment he starts to squirm, I immobilize him with a firm hand on the back of his neck, squeezing lightly, threatening playfully. He melts into my touch, and my tongue invades his mouth immediately. He moans when I slip my hand between us, gripping his cock and pulling him closer. His face is still wet with tears, but he's responding to me, rubbing his body against mine. Without another word, I move my hand from his cock to the pants he's wearing, shoving them down roughly so I can feel his skin on mine. I palm his cock and he arches into my touch, moaning.

I laugh, low and evil. "Don't think you're coming just yet," I warn. "I'm planning to fuck you good and hard, and don't you dare come before I tell you to."

He can do nothing more than whimper.

I barely let go of his neck as I finish undressing him, and myself. He helps me, his eyes never leaving mine, my hand never moving from the back of his neck. I never want to stop touching him.

We're naked, and the feeling of my skin touching his is getting me worked up. I touch him everywhere, his chest, his legs, his stomach, his cock. I want his entire body to yearn for me.

I pull him close again, kissing him just as roughly as I did the first time, until I feel his body threaten to collapse underneath of him. Finally, I break off the kiss, turning him around and pressing him face-first against the dining room wall. Immediately, his body aligns with mine, pinning him close, making him writhe in excitement. My fingers graze his ass, rough and purposeful, and within seconds I prod at him, demanding entrance. I don't want to hurt him, not like this, but I bite at his neck and shoulders. I smile as I bring my hand up, placing my fingers on his lips.

"Suck," I order, and he takes my fingers into his mouth immediately. He ruts against me as he does, tempting me with his cock, enticing me with the warmth of his flesh against mine. He works my fingers as carefully as he would work my cock, desperate, like he can't get enough of me. He stays close, struggling every time I come close to breaking contact with his body.

Suddenly, I withdraw my fingers from his mouth and work them into his ass instead, quickly and firmly, giving him no chance to argue or resist. I doubt he would, anyway, if the sounds of pleasure he makes are any indication. He thrusts himself down on me, hard and fast, and I realize that I'm going to hurt him if I fuck him like this. He seems willing, but I'm not going to fuck him dry after missing him for a week.

I remove my fingers from his ass, and feel my cock harden when he whines in response, low and needy. I slap his ass lightly and order him to stay. I am gone and back again in a moment, fingering his ass again and dragging my teeth along his neck. I shift positions, aligning myself in the perfect position to drive deep into him, and I can feel him tense for just a moment before relaxing. I've lubed up, but he must not realize it, because he cries out in surprise and ecstasy as I slide into him, slick with lube. He rakes his nails against the wall.

"Fuck, Cash, fuck you feel so good!" He whimpers, but it's a good whimper. Sexy.

"Missed you, Sascha," I whisper in his ear, my voice raspy. "I didn't know that I'd ever do this again."

He goes quiet, but he's rocking against me as much as he can. I'm pinning him to the wall. I reach around him, grabbing at his cock as I fuck him. He makes a high moaning sound, desperate to come, but I whisper "shh," in his ear, slowing the pace a little.

"Not yet," I order. "I am far from done with you."

I continue fucking him until he is reduced to nothing more than helpless mewling noises, until his legs start to shake from the pressure and he can barely hold himself up, much less thrust back against me. I want to make him mine again, take all the control away from him until all that is left is the sensation.

"Please," he whispers. "Cash, it hurts. My legs hurt."

"Good," I reply, speeding up the pace. I know just how much he gets off on the pain, how much he needs it. I know I'm hurting him, but I can tell that it's in a good way. I thrust harder as he begins to sag, lifting him up and down as he whimpers. It's one of the best feelings I have ever experienced. How could I ever have let him go?

"Who do you belong to?" I growl in his ear, my hand tightening around his cock. "Tell me who you belong to."

"You," he manages, in between panting. I tighten my grip more. I want to hear him say it. "I belong to you, Cash. And I love it."

"That's right," I growl, slamming into him a few more times. "Now, come for me."

Sascha comes across my hand, and the wall, and I keep fucking him at frantic speed as his muscles contract around me. I come when I hear him start to scream, filling his ass and holding him there, pinning him up in the air.

We come to a halt slowly, panting together, hot and sticky and shuddering. I gently ease him back down to the floor, steadying him with my body as he wobbles unsteadily on his legs. I pull out and start to move away, returning just seconds later to catch him as he nearly falls, looking exhausted and satisfied.

"I suppose we should get you to bed," I suggest, keeping my voice soft.

He relaxes into my arms for a minute before I place him on his feet.

"Come on," I encourage him. "Shower first. I'm glad you're back, but we're still not getting into his bed like this."

He gives me a little smile, and he's putty in my hands as I guide him into the shower, stepping in next to him. He stares up at me in awe as I quickly soap us both up. I'm silent until I shut off the water, reaching out for a towel to dry us. I just want things to be calm and peaceful and safe for him, but he keeps staring up at me.

"Keep looking at me like that and I'm going to get a god complex," I say lightly, drying him off.

He just smiles at him. He's safe, and I'm not letting him go anywhere.

I pull him into bed, still holding him close. I don't say anything more as I reach across him to shut the light off, but I don't let him go, either. Neither of us is usually big on cuddling, but I want him close tonight. I've already let him go once, I won't do it again. For the first time in more than a week, I sleep peacefully.

Chapter 15

Family

It's after lunch when Abriel comes for me. I'm a little surprised, because I figured he would have come sooner, but maybe he went into work or something. He's always been like that, reliable when he's made a commitment. And now I know where his loyalties lie, and they clearly aren't with me.

Cash answers the door, because there's been an unspoken agreement that I would not be doing this, at least until things get straightened up. Well, as unspoken as, "Sascha, do not go near that door," can be.

It's his way of showing he cares.

Still, I'm not far behind.

"Mr. Gabbamonte, it's nice to see you again. I hope you're well." Cashiel is as cold as he is polite.

"Is he here?" Abriel asks, heedless of social niceties. "My wife came by yesterday and said you wouldn't even talk to her. Is Sascha here?"

"Yes." I can tell by Cash's voice that he'd rather not speak with Abriel, either. "It was unfortunate that your wife wasted the trip out here."

"She —" he stops himself, realizing he's got no chance in this argument. Abriel has always been good at reading people who aren't his wife. "Is he okay? I'm sorry if he's put you out; I'll take him home right away."

"You may speak with him. He'll meet you in the living room."

I stay hiding in the office until Cash comes to get me.

"I know you were listening. Come on; go talk with your brother."

I look at this man who means so much to me, suddenly afraid. "Cash, what do I say? I want to stay with you." Good god, I am whiny!

"Just talk with him Sascha," he orders firmly. "You know you have my support. Try and work things out."

For a moment I'm scared, because what if what he really means is that he doesn't want me to stay, that he wants me to go back with Abriel and his wife? I can't do it, I just can't.

"Today, Sascha."

The warning tone gets me moving automatically, although I hesitate when I walk past him. He raises an eyebrow and gives me one of his rare half-smiles, encouraging me.

I walk into the living room alone.

"Sascha, Jesus Christ, what were you thinking!" Abriel stands up as he yells at me.

I draw back toward the door, his body language and tone triggering my instinct to flee.

"Do you know how worried I was about you?" Abriel sits down, helping me to relax a little. "I had no idea if you had been stolen or where the hell you would have run away to! I never expected you to turn up here! I bought you to get you away from here!"

I shrug, awkward. He doesn't know me that well, and he has no idea what Cash means to me.

"You can't just run off like that! I know Lisa was harsh with you, but that's no excuse to—"

"I'm not a goddamned child, Abriel, I didn't just 'run off' because I got yelled at!" I snap, the fear replaced with rage. "The way she treated me—the way you *all* treated me—it was unacceptable!"

"Sascha, I am doing my best."

His best? Letting me get hit and starved and threatened was his best? "It's not good enough!" I snap.

Abriel shakes his head. "You know, Sascha, I spent the last four and a half years *hunting* for you. Every chance I got. Between school and marriage and work and raising Bella, every spare minute was spent finding you."

"So you could bring me home to treat me like shit? Sorry if I'm not kissing your ass like a humble slave."

"I wanted to make sure you were safe! I care about you; I worried about you! I saved you from slavery and this is the thanks I get?"

"Saved me?" I ask, incredulous. "It was about damn time you found me, if you were really trying. You act like I'm so fucking ungrateful—the only reason I was ever Demoted in the first place was to save *you!*"

My brother is quiet for a moment, and I wonder briefly if he's never really made the connection before. When he finally looks up at me, the look on his face tells me otherwise.

"Why the hell do you think I tried so hard to find you?" he asks, glaring. "I had to make it up to you."

"Then why didn't you make it up to me!" I yell back, exasperated. "You bring me home and treat me like shit! I was miserable living with you."

"Yeah, well, the past few years haven't been that great for me either," Abriel mutters.

"What do you mean? You got to go to college, have a family, have a job, have children—you got it all, Abriel, I made sure of that. And this is the thanks *I* get?"

"Yeah, well did you ever think to ask me?" Abriel looks hurt. "Or did you just think your stupid little brother would mess up your perfect plan?"

"What?"

"Come on, Sascha. Did you really think it would be all goddamned unicorns and rainbows after the Assessment?" Abriel shakes his head. "Everyone knew. Everyone at school, all my friends, all *your* friends. Our family. Mom and Dad. It was obvious that something had happened, you were just too damn good to get caught."

I shrug. "I didn't want to risk you being Demoted."

"So you fucking took my place! Sascha, I didn't want to do all this. I didn't want to have to struggle through school, to be asked to do things that I'm not capable of every day. I never liked learning like you did. That was *your* dream."

Sure, it was my dream, but it's better than being Demoted. "It couldn't be that bad," I insist. "At least you still have your personal life."

"A lot of good that does," Abriel shakes his head, looking bitter.

"Mom and Dad won't talk to me. They haven't since the Assessment. The second they shipped me off to college with your savings they washed their hands of me. When Lisa and I got married, they sent a postcard, and when Bella was born, they didn't answer my com calls or emails. That's why I'm so close with Lisa's family; I don't have any other ones."

I stare back at him, confused. "But... but they had you!" Abriel was supposed to be the golden child once I was gone! All the love and support they had always given to me was supposed to go to him.

"God, you don't get anything, do you? They didn't want me. They *never* wanted me." Abriel stops for a moment, letting the words sink in. "You were the one they put their hopes into, the one they cared about. I was just something they could use to make you happy or to bribe you into doing things. They had given up on me so long ago, by the time you were Demoted it was like you had died and there I was. Mom tried to blame me for convincing you to do it, but Dad reminded her that I wasn't bright enough to come up with a plan like you had. And it was true. I couldn't even pretend to know what you did, or how you did it."

I feel my eyes starting to water. This isn't right. It wasn't supposed to be this way. I sacrificed myself so that my brother could have the life I couldn't, the one that he deserved.

"I got pretty fucking depressed in college, spent a lot of time drinking and partying," Abriel admits. "That's how Lisa and I ended up with Bella, and why Maggie and I broke up. I was a stupid freshman, Lisa was two years older and rebelling against her parents, and Bella was conceived on a fucking rooftop after we split a bottle of vodka. Lisa's parents took care of Bella while she finished school, and they got me a job while I was still in college so I wouldn't have time to party any more. If I didn't agree, I wouldn't be able to see Bella, and I know that they will still pull her from me if I make waves. I love being a dad, but I know I'm nothing more than a hindrance to my little girl. It's why I let her mom raise her. She's like you were as a kid, Sascha, all bright and curious and shit. Daddy's just her playtoy when she wants to have some fun, or when Lisa won't give her something."

"You're better than that," I argue, my voice barely even a whisper. "You're kind and funny and you care about people, and you work hard—"

"And that's not what matters."

It had all seemed so clear when I was a kid. But I think of Cashiel, and the business we do, and try to picture someone as gentle and easygoing and compliant as Abriel in this world. He'd never cut it. The snarky jokes and quick interactions would leave him behind.

"You never even asked me." My brother is staring at me looking lost and confused. "I can't believe you thought I'd screw it up."

"I didn't think that," I argue, finally finding my voice. "I didn't think that at all. I just knew that you'd try to convince me not to, and I didn't want to be convinced. I was so sure I was doing the right thing. I didn't want you to have to go through what I've been through."

"Of course I would have convinced you not to do it! Don't you get it—from the moment you told me what being Demoted was when we were kids, I accepted it," Abriel shrugs. "It fit, really, I've never been much of a leader, and I don't like to have to make decisions. I like to do as I'm told, and I'm *good* at doing that. I'm easy enough to satisfy, what's wrong with belonging to someone else? I wouldn't have gotten beaten up like you did; I'm not so damn confrontational, for starters. I like to keep peace."

"Yeah, I'm sure that's served you real well with Lisa," I mutter, my mind blown from what I've just heard. "Follow at her heels like a loyal puppy."

"Sascha, it's what I did with *you* my entire life," Abriel informs me. "Jesus, are you that dense? Since before I could remember, I followed you around, did whatever you told me, trusted your decisions without question. What the hell made you think I'd be all right without you?"

I let my head drop, willing myself not to cry. This was all for nothing. "I thought I was giving you the life you wanted."

"I'm not you, Sascha!" Abriel snaps. "I've spent my whole life trying to be as good as you at everything, and I've never been able to! Even finding you—all I could think was that if I had been Demoted and you had passed the Assessment, you would have found me the second I left the re-education center. It wouldn't have taken you two and a half more years! You wouldn't have let me get passed around and hurt, and when you brought me home—fuck, you would have done better at this than I'm doing! You would never let someone treat me the way that I let Lisa treat you! But leaving her would mean losing Bella, losing my job... I'd have nothing left, Sascha, and neither would you. As usual, my best isn't good enough."

A part of me wants to go to him, to hug him and tell him that it *is* good enough, that he's worked hard enough to make it okay, but it's not true. We're not five anymore, and this isn't a low grade on a report card.

"Abriel, I'm sorry," I say, feeling the inadequacy of the words. "I thought I was doing the right thing."

"I know you did. Why do you think I had to find you? Everyone told me for years that it was stupid, but I knew why you did it. I just wish you knew why it was so wrong."

I can't let him think it was wrong, I have to convince him. "They do things to you. They beat you. They rape you. They control every move you make. They sterilize you, make you do stupid, repetitive tasks—"

"I know that." He must see the disbelief on my face. "I was okay with that. I wasn't looking forward to it, but I know some slaves have it better than others. The ones who don't cause problems, who don't talk back. They can have decent lives. That's what I was preparing for. You make as good a slave as I do a free person."

He's trying to joke, but it's not funny. It's not funny because it's true, he would have done well at the re-education center. He would have been assigned to some friendly master or mistress who would have treated him kindly, like a family pet.

"I just... I just didn't want you to have to go through that," I say feebly.

"I know," Abriel forces a smile. "You've always looked out for me. And that's why I'm looking out for you. Rescuing you is the only thing I've ever gotten Lisa to back down on, and I'm going to make this work. I'll do a better job in the future, I swear."

"It's all right," I shrug. Honestly, there's nothing else I need from Abriel.

"No, it's not all right, I shouldn't have let Lisa go as far as I did," Abriel confesses. "We've talked about it. Hell, she wanted you whipped and branded as a runaway, like protocol requires, but I convinced her that we should just keep a closer watch, maybe bring you into work with me—"

"Abriel, I'm not going back with you." I had intended to tell him this all along, but his plan to babysit me confirmed it.

"What?"

I take a deep breath. "I came back here for a reason. I'm comfortable here. This is my home. I want to stay here."

"Your home is with your family!"

I choose my words carefully. "Lisa and Bella are not my family. Lisa hates me and Bella refers to me as 'Slave Sascha' and threatens to have her mother hurt me if I refuse her requests. They don't know me and they never will, and you... you've moved on."

God, it hurts so bad to admit that.

"No. This isn't okay. I didn't spend years finding you so you could run off and leave at the first problem," Abriel protests. "You have to at least come home and try to work this out."

A shudder of revulsion and fear catches me. "I'm sorry for what I did at the Assessment, and if I could take it back I would, a thousand times, but if you care about me at all, you'll let me stay here. You *can* fix this mistake."

My brother glares at me for a moment, a haughty expression on his face that looks completely unnatural. Lisa's family must be rubbing off on him. "Is it the rich guy, then? You like his money? Is he fucking you?"

The questions are a low blow, but I can tell I've wounded him by rejecting his offer. "It's not about his money, and it's not about fucking. He cares about me, Abriel. He needs me and he treats me like a person."

"I treat you like a person!"

"You treat me like a childhood toy that you keep in the back of your closet because you can't bear to part with it!" Now I am crying. "There was no reason for me to be at your house, nothing for me to do, nothing to challenge me. I was so goddamned bored that I wanted to kill myself, and you contented yourself with spending twenty minutes talking to me about the good old days and pretending nothing had changed when *everything* has changed. I do things here that keep me occupied and interested and alive. I will never have that opportunity with you. I will never have *any* opportunity with you."

Abriel switches from looking haughty to looking desperate, pulling at my emotions again. "Sascha, just give us one more chance. I want this to work out."

I ignore his plea. "Cashiel will buy me back," I say, sticking to the plan, forcing my voice to stay steady. "I already discussed it with him."

"You always do get what you want, don't you," Abriel muses.

"You can't want this," I counter. "Admit it. This isn't at all what you thought it would be. This has to be just as uncomfortable and sad for you as it is for me, and your wife is angry, and your kid is probably feeling neglected… just let me go. It's okay."

We sit in silence for a while, contemplating it. My heart is pounding, because it suddenly occurs to me that Abriel has the legal right as my master to grab me and drag me out of here kicking and screaming.

"I'm not going to be able to convince you otherwise, am I?" Abriel asks, finally.

I shake my head. I wish I could say otherwise, but I can't.

"And you're sure you're treated well here?" he checks. "I mean, if you really just don't want to stay with me, I can probably find somewhere else—"

"I want to stay with my master," the words fly out of my mouth before I realize how telling they are. I clarify, "I want to stay with Cashiel."

Abriel nods, his lips tight. "I guess if that's what you want."

I can't say anything, because it is what I want, more than almost anything in the world. All I want more is for my brother to be like he used to be, for him to get along with mom and dad, for everything to be simple and for none of this to have ever happened. But what I can realistically have is my life with Cashiel, so I'll take that. I get up and walk out of the room, finding the man standing right outside the doors. It's all I can do not to fall to my knees.

"He's amenable?" my master asks.

I nod, unable to speak.

Cashiel walks into the room and I follow on his heels like a sad, lost puppy.

"I've drawn up a check returning the money you paid for Sascha," he says coolly. "I included some extra to cover the expense of fuel and housing and food and time off work. I'm sure you'll find the offer more than reasonable."

Abriel takes the check, staring at it silently. "Yeah," he mumbles. "I guess I can have his things shipped, or maybe I can bring them —"

"Donate them or sell them or throw them away," Cash dismisses him. "It's not an issue. Besides, I hear your little one could use a tablet, anyway."

A low blow, and Abriel doesn't even catch it.

"Right, sure," he mumbles. "This is more than enough."

"I've grown very fond of your brother," Cash says, glaring at Abriel in a way that would have made me flinch, if not cower. "You can rest assured that he will be treated well here." He hands over the transfer of ownership paperwork with an expectant look.

Abriel hesitates for just a moment, glancing from me to Cash and then back again. Finally, he signs them, and I feel some of the pressure on my chest starting to lighten. My ownership is back where it's supposed to be.

My master grabs the papers quickly. "I'll show you to the door, Mr. Gabbamonte."

Abriel follows silently, as do I.

He pauses at the door, just as Cash is ready to shove him out. "Can I see him some time?" he asks, a touch of desperation in his voice. "I mean... this didn't work out, but can I see him? I just found my brother. I don't want to lose him again."

"That is up to Sascha," Cash answers easily. "But I think it best that you give it a while. There's work for him to catch up on. I have your information; I'll have him send you a message from his new tablet once he's ready."

"Thank you." Abriel looks at me, sad and disheartened.

I push past Cash and wrap my arms around my brother. Maybe it's not appropriate for a slave, and maybe it's not appropriate for me, but I don't care and Abriel doesn't either.

"I'm sorry, Sascha," he mutters. "I did my best."

"You did well enough," I tell him. We both know it's a lie, but we always have. It just never meant this much before.

He leaves without another word, and the latch on the door has barely finished clicking shut when I fall to the floor and start sobbing uncontrollably.

Cash lets it go on for a while, longer than I thought he would. Finally, I can tell he's had enough, and there's a sneaking suspicion in my head that he might be worried about me.

"Come on, Sascha," he orders. "Get up."

I obey, only a little surprised to feel his hand around my upper arm, pulling me up and closer to him.

"You're all right," he says, his voice gravelly. "It's better for both of you that he could give you up."

"What if he didn't, though? What if he had said no? I couldn't have handled going back with him, Cash!" The admission starts another small panic attack, which I know is stupid, but I held it together so well, all of this terror needs an outlet.

"You shouldn't have worried about that," he dismisses my concerns. "Asking him was only a formality. I didn't mention it, because he's your brother and you care about him, but I could buy and sell him like a low-quality hov-car, and I would destroy his family with a smile on my face. You were never in danger of having to go with him."

I'm simultaneously touched by his devotion and offended by how easily he dismisses my brother. It's true, sadly, but sometimes I forget how ruthless this man can be.

"What do you think I've been doing since you showed up at my door in the middle of the night?" he asks. "I know every dirty secret that family has ever tried to keep, and I have a good idea of exactly which buttons to push to get what I want. Your brother didn't stand a chance of taking you home with him."

He's a ruthless man, but he's ruthless in protecting *me*, so I can't complain. "Thank you."

He just nods. After a moment, he raises an eyebrow at me. "Why did you lie?"

"Sir?" I'm a little scared, because his voice has taken that dark tone again, the one that means he's not particularly pleased with me.

"You switched Assessments with your brother," he clarifies. "I heard you. Why did you lie and tell me you were high?"

My last secret, the last part of me that I have kept from him. "I never wanted it to come out," I admit. "It might have put Abriel in danger."

He nods, appraising me like he's just seeing me for the first time. "It makes a lot more sense than you being high. Maybe one day, you can tell me how you did it; I'd be fascinated to know. You don't need to lie to me anymore," he admonishes mildly. "Come on, let me catch you up on what you missed."

Chapter 16

Possession

It's business as usual, like it always is with Cash. He's quick to catch me up on everything. If I wasn't sure he'd smack me for suggesting it, I'd say that he might have been a little less productive than usual. He missed me. It's strange to realize that, but it makes me all warm and happy when I do.

"Torenze remains our biggest problem," Cash informs me. "I can't quite figure out what his endgame is—I wonder if he just wants to toy with me. That, or he's still playing some part for my mother's business, but it seems highly unlikely, given their history. He's never been one to play both sides; he plays his own side, and he destroys the competition when he can. He was quite perturbed by the fact that I had sold you without letting him borrow you—he even threatened to reveal my secrets to my mother, but I think that was just to intimidate me. He's not usually one to resort to threats like that, but he saw it as a slight. He asked to borrow you, publicly, and I refused. He isn't accepting it."

I smile, pleased that the bastard was made unhappy.

"Don't look so thrilled," Cash advises. "He can't be underestimated—he's one of the few who's able to blow my cover. He could destroy the whole project. We've only just started to bring back the research and assemble a team; it will be a while before anything really comes of it. So much time for him to be pissed off, especially now that you're back."

I hadn't really thought of it that way. I wish the asshole would suffer some sort of unfortunate accident.

"I'll figure something out. Just keep it in mind," Cash assures me, directing me to the next concern. "We need him on our side."

I make dinner, pleased to go back to some sort of normal routine. That, and Lisa's cooking sucked by comparison. I've been spoiled, living with Cash; we can afford higher quality ingredients, and between his money and my ability to bypass government-imposed health restrictions, we have considerably more variety and taste in our food. It's good to be back.

It's when we're sitting down eating that it finally hits me how good it is to be back home, how amazing it is that this has even become home for me. The things, the food... the man sitting across from me.

"Thank you," I say suddenly, the words feeling inadequate.

Cash raises an eyebrow at me.

"For getting me back," I mumble, feeling stupid. "I know you didn't have to. Hell, when I first got here you would have been glad to dump me off on my brother. I caused you enough trouble."

He smiles at me. "What can I say? I have grown fond of you. It was lonely without you here, and I worried about you."

"You won't regret it," I promise him. "Getting me back. I'll work hard, and be helpful, and—"

"Of course not," he waves his hand, dismissing me. "And it's not about any of that. I've developed what some might call 'feelings' for you. I'm happy to have you back."

"Oh." I wasn't really expecting this. I don't know what I thought he felt about me—I knew he cared about me, but I didn't exactly know how or why, and I certainly didn't expect him to come out and tell me like this. He's not usually much for talking, and especially not about touchy-feely stuff.

"Sascha, I didn't get rid of you because you caused trouble," Cash confesses. "I thought you would be safer with your brother. Between my mother and Oliver... I didn't want to see you get hurt. I didn't want to have to hurt you again. My feelings for you have been growing for a while. Once I stopped resenting you, I started liking you more and more. The thought of seeing you hurt made me panic. I tried not to let it cloud my judgment, but I can be hasty when it comes to you. I should have talked to you before shoving you out the door, but I didn't think I could go through with it. I'm just glad you're back where you belong."

I nod, shocked at his confession. It's so typical Cash, all calm and quiet and matter-of-fact. "I'm glad, too."

"It was a bold move, coming here. I'm not surprised, but I'm glad you did it. I'm surprised it worked. Keep in mind, though, if you *ever* take off like that while I own you, I will track you down with a team of slave hunters and I will beat you within an inch of your goddamn life."

I grin. I wouldn't run away from him, but it's amusing to see how strongly he reacts. "You wouldn't," I challenge him.

He smiles back. "No, you're probably right. I wouldn't need a team."

I don't miss the part where he didn't deny the threat, but it doesn't bother me. If I run away from Cash, I probably deserve to be beaten within an inch of my life.

"You'll really let me talk to Abriel?" I ask. It's such an uncommon thing for a slave to be allowed to do.

He nods. "As long as it isn't interfering with anything else. I wasn't sure if you'd want to or not, and I didn't want to put you on the spot. You can tell him that I won't let you if you don't want to."

So now he's not only protecting me, he's protecting my pride. "Again, thank you."

He shrugs. "You're welcome."

We're mostly quiet through the rest of dinner, enjoying one another's company. Was it really awkward with him before? It was so long ago, I can barely remember. The absence has highlighted how different things are now, how close I feel to him. I guess it snuck up on me, but I do.

"Maybe we'll go shopping tomorrow," he muses as I clear away his plate. "About time to get you some new things, anyway."

I just smile. Honestly, I probably left enough things here that I don't *need* anything else, but if he wants to shower me with gifts, I'm not going to complain.

He's gone by the time I return from doing dishes, and I wander down the hall to find him in the bedroom, reclining in bed and reading something on his tablet. I pause in the doorway, taking in the sight of him. He's every bit as handsome as he was when I first set eyes on him.

"Finally finished?" he asks, not bothering to look up.

"Yes, sir." His voice alone is enough to get me turned on.

"Come over here and kneel," he orders, sounding casual.

It's an unusual request, but I do as he asks, dropping to my knees next to him, waiting for his next command. He takes his time, finishing up whatever he's doing, before setting the tablet down and glancing at me.

Without a word, he stands up, pulls his shirt over his head, and strips off his pants and boxers. Naked, he sits back down on the bed, his legs resting on the floor.

I go to him, prepared to move between his legs and take his cock in my mouth, but a firm hand on my shoulder stops me.

"Don't move unless I tell you to."

His tone is calm, but it still carries the edge of a threat, and I feel my heart start to race. I freeze in position, and he waits until I start to tremble before he delivers the next order.

"Put your arms above your head."

I obey instantly, curious of what will happen next. I'm rewarded by a soft ripple of fabric brushing over my stomach as he lifts my shirt, removing it without touching me. I shudder.

"You may lower your arms," he says quietly, his eyes fixed on mine. "And then stand up."

I do exactly that, standing in front of him and feeling strangely exposed. The feeling only increases as he unbuttons my pants and slides them down, his thumbs barely grazing my hips.

"Step out of them," he orders, and he offers me his arm to support me as I do so.

Lightly, he touches my legs, starting in the front, and then working his way around to caress my ass. He's driving me crazy, barely making contact, definitely ignoring my cock. I want to jump on top of him and fuck him.

"Cash," I moan, needy and desperate. I reach my hand out to him, startled when it is slapped away.

"I told you not to move unless I told you," he reiterates. "Now, turn around."

My breath becomes shallow and tense as I do as he asks, suddenly afraid of what he might do to me. He doesn't seem angry, and he's never hurt me in a bad way during sex before. He's certainly never punished me for anything. But I'm scared, scared that maybe he wants some sort of payback for the time I was gone, or the hassle I've caused him. I'm scared that I overestimated him, that I overestimated myself. After all, I am just a slave.

I'm trembling for real, now, not just because I'm horny, and my arousal is fading just as quickly as I start to spiral into terrible possible futures.

A sharp voice draws me back to reality.

"Turn and look at me."

I cower at the tone, even as I turn, and I'm relieved when I see that my master's face has softened. He reaches out, gripping me tightly with both hands on my waist.

"I'm not going to hurt you, Sascha," he says, resolute. "I'm just playing. I'd like you to play along, but I won't be angry if you don't. You can ask me to stop, and I will. Are you all right?"

The trembling stops, and I feel my body relax into his hands. "Yes, sir. Sorry." I make such a big deal out of things sometimes.

"You're mine," he says, his voice dangerously possessive. "Your body. Your movements. Your pleasure. Every part of you belongs to me, and I want you to remember that."

I stare back at him, nodding slightly. I wonder if nodding is considered movement.

"Now, I believe I left off here..."

He resumes the light touching where he left off, his hands grazing my ass, coming together to cup it lightly before sliding back around to the front. He explores between my legs ever-so-briefly before sliding up, across my chest. I'm dying to just throw myself on top of him, to thrust into his hand, but I don't, I keep up with the game he is playing, letting him control my every move.

After an agonizingly long time, he grabs my cock, stroking it quickly and roughly, too roughly, and I bite back a cry. I can't tell whether it feels good or painful.

He strokes me with one hand and reaches around to grope my ass with the other. It feels so good, so perfect after waiting so long, and I move in time with his hand, thrusting twice before I feel the warmth of his skin disappear.

I open my eyes and look up at him, checking his face for a reaction.

His face is stern, and he raises an eyebrow at me. "I did not tell you to move." But this time, there's a slight smile at the edge of his lips. "Turn around."

I feel much more calm as I turn this time, secure in the knowledge that he's not going to do anything awful to me. More than anything, I'm curious, waiting for his next command. My curiosity grows as I hear him get out of bed, standing behind me.

I don't dare speak or turn my head, but my breath catches as I feel him close to me, so close I can feel the heat from his body, but not close enough to touch. I feel the hairs rise on the back of my neck as he leans in, his breath tickling my shoulder, and then his lips touching my skin ever so lightly.

He's gone as soon as he appeared, and suddenly he's in front of me, a devious smile on his face. I bite down on the inside of my cheek to keep from begging him to fuck me.

"You will stay *very* still, is that clear?"

"Yes, sir," I reply, not caring what I will be staying still for. I'll wait for it. It's not like I have another choice, not in this game we're playing. It feels so good I don't even dream of calling it off.

He waits, staring me down for a moment until he's satisfied. Then he drops down to his knees, wraps his arms around my legs, and wraps his lips around my cock.

There have been times in the past where putting up the effort to move in bed has been difficult, but the effort it takes to *not* move is tremendous. I'm suddenly aware of every inch of my body, the way it feels, the parts that feel good, and the parts that are a little sore, and the parts that feel *amazing*, like I'm going to explode at any moment.

I blink my eyes, feeling a little bit like I'm cheating as I fight the urge to thrust, to hold onto something, to cry out in agony and joy and defeat. My legs start to feel weak, and I struggle to catch my breath as I feel my master's head bobbing up and down over my cock, his tongue swirling patterns across the tip. The slightest whimper escapes my lips, but I force myself to remain standing.

"Put your hands on my shoulders," he says, leaning back from my cock just enough that I can still feel the little puffs of air with every word. "And stop locking your knees. You'll pass out and break my neck."

I stifle a laugh as I do as he says, rewarded by more insistent sucking on my cock. I let myself relax into his touch, squeezing ever so lightly on his shoulders to keep myself grounded. The man is a genius with the things he does.

All too soon, he stops, dragging his tongue up over my cock and trailing a thin, sticky line along with it.

"Put your arms at your sides and stand up straight."

I want him to fuck me now!

"Close your eyes."

My world immediately goes dark, and it's strange how powerful the sensation is. I know I could simply open them, but I won't. He's given his order, and I intend to comply.

I startle when I feel something cold and wet on my ass, which I realize a second later is lube. The tension and the lack of sight makes it feel different, and I shudder as my master's hand creeps in closer, spreading the slippery stuff around as his other hand steadies me by my hip.

"Spread your legs."

I gasp as his finger enters me the second I do so, and it's all I can do to keep from rutting against him.

"Farther."

A second finger joins the mix, and I lose what little control I have, pushing back against him desperately, needing to increase the contact.

He withdraws his fingers and slaps me lightly on the ass, barely enough to make me jump.

"Turn around."

The command is becoming annoyingly familiar, but this time I turn toward him, rather than away. I open my eyes to look at his face, and the crease in his brow indicates his disapproval. I close them immediately.

"Lean across the bed," he orders, his voice stern. "Then reach back and hold yourself open for me."

Jesus Christ. I move quickly, situating myself as comfortably as possible, and struggle to follow his orders due to the amount of lube spread across my ass. I wait for him to fuck me.

He keeps me waiting. I lie there with my eyes closed, listening to his footsteps going away, the sound of water running, a cabinet being opened. I'm confused, but no less aroused. I know he won't leave me like this.

A soft piece of fabric touches my eyes, and it takes all my self-control not to pull away from it. He's blindfolding me, and it's more threatening than keeping my eyes closed myself, even though I can remove it as easily as I can open my eyes.

I've barely adjusted to this when I feel something warm on my ass.

"Move your hands," he orders. The second I do he is wiping carefully at my skin, wiping away the slick lube that was giving me such difficulty. "Put them back."

I do, waiting for his next move.

I feel the bed compress next to me, and my master's hands are in my hair. "You should really see yourself like this, Sascha," he says conversationally. "You're always beautiful, but there's something about this—you're arranged like a piece of art. I could look at you for hours."

I hope that's not in his plans, because I could imagine getting sore in a while, not to mention dying of lust. Still, the thoughtfulness behind the compliment is appreciated, as is the gentle touch he's gracing me with.

He lets me sit there for a while longer, until my arms start to get sore. Without a word, I hear him get off the bed, standing behind me again. The telltale click of a lid gives me a slight heads-up, but I still yelp with surprise as his fingers thrust inside of me again. It's all I can do to stay in the position he's given me.

A few agonizingly pleasurable minutes pass as he continues to work his fingers into me, starting with careful stretching and preparation, then escalating up to calculated teasing, then fucking me with them until I want nothing more than to feel his fingers replaced with his cock. Finally, he stops, filling me with sadness as much as relief. I await his command.

"Stand up, but keep your hands where they are," he orders.

It's strange and uncomfortable, but I do it. I'm caught off-guard when he thrusts his fingers back inside of me while I'm standing, the position making me extra tight. I whimper.

"Hands at your sides," he orders, his fingers still inside me.

The second I drop my arms, he reaches around me, grabbing my cock and stroking it as he works my ass with his fingers. I want to squirm, want to move, but I force myself to stay still, waiting for his next command.

"Good," he whispers in my ear, stopping suddenly and withdrawing both hands. "Now, get on the bed, on your back, and pull your legs up."

I do as he asks, trembling like a goddamned virgin. I feel him joining me, between my legs, his arms coming up to trap my legs.

"Relax your arms," he orders. "You can let your legs rest on my shoulders."

I'm surprised by how comfortable I am. The sensation is only increased as he leans forward, brushing his cock against my ass, and removes the blindfold.

"Open your eyes."

He's half-smiling, the playful look I've come to associate with good sex and a happy master. I want to smile back, but I'm not sure if it's allowed, and I definitely don't want this to stop.

"Stay still," he warns, gripping my legs as he enters me in one long, slow motion.

I manage to stay still, but a strangled noise emerges from my throat anyway. The noises only get louder as my master starts moving in and out, slowly at first, letting me get used to the fullness he's created. It's a monumental effort to stay still.

When I think I can't handle it anymore, I sink to begging.

"Please," I whimper, my cock aching as it presses against my master's body. "Please, master."

"You want to come?" he taunts, his movements slowing to almost nothing.

"Yes!"

He stops moving completely. "All right, then. Go. Your turn. Keep moving until you come."

As hot as the orders not to move had gotten me, the order to move is even better. I thrust my hips, squirming and writhing underneath of him, growing more and more frustrated as I struggle to find the exact right angle.

"You're gonna have to do better than that," he teases. "Move it, Sascha. Show me how bad you want it."

I renew my efforts, uncertain whether to try to take his cock deeper inside of me or to increase the friction between him and my cock. I wonder if he's purposely making it difficult, and I groan in frustration.

"I can't," I whine, feeling a little humiliated. "Please, just fuck me?"

"It would be very unfortunate for you if you can't," he observes. "Because you are going to lie there and continue to fuck yourself on my cock until you come."

The casual indifference in his voice is offset by the smirk on his face, but the statement is enough of a threat that I take it seriously. I work myself up and down on his cock, his eyes never leaving mine as I struggle.

My hard work finally pays off, and I feel the familiar sensation as I'm about to come. I keep going, following his orders exactly and continuing to ride him as my orgasm approaches.

"When you come, you will continue to work yourself on my cock," my master informs me. "You will not stop until I finish."

I nod slightly in acknowledgement, his words barely understood as ecstasy rips its way through my body, threatening to reduce me to a limp pile of mush. But my master's orders ring in my ears and I force myself to keep going, keep raising my hips and grinding into him as he starts to thrust into me, meeting me at every stroke, filling me deeper than before and drawing whimpers of pain and pleasure.

After what seems like forever, he comes, and in my haze I keep going, rocking up and down on his cock even as the warmth of his come fills me.

"You can stop, Sascha."

I freeze, shuddering and panting beneath him. A part of me wants to go on fucking, now that I've gone on this long, even though I know it will be a while before I can even think about coming again. I don't ever want this to stop.

Still, my master slips out, gently easing my legs down. "Relax," he orders, noticing my tense muscles. "And don't move."

He gets up, returning with a towel to clean me up. I stay where he ordered me to stay earlier, unsure of whether we're still playing this game or not. That, and I seem to have lost all voluntary control of my muscles.

Once we're cleaned to his satisfaction, he lies beside me in bed.

"Come here," he beckons, tugging on my arm to prompt me to roll toward him.

I curl into his embrace and he kisses me, slow and sensual, his hand coming up to cup the back of my head. I hesitate briefly before kissing him back, deciding that I'm done with the fucking game, I just want to kiss him. He doesn't complain, just keeps going until we're both breathless.

"I'm never letting you go again," he mutters when we finally move apart. "You're mine for good."

At some point, long ago in my past, those words would have driven fear into my heart. Now they just feel right and safe and comforting.

"I like being yours," I admit, wriggling closer to him, wanting to feel him this close to me all the time. I drift off to sleep, secure with my master's arms around me.

Chapter 17

Volunteer

I wake before Sascha the next morning, taking a moment to run my hand through his hair. He used to wake up when I did this; now, he just leans into it, peaceful and content, falling back asleep instantly. I am so glad to have him back, and I am determined to keep him safe in the future.

By the time I emerge from the shower, he's awake, and I smile at the sight. I missed him so much while he was gone.

"Cash, I want to do it," he spits out, quickly, like he might reconsider.

"If you're using that term in the vulgar way I think you are, I doubt we'll have time for much more than a quickie," I point out, selecting an outfit from my closet. "I have a meeting this morning, can't be late."

He grins at me. "No, well, yes, but that's not what I was talking about. The thing with Torenze. I want to do it for you. For the project."

I freeze for a moment before turning to face him. "You don't have to do that," I assure him, turning back and picking out a shirt. I've just gotten him back; there is no chance that I'll let him be put in danger again. Oliver won't just fuck him, he'll torture him, and he'll enjoy every minute of Sascha's screams.

"I want to," he insists. "It's important. It could help."

I turns toward him again as I slip my shirt on. "It *will* help, that's a given. It may even secure him on our side. But we don't know yet if there are other ways."

He stares at me, resolute.

"He'll hurt you, Sascha." It's not a threat or a warning, it's a fact. I don't want to scare him, but if scaring him keeps him safe, I'll accept him being scared.

"I know," he says, shrugging like it doesn't matter. "I've been hurt plenty before. I can handle it."

"You shouldn't have to," I tell him, shaking my head. Sascha thinks he can handle it, because all he's seen is a businessman with a fetish for humiliation. I've seen the full extent of Oliver's interests. He was my mother's right-hand man, her best torturer, the one she sent her most disobedient slaves and her disobedient son to for correction.

"I won't ask this of you. Besides, I thought you were rather opposed to being lent out?" I remind him, hoping to change the subject. "I won't have you miserable like you were last time."

"I didn't think I had a choice last time," he reminds me. "This time I know I have a choice, and I want to do it. For you. For the project. I've worked on it for months with you; I'm invested in this, too."

I don't have time to argue with him, and I do appreciate the offer, so I come to sit next to him, taking his face in my hands. I stare into his eyes, amazed to see how completely dedicated he is to this. Stubborn boy. I sigh, brushing my lips gently against his.

"We'll talk about this tonight," I concede, fully intent on scaring him away from the idea. "Limits, boundaries, goals. I want you to think *very* carefully about this; once I've made the offer to Torenze you will not be allowed to back out. If it means tying you up and dragging you over there, I'll do it."

"You won't have to," he promises. "I'm in."

"Just take the day and think about it," I reiterate. I know Oliver, I know the sorts of things he'll do to Sascha. I saw the way he looked when I beat him that day; the lust, the desire to hurt him more. He'll do that and so much worse if I let him.

I receive a disturbing com on my lunch break. My mother has befriended our secretary, who is more than happy to tell her I'm on my lunch break.

I wish I could get our secretary fired.

Instead, I answer.

"Cashiel, does the name Lisa Dover-Gabbamonte mean anything

to you?" my mother asks, as if it's nothing out of the ordinary for her to com me in the middle of the day and harass me about my slave's evil sister-in-law.

"No," I reply, because she knows I do.

"Don't lie to me, Cash," she cautions, her voice thick with threat. "I'll have to come over and wash your mouth out with soap."

As if she didn't do that enough when I was a child.

"What do you want?" I ask, tired of the game. "What did that little bitch say?"

"Language, Cashi," she chastises me, making me wait before revealing the purpose of her call. "It seems that Ms. Dover-Gabbamonte recently acquired a slave who she thinks fails to meet the high standards of the Miller System. I assured her that our standardized program was guaranteed to produce high-quality personal attendants, and that any deviation from the normal quality was likely a product of the slave being improperly handled by its owner."

I seethe, contemplating who I'd like to hurt more, Lisa, or my mother. "Perhaps you should advise her to lodge a formal complaint with the licensing agency," I reply.

"I have friends on that advising board," my mother reminds me. "I could exert some influence."

"What do you want?" I repeat.

"I want you to stay away from my business," she replies, just as cold as she's always been. "There are rumors, Cash. I want you away from my business, and away from the other people who are involved in the industry. That includes Oliver Torenze."

She's threatened. I'm actually threatening her and I haven't done anything yet. If she wasn't so terrifying, I'd be thrilled. "Or what?" I challenge her. "You'll get all the people who hate me into a room to yell at me at the same time? I'm not a child, anymore. You have no say over my life."

"You're awfully attached to that slave of yours," she comments. "It would be a pity to see your little toy get taken away. After all, an uncontrollable slave looks bad not just for the Miller System, but for the country. We are built on the backs of the Demoted."

"Sascha is not uncontrollable!" I snap.

"An investigation of your home would answer that far more objectively, don't you think? What would your little research associates say about that?"

"You've already demanded entry into my house," I reminded her. "What, are you sad you couldn't find anything that time? Or are you planning to plant some sort of evidence. You couldn't get me locked away last time; it won't work this time, either. You have no say in the licensing process—you're nothing more than a corporation, selling a training project. You might think you're important, but legally, you're no better than I am."

"I'd make sure to bring a friend with me, this time," my mother warns. "You've never been very good at making friends, but I am. There's a certain judge who just adores the slaves I produce, and who would be thrilled to help one of his idols strengthen her position. Perhaps he could accompany me?"

I slam my com device down and block her from comming me again. It's childish, but I can't tolerate her taunts. Investigations are usually reserved for cases of hoarding or money laundering, but with the right influence, she could arrange it. The only thing that makes me slightly less afraid is the fact that I know she would take it public, destroying my image again instead of focusing on real legal repercussions. She claims to love me too much to see me locked away forever, but I just don't think she can stand to have her name associated with real crime.

Still, I need make sure my project is safe. More importantly, I need to make sure Sascha is safe. A few months ago, it would have been easy, but there are so many records and half-funded accounts sitting around. I consider my options, and I am left with only one. I pick up my com device again and make the connection.

"Cashiel, my boy, I wasn't expecting to hear from you."

I feel sick as I hear Oliver's voice, too friendly over the phone. I explain my dilemma; the mess with Lisa, buying Sascha back, the threats from my mother, the issues with the project. I hear him laughing.

"I can have it all taken of, Cash," he says soothingly, the way he used to talk to me when he was teaching me the philosophy of the re-education center. "Kristine won't bother me; I'm too high-profile, and I don't have a little pet to worry about. You want a partner; I've always enjoyed working with you. Far more than your mother, especially after she put me out on my ass. Let's do this together."

It's so easy to let him carry me. "What do you want in return?"

"A small cut of the profits, when they come in," he suggests. "Say, a quarter of them. And part ownership of our brand. I think Torenze & Michaud sounds nice, don't you? Or even the other way around. This is your baby. I'll let you have first billing."

"Okay," I agree. Suddenly, it doesn't sound so bad. Partnering with Oliver has never been as painful as fighting with my mother.

"But I want a little symbol of your trust," he adds. "I scratch your back, you give me something to scratch mine."

I'm silent. I will not give him Sascha. He must realize he's gone too far, because he laughs again.

"Not give, I misspoke," he says quickly. "Just borrow. Just for a night."

Sascha offered this morning. Can I really make him go through with it? "Let me think about it," I say, torn between the paucity of options. But I'm not dismissing him like I normally do.

"I'd make sure my alliances were established before doing things that could get me into trouble, Cash," he cautions. "Haven't you learned not to show your hand so early in the game?"

"I'll com you tomorrow to discuss the details," I promise, committing to a time. "Will you wait that long?"

"Of course," he replies, like we're friends. "I look quite forward to it."

I'm tense when I come home, picking at my dinner and snapping at the single person who dares to com me with a question about work. I don't quite snap at Sascha, but I come close a handful of times, enough that he starts getting nervous.

"Torenze?" he asks.

I scowl as I nod. "Him. My mother. Mostly my mother."

Sascha looks at me, questioning. I don't want to lie to him, but I don't want him to worry about this either, not when it might blow over.

"She's heard rumors of what I'm working on, and she's trying to make trouble," I explain vaguely, leaving Lisa out of it for now. "Oliver could shelter the data and the funds that we've collected; even if there was a formal investigation, there would be nothing to tie back to me. The problem is, he's not sure he wants to partner with me just yet."

"So make him an offer he can't refuse," Sascha encourages me. "Me. You know he wants me, and you know that him getting his jollies off is worth far more to him than exposing you. He's pestering you because he can, and because you have something that he wants. Get him to join you, like you said, and he'll be in your pocket."

"Friends close and enemies closer, huh?" I muse.

"It's the logical solution," he says, like it's that easy.

It would be, if I didn't know Oliver's history. He worked with my mother to break down even the most difficult of slaves, zeroing in on their biggest fears, humiliating them, torturing them until they broke, often in more ways than one. I know I should tell Sascha what he's getting into; my plan for tonight was to terrify him with stories of what Oliver did to the slaves, and to me, but that was before I thought I'd really need him to go through with it. The stubborn boy will probably continue to insist that he can do it, and he'll be so much more anxious. Being made to wait can be its own form of torture.

"It's putting you in danger!" I protest, feeling weak for being unable to tell him the extent of that danger.

Sascha sighs, like I'm an overprotective lover. But he doesn't know what Oliver is capable of. "Look, I won't be in real danger," he points out. "Do you really think he'd lose control and kill me or something? That's not socially acceptable. It would reflect too poorly on *him*. Hell, I doubt he'd mind it if you waited right outside his door."

"I *would* wait right outside his door," I growl.

"He's not going to kill me, and he's not going to steal me away," Sascha points out. "So what's the worry?"

"There's other things he can do," I mutter.

"Yeah, and I've had them done before. I can take it, Cash."

I fix my gaze down at the table, avoiding his eyes. I need to be strategic about this, to separate my feelings from my plans. "Go get me a drink."

Sascha sits there, defying me. "You can't just—"

"Sascha, get me a goddamned drink now or I'll tie you to that chair and leave you there all night!"

He's on his feet instantly, the hurt and anger clear on his face. We were supposed to discuss this, not fight about it, but the stakes are so much higher, now. I'm furious at myself for letting this be my only option.

He returns with my drink and slams it down in front of me, making it slosh over the edges.

I grab his wrist, twisting it until he cries out in pain.

"Like that?" I snarl. "That's what he'll do with you. He'll hurt you and torture you from the moment I leave you with him until the moment I pick you up, and that's if I can get him to agree to not do any permanent damage. I've seen him do it; he's twisted and evil and doesn't give a shit what he does to hurt someone else's property, or his own. Do you understand what you're volunteering for?"

I'm trying to scare him, and it's working, but the look on his face is even more resolute.

"Let go of me," he whispers, half-pleading. "Cash, you're hurting me."

I drop his arm and turn away, still fuming.

"I don't want him to bring us down," Sascha says, rubbing his wrist where my fingers bruised it. "I want him controlled, and I want to help to see this project go through. Let me, please."

"Fine," I mutter, shaking my head. I glance at him, the picture of a hurt slave. "Give me your hand."

He obeys, despite the fact that I just hurt him. I wanted to scare him, wanted to have an excuse to stop this whole thing. I would rather abandon this project than see him hurt, but he's so committed to it. I can't deny him the opportunity, not if he wants it this bad. Telling him what Oliver will do to him will only make it worse.

I hold his hand gently, rubbing the spot I bruised. I lift my drink, pressing the cool glass against his skin. I'm too ashamed to look at him, or to speak. I should apologize, but I can't, yet.

"One night, twelve hours, uninterrupted," I say, still looking at his wrist. "I'll stipulate that he is not to do anything that would cause permanent damage, disfiguration, or scarring. He is not to leave the house with you. Aside from that, you will be his to do as he pleases with — anything that he wants, fucking you, hurting you, humiliating you — for the time he has you."

Sascha shudders.

"In exchange for borrowing you, he will join me on the project. He'll sign the papers redirecting a quarter of the startup funds, sign the nondisclosure agreement, and take part ownership of any proceeds that come from it. He'll be partially responsible for anything that comes from the research, so he'll have motivation to keep it to himself. From then on, I'll deal with him, and hopefully, you never have to see the bastard again. It will be exceedingly clear that this is a one-time offer."

I finally set the glass down, allow Sascha to take his arm back. He cradles it to his chest, and I finally look up at him. "Sascha, you don't know what this means to me. I could never ask you to do this."

"That's why I offered," he reminds me. "And in the future, the polite way to say 'thank you' is *not* by almost breaking my wrist."

I am utterly ashamed. I lift my drink and hand it to him. "Here, drink. Maybe it will help you forget that I can be an absolute asshole at times."

He takes a sip, smiling. Alcohol isn't really permitted for slaves, but, then, we're breaking so many rules already.

"I've known you too long to forget that, sir. But stop trying to scare me. I'm scared enough already."

"He's the only one who can offset my mother's influence," I admit, still not revealing the extent of it. I don't need Sascha any more terrified. "It's unfortunate that I have to hand you over to him just to get on our side."

"I'll recover," he says, finishing the drink. "But what happens after that? What do we do?"

"We wait," I explain, shrugging. "I know, it's a little anticlimactic, but we take the funds, find partners for research, and go from there. It won't be a long wait—there are plenty of people interested in the project already, we just need a strong backer. That's Oliver. Once he announces his support of the project, it will go quickly."

"How long will it take?" He asks. "The research... whatever comes from the research?"

"Hard to say. Last time I did it, it took about a year for the research and analysis," I recall. "It should be quicker, this time. It won't just be me using my mother's money on the side. Nice thing about slaves, they don't need too much time to prepare and plan things. No other schedules to work around. The big point will be when the research is made public — after that, it will be a lot of media attention; news stations covering it, politicians debating it, that sort of thing. After that it should take on a life of its own. If the right people buy into it, the Miller System will get replaced by Michaud & Torenze."

Sascha nods, looking pleased at the thought. "Do you think that it would go beyond the re-education centers? I mean, you said that you compared slaves from different re-education centers; did you ever compare them to free people? What if people were wrongly Demoted?"

I raise an eyebrow at him. "Do you *want* me to go to prison? What I'm doing is fringe research on a very specific business model. Nothing too subversive or radical. Stuff like that... no, I haven't looked at it, and I won't. Not officially. I'd be thrilled if someone else picked up and did it, but it would be far too risky for my liking. I'd lend them my research, you know, from an academic standpoint, but I wouldn't risk getting involved any further. Policymakers love the Demoted system, it solved all their problems — poverty, crime, drug use — all those things dropped by huge percentages once the Demoted system was put in place."

"The same would have happened if they just shot the same amount of people they Demoted every year and still counted them in the census," he points out.

"Yes, but then where would wealthy people get free labor to make them more wealthy?"

Sascha grins at me, looking amused by my very realistic interpretation.

"I accept the Demoted system, Sascha. It's law, and it's deeply embraced by the people who matter. The only way to have any effect at all is to play by the rules and work within the framework, not against it. But then, you should know that, that's how you got your brother free."

He draws back, flinching a bit. It was intended as a casual statement, but he takes everything as criticism. I didn't mean to scare him, not like earlier.

"Relax," I say softly. "I'm impressed that you were able to do it.

Your strategy was brilliant and amazingly selfless. I'd say he doesn't deserve it, but maybe he did, then." Of course, if it wasn't for Abriel and his wife, Sascha wouldn't be faced with Oliver's torture methods.

I listen as Sascha explains the details of how he cheated the Assessment. I'm fascinated by his dedication and attention to detail. "Most people wouldn't do that, someone still gets Demoted."

He shrugs. "It was worth it."

"Still?" I ask. "After how he treated you?

Sascha considers it for a few moments. "He would have been happier if I had left well enough alone. He's married to that evil bitch, and our parents lost both their sons," he admits. "But I'm still glad he didn't get Demoted. I just wish he had never found me. He took a risk, contacting me. He cheated the Assessment; he could still be put in prison, even though he knew nothing about it. Or even if not, his life would be destroyed. Everyone knowing that? Wouldn't sit well. He took that risk because he thought I was in danger."

I nod. This is all true. And it is all exploitable. I don't know how to tell Sascha that I might blackmail his brother. He will hate me for doing it, but I'd rather have him safe and hating me than confiscated.

"I'll set up the deal with Torenze," I tell him. I hope it's enough.

Chapter 18
Trashed

Torenze requests me on a Saturday morning, because he wants to be "refreshed" when he gets to spend time with me. He manages to destroy any hopes of enjoying my weekend with Cash, but I don't complain. I guess I did ask for this.

Over the past few days, my master and Torenze have commed back and forth, worked out the details. In the end, Torenze agreed to do no "permanent" damage—which was defined as something that wouldn't heal in a month.

He can't break any bones, but he can bruise and hurt and draw blood, as long it doesn't scar. I don't scar easily.

The ride over is tense, and Cash keeps cursing. Not at me, not to me, and he grips the steering wheel harder than he gripped my wrist the other day. I try talking to him, but he brushes me off.

No, I wouldn't have appreciated some reassurance or anything.

We're silent as we walk up to the house, and Torenze greets us with a greedy smile.

"Welcome, boys!" he teases, including my master in the statement.

Cash is not amused.

"Are we doing paperwork before or after you borrow the slave?" he asks, cold.

"Now, you don't think I'd back out, do you?" Torenze laughs, ushering us inside. I fight the urge to cling to my master.

"I'm trying to plan my day."

My master keeps his face emotionless, trying not to let on to Torenze how much this bothers him.

"I'm good for my word, Cash," Torenze points out. "You've known me long enough to know that."

My master nods. "Of course," he agrees, looking down. "I just wanted to stay on top of things."

Torenze laughs. "Your mother would be proud of you. I'll sign now, that way you can pick up the boy tonight and head straight home. I expect he'll be tired out!"

His laugh makes my stomach twist, threatening to throw up the light breakfast Cash forced on me this morning.

Cash just nods, waiting expectantly.

"Muffin," Torenze calls, prompting a young man to come rushing out from another room. He looks like he's fresh from the re-education center, wide-eyed and terrified.

"Yes, master?"

"Bring me what we discussed earlier."

"You didn't mention anyone else being involved," Cash says, guarded.

I can hear the rage building inside of him and it frightens me.

"It's a slave, Cash," Torenze points out. "Muffin won't hurt your boy. You wouldn't question me using a pair of handcuffs on him, what does it matter that my new toy is human?"

I can tell Cash is seething, but he nods. "Of course."

Muffin, god help the name, runs in with some tablets, and I tune out as the free men go over details and place signatures. I try not to think of the fact that my master is going to be leaving soon, and I try not to notice the heavy bruising that covers the other slave's face, and I really try not to notice the way Torenze eyes me up. I fail on all accounts.

Suddenly, my master is gripping my arm, looking at me expectantly. "Master?" I question, missing what he said entirely.

He frowns. "I'll be back to pick you up at ten tonight. Make me proud."

I know I already have made him proud by agreeing to this, but I still need to carry out the agreement. "Yes, master," I whisper, wanting to back out.

He doesn't give me a chance, walking out without a word.

"Muffin, get the boy some water."

I stand there awkward and afraid, wondering what he's planning to do to me. At least he doesn't plan on keeping me dehydrated.

The boy returns with a few bottles of water, looking terrified, but that's the only way he's looked since I first saw him.

Torenze takes one and opens it, handing it to me. "Drink," he orders.

I obey, staring at him with uncertainty clear on my face. I won't speak out of turn, but I'll let my confusion show.

"All of it."

I finish the bottle, still confused. Has he drugged it? It's not like he needs to, but it might be a nice change. Alter my consciousness; maybe he'll give me too much and I'll pass out.

He opens another bottle and hands it to me. "This one, too."

My breath catches as I get a clue of his game. I drink it all without stopping.

"Good boy," he smiles at me. "Now, take those clothes off. Slaves in this house do not get to wear clothes."

He's like a walking cliché of a bad S&M novel.

I strip, reminding myself to keep my eyes down, not to glare at him like I'd glare at my master if he gave this order. I let my clothes fall to the floor, earning a backhand that sends me stumbling.

"Pick them up neatly, boy," he growls. "Fold them and set them over there."

My lip smarting and tasting of blood, I follow his orders silently. I return to stand in front of him, waiting.

"Get on your hands and knees."

At least I won't wait long. I comply instantly feeling a sharp, stinging pain as he slaps my ass. I stay still as a few more blows land, biting down on my lower lip to keep from crying out.

No amount of self-control can keep me from crying out when I feel something thrust into my ass, dry and without warning.

At Cashiel's reluctant suggestion, I lubed up before coming here, and I'm grateful for it now. Whatever he's forced into me is big and heavy and painful. I yelp as he works it in and out, deeper than is comfortable. I don't turn to see what it is.

"You're starting to look better," Torenze comments. "Muffin, look at this slave."

"Yes, master."

"Tell me what you see."

"I see a lot of scars, master." The boy sounds terrified.

"That's right," Torenze agrees. "A lot of scars for being a disobedient, naughty boy. I'm going to do his master a favor today by reminding him that he's a dirty slave. You might get to help, Muffin. Would you like that?"

"If it pleases you, master."

I can hear in the boy's voice that it doesn't please him, probably like being called "Muffin" doesn't please him. I stay silent, resigning myself to the humiliation games.

"Muffin, what else do you see?"

"I see a dirty slave who has a cleaning brush stuck up his ass, master."

So that's what it is. I hope it's clean; Cash will be annoyed if I'm infected with something.

"That's right, Muffin," Torenze says. "And that's what little Trash-Boy is going to use to clean the bathroom, isn't it, Trash-Boy?"

"Yes, sir," I mumble, flinching when I realize I failed to keep the disdain out of my voice.

"Do you like your name, Trash-Boy?"

"No, sir," I answer honestly.

He slaps the brush in my ass, jarring it and making me gasp in pain.

"Tell me how much you like the name, Trash-Boy," he orders. "Beg me and Muffin to call you that all day."

I want to tell him to get fucked. "I love the name, sir," I lie. "Please, call me Trash-Boy to remind me what a trashy boy I am." The words come out mechanically, but he seems satisfied. I guess his fantasy is driving the situation at this point.

He drags me into the bathroom by my hair and orders me to clean the floor with the brush in my ass as Muffin sucks his cock. I'm not looking forward to servicing him, but scrubbing the bathtub with a brush sticking out of my ass isn't so pleasant, either. I try to make a game of it, attempting to actually clean well and not paying much attention to this man who's successfully humiliating me.

I'm caught off guard when he throws me to the ground, rips out the brush, and shoves himself into me, rutting and thrusting while holding the brush frighteningly close to my face. I'm relieved when he lets it drop after coming inside of me.

He leans back against the wall, smiling and sated. He hands another bottle of water to me. "Drink it and take care of Muffin," he orders, a lazy smile on his face.

I down the water quickly and then get up to go to the slave, unsurprised when a hand grabs my balls and jerks me down.

"Crawl."

I crawl to the slave, who looks terrified. I smile up at him, hoping to be encouraging, and I place my hands on his thighs gently. I wish I could say something to him, but I know better.

"Get to it, Trash-Boy!" the order comes, so I take the other slave's cock into my mouth.

He doesn't fight me, but I can tell he's not into it. I use all my skills to find something that turns him on, sucking hard, fast, slow, soft, caressing his legs and ass with my hands. I have a feeling it will go badly for both of us if he doesn't get excited.

Finally, I feel him getting hard. I hope he comes quickly.

No such luck.

Torenze suddenly grabs his slave by the ear, jerking him away from me and making me fall forward, barely catching myself.

"Did you almost come from that dirty trash!" he demands, slapping the other slave with every step he drags him away from me.

"No! No, master, I swear, I didn't!" The slave starts sobbing, going into hysterics. I feel bad for him.

"You did, and so now you're going to be punished along with him!" Torenze decides.

It's less of a punishment and more of a sick game. The slave must be awfully new if he hasn't caught on to that yet.

"Trash-Boy, come!"

I follow with a sigh, shuddering as I feel the evidence of my previous fucking leaking out of my ass.

He takes us into what can best be described as a dungeon. I idly contemplate which promotion he purchased it with, and I'd put bets on the first one. He probably had the spanking bench before he had a matching bedroom set.

He ties his slave to a whipping post and selects a whip. I'm bored by the display, but bored is better than what I expected.

"Trash-Boy, get over here!"

I wish I could still be bored.

"Yes, sir?"

"You will beat this disgusting slave until he comes," Torenze orders, shoving the whip into my hands. "There will be a penalty if he doesn't."

"Yes, sir," I reply, certain it won't work. It's just more of a setup.

Nonetheless, I get started, hitting the poor kid hesitantly, and wincing when he screams. It goes on for a while, and I'm hesitant to hit him very hard or break skin, but the fact that he's turning lobster red indicates I'm doing something.

"Tell him just how much you want him to hit you, Muffin," Torenze orders. The poor boy starts on a senseless rant about how he loves it and how he wants it harder. The humiliation this man is piling on his slave is almost worse than the humiliation he was about to pile on me, but it's not something I can control.

After a while, Torenze stops me and turns Muffin around, showing me his tear-streaked face and hard cock.

"Taking a long time isn't he?" Torenze asks. I realize he's not talking to me.

"Yes, master," Muffin whimpers.

Now Torenze turns to me. "Get over here and suck this cock."

The second I'm down on my knees, he starts whipping me as well. He's not nearly as gentle as I was with his slave, and I know he's leaving marks with every lash. The next few weeks will be miserable. I struggle to keep up the rhythm on Muffin's cock, cursing myself when I falter and his erection droops.

The next few lashes wrap around to my chest and stomach, and I refocus on the rhythm I had established, relieved to bring the boy back up. I want to keep going, but I'm stopped again, handed a bottle of water and ordered to drink. I comply, unable to stop myself from watching as Torenze rams himself into his slave ruthlessly. He pulls out before either of them finish.

"Muffin, keep yourself hard," he orders, smirking at me as he says it. "And you. Beg me to suck my cock, Trash-Boy."

If he thinks he's going to break me with a little ass-to-mouth, he's got another thing coming. It's not my favorite thing, but I've done much worse. I beg him, half-convincingly, until he "lets" me suck his cock. I nearly choke as he rams down my throat and comes, holding me there unable to do anything but swallow.

"Now get up and beat that boy until he comes," he growls.

I resume my task, despite Muffin pleading for me not to. I've never been in this position before; it's harder to follow orders to hurt someone else. I realize with a shock that I'd rather be in his place.

A few more minutes pass. We're getting nowhere, although Muffin is getting hysterical.

"Make him come and I'll let you use the bathroom," Torenze teases.

Fucker. I had been trying to ignore it, but the second he makes the offer, I want to. I want to so badly. Four bottles of water suddenly make their presence known.

The desperation brings out an ugly side of me, one where I'm hitting harder and even yelling at the poor boy, who's sobbing at this point. I don't stop until I break skin. The sight of blood nearly makes me throw up. And Muffin is still frustratingly hard and not-coming.

"Problem, Trash-Boy?" Torenze asks, laughing. "I see you've made some progress."

"Is he trained to respond to pain at all, sir?" I ask, realizing my mistake might have been trying at all.

Torenze laughs. "No, not a bit. But I bet if you keep going, he'll get there eventually."

I seethe. "Is there another option, sir?"

Torenze laughs, evil and terrible sounding. "Oh, yes! It's simple. You give him, say, twenty more, as hard as that last one, no harder, don't want him all scarred up like you, or you can stop now, and I'll give you the beating I've longed to give you since I first saw you acting haughty at that slave auction. Oh, and if the boy comes, you get the bathroom."

I can hear Muffin begging me not to do it. I can also feel the pressure in my bladder increasing. I want to be the bigger, braver person here, but I'm not. Muffin begs his master as well.

I stay silent, but turn and began to lash at the other slave, feeling my resolve crumble as he pleads with me.

The twenty lashes fall and he does not come. I am defeated, and Torenze's laughter in the background confirms it. I stand there, uncertain.

"Now, you take his place!" Torenze orders me, a delighted look on his face.

"But you said —"

I'm cut off by another backhand as I stupidly try to contradict him.

"You were going to be whipped anyway, boy, I just wanted to see if you were stupid enough to hurt this boy even more before you did!"

The realization that I've been had hurts worse than the bite of the whip will. Torenze grabs me by the hair and drags me to the whipping post, where he glances casually at his slave.

"You may come now, Muffin."

The boy comes instantly, sobbing as he does.

"I forgot to mention," Torenze whispers in my ear. "Muffin only comes when I tell him to. Such a wonderful feature."

I beat the boy for no reason. I've never been this complicit in someone else's abuse.

I'm numb as Torenze beats me senseless, drawing drops of blood, but nothing to void the agreement he has with my master.

Finally, it's over, and he pushes another bottle of water at me. Muffin must have retrieved it while I was being beaten. I drink, knowing fully well that I've had far too much already. My bladder makes its demands known.

"Let's go to the bathroom, shall we?" Torenze asks, suddenly sounding inviting. I want it bad.

I've never seen a more inviting toilet. He makes Muffin beg to use it, and when he's satisfied, orders him to go, right there in front of us. I envy him.

"Now, Trash-Boy," Torenze considers me. "What would you do to earn that privilege?"

Pretty damn much anything, at the moment. "Whatever you wish, sir," I reply honestly for once.

"Dance for me."

I dance. I don't know what the hell I'm doing, but I dance.

Torenze laughs. "That was entertaining," he admits.

I look hopefully at the toilet.

"Oh, no." He shakes his head. "Stupid whore. That's not good enough."

Fuck him.

"Fill up this bottle with water and drink it."

I sigh, filling the bottle in the sink and drinking it obediently.

Torenze looks at me, curious, then at his slave. "Muffin, you think Trash-Boy deserves to drink from the sink?"

"No, master."

Torenze looks back at me, pointedly. "Where does trash drink from?"

"Probably the toilet," I mutter, clenching my jaw.

Torenze makes a clucking noise with his tongue. "What a pity you have such an attitude, Trash-Boy, I was about to let you use the toilet."

I curse myself for my stupidity as my chance is ripped away.

"Now you will drink from it."

I glare at him. "Should I lick it out or use the bottle, sir?"

He cuffs me and I fall to the floor, still glaring. He fills up a bottle of water from the bowl of the toilet and shoves it in my face. When I reach up to grab for it, he smacks my hand away and motions for his slave to come over.

"Pinch his nose and hold his mouth around the bottle," Torenze orders his slave. "He will continue to drink until I finish fucking him. He can breathe when you refill it from the toilet."

I start to panic as I realize just what this entails, and suddenly I'm begging, incoherent, pleading that I will do anything, fuck or suck or drink or piss anywhere. It's useless.

Within seconds, I'm faced with the option of drowning or drinking the water in front of me, so I gulp quickly, the pain in my stomach compounded by the rapid fucking that Torenze is subjecting me to. The slightest reprieve comes when I finish the bottle of water and Muffin refills it, allowing me to breathe until he returns. I can see the slightest indication of apology in his eyes as, but mostly I see pity. I realize what I've been reduced to. I force the muscles in my ass to cooperate with the fucking, and I've never been happier to feel someone come inside of me.

Six bottles of water slosh around inside my stomach.

Torenze stands up calmly. He takes Muffin by the arm and leads him to the bathtub, ordering him to lie down on his back.

I make a break for the toilet, throwing up before Torenze can stop me. I need to piss, but throwing up seems so much more important. As it is, I'm throwing up nothing but water.

"Get in the shower!" he barks, and I step in, awkwardly placing my feet to either side of Muffin, who is lying on the floor in tears. He grabs my hands and ties them above my head, hooking them to a bar at the top of the shower. "You have one hour. If you need to urinate, feel free. But neither of you moves an inch."

He slaps me a few more times for good measure, and I realize the new predicament he's placed me in. I can piss, if I piss on this poor boy.

The next hour is excruciating. I writhe and squirm, wishing I wouldn't hate myself so much. The other slave, who whispers to me that his real name is Mark, even tells me it's okay, but it's not. I'm better than this, I can't bring myself to do this to another person. My bladder aches and so do my wrists and shoulders by the time Torenze returns.

"Such a strong boy," he laughs, slapping my ass and making me stumble, stepping on Mark and making him gasp. "Let's see how strong you really are."

He punches me in the stomach, repeatedly, in the bladder and kidneys. I start to cry as I feel the warmth start to dribble down my leg, and I fight it. After what seems like forever with this torture, he grabs my hair, jerking my head back as I still try to beg him.

"Still so stubborn, aren't you?" he hisses. "We'll see about that."

He leaves, returning a second later with an assortment of dildos. Perhaps he's finally grown tired of fucking me. He shoves a large one into my mouth, and I do my best to lube it up with my own saliva.

I still scream when he puts it in me.

Years of training don't go to waste, and I feel my cock hardening. Torenze laughs, cruelly, and motions for Mark to get on his knees. It's worse, somehow, thinking of him as "Mark" instead of "Muffin." He follows his master's orders and starts sucking my cock.

"You can piss right now if you want to," Torenze taunts, knowing fully well how hard I am. I couldn't piss right now if it would save my life. "Don't you want to?"

"Yes, sir," I whimper, hating myself for sounding so weak.

"Oh, you do?" Torenze acts surprised. "But poor little Muffin has his mouth wrapped around you trashy little cock, and it's going to stay there until I tell him to move it. Wouldn't that be disgusting?"

It's gone on long enough that I'm sick enough not to care. "Yes, sir," I mumble. "But I'd do it."

"Tell me what you'd do," Torenze growls in my ear, still fucking me. Goddammit, this is turning him on, and as much as I want to vomit, my body is responding to the stimulation, my cock getting hard, aching for release, both of come and urine.

"I'd piss in your slave's mouth, sir." I give in, crying as I feel Mark tense underneath me. I feel awful. "I'd come down his throat and then I'd piss in his mouth, so he could swallow it or choke on it. I'd love it, sir. I wish that I had done it earlier, but it will be even better now. Right into his mouth."

"And why is that, Trash-Boy?" Torenze grunts, about to come.

"Because..." Because I need to piss so bad I'm afraid my bladder will explode, because I'm trained to get off on pain, and once I come, I know I won't be able to hold back anymore. "Because I'm a dirty, trashy whore, sir," I admit, feeling the truthfulness of it. Fighting is too hard. I'm too weak to protect myself and too selfish to protect this boy. "I'm a dirty slave whore who loves cock, and who doesn't care who he hurts or who he pisses on."

The words bring Torenze over the edge, and I can feel him coming inside of my ass again. At the same time, he reaches around to grab Mark by the hair, jerking him down hard on my cock and ordering me to come.

As I'm shuddering and Mark is struggling to swallow, Torenze laughs again. "Now, you can piss in his mouth."

I'd like to say I'm strong enough to resist.

I'm just not.

I fight the urge to be sick again as I let go, feeling relief mixed with shame that I've never felt before.

The relief is spoiled as soon as it starts, as I feel my own piss being spit back out at me, covering me as Mark chokes and Torenze holds his head down on my cock. I want to sink to the floor, but I'm still held up by my wrists, tied to the shower bar, and I finally remember how to check out like I used to.

The rest of the day is a horror-movie blur. I'm fucked multiple times, both by Torenze and his slave. Maybe I even fuck the slave. Torenze could have ordered me to fuck the wall and I would have. There are bodily fluids everywhere, curses for being dirty, beatings, restraints, bruises. Various methods are utilized to make me "clean" again, but they are all much less about actual cleanliness and much more about furthering the pain and humiliation that gets Torenze off. It doesn't matter, though, because I'm done, gone, checked out.

Chapter 19
Dirty

The only reason I'm aware my master has come for me is that the suffering stops. I hear knocking, and I'm left alone with Muffin or Mark or whatever the hell his name is, and I wait for the suffering to start again.

It does to a minuscule extent; Torenze drags me by my hair to the foyer where I last saw my master.

I have been fantasizing about this moment so much that the sight isn't surprising or relieving. I expect it to be a fantasy that gets blown away with some new torture. That's what's been happening for the past twelve hours, except when I forget to fantasize about anything at all.

"Oliver, if I let you borrow my hov-car and you returned it in this state, I'd insist you take it for a tune-up first."

It's the cynicism and careless disdain in my master's voice that cuts through the haze, convincing me that it's actually him. Fantasy-Cash always pulls me into his arms and carries me to safety.

"I could always keep him overnight for observation," Torenze suggests.

I jerk away from him and fall at my master's feet, too weak to stand. Being tied up, forced to stand on the tips of my toes or face worse damage to my arms and shoulders, has taken a toll on the muscles of my legs, as have the beatings. I don't beg, but I lie there, pleading silently. Everything is blurry, and I'm still scared that it's not real.

"You used him hard." My master's voice is carefully void of emotion.

"I use all my toys hard, you've known me long enough to know that."

"I hope I can say I've known you long enough to trust that you haven't broken any of the terms of our agreement?"

"Of course," Torenze agrees. "He'll be just fine in a month. Probably even less than a month."

"Good." My master finally looks down at me.

I turn my face away, unable to meet his eyes. I don't want to see it, the pity, the disgust, the horror that he must feel looking down upon me. I'm miserable, covered with my own blood and piss and Torenze's come and all sorts of other repulsive things. I can't look at him and see that. I look down at the floor instead. It spins.

"We'll be going, then," my master says calmly, as if nothing has happened. "Like you said earlier, I'm sure you're tired out."

"In the best of ways," Torenze says, laughing his sickening laugh. I gag, praying that I don't throw up again.

"Your cooperation on the project is most appreciated. Welcome to the team," my master says cordially. "Come, Sascha."

I try to follow him, but all I can do is crawl, and even that hurts. Fortunately, I'm too addled to realize what's happening, because before I know it, he's picking me up and carrying me. I want to protest, badly, but the exhaustion shuts me up nearly as much as the firm grip. I let myself sag as my master carries me to the hov-car.

I can't avoid crying out when he sets me down on the seat, and I can feel my face contorting with pain as he reaches across me to fasten the seatbelt. My master says nothing, but the disgust is clear on his face.

"I'm sorry," I whimper, starting to cry again. Or was I crying already? My face is wet, but I don't remember starting to cry. But I don't remember going outside, either.

He says nothing until he walks around, getting in on his side and putting it into gear. "Don't be ridiculous, Sascha."

Right. It would be ridiculous to hope he'd still want me. That's why he didn't want me to do it in the first place. He knew I'd come back like this and be nothing to him. I cry more.

"Son of a bitch!" my master snaps, slamming a hand down on the dashboard and making me jump. "I'm taking you to the hospital."

Just when I thought I was unhappy enough, he wants to let other people see me like this?

"Please, master, no!"

"I'm taking you to the goddamn hospital," he insists. "You look terrible! I don't know what the fuck he did to you, but you need a doctor!"

"No. No hospital," I moan. I can't. I can't handle it. "I promise there's nothing permanent. Please, Cash, just take me home?"

He glances over at me and I can see him soften. He thinks about it for a moment before responding.

"All right. We'll go home, but if I check you out and anything looks suspicious, we are going to see the doctor first thing in the morning, is that understood?"

"Yes. Thank you, sir," I mumble, slumping over in the seat. I flinch away when a hand reaches out toward me, but I realize it's Cash, and I clutch it to me, holding on to him. For once, he doesn't seem to mind.

We get home and I struggle to unbuckle myself and open the door. By the time I've finished, Cash is already at my side, about to pick me up again.

I pull away. "Don't," I beg. "I'm dirty and disgusting, and covered in—"

"I know what you're covered in, and I have a pretty good idea of what he's done to you. We can get you taken care of more quickly if you let me help you," my master insists, grabbing me firmly and pulling me out of the car.

I try not to think of how dirty I'm getting him and his car. "You're never gonna get that smell out of your car," I mumble, only aware of how strange it sounds after I say it.

"I know a good detailer." Cash's jaw is set, his face looking grim.

He helps me into the house and takes me straight to the shower. Not that I blame him, I know how awful I smell and how terrible it must be to touch me. He deposits me on the edge of the tub and turns the water on, ordering me to wait while it warms up. I lean against the wall and fight the urge to be sick again.

He comes back quickly with a chair from the kitchen and a drink bottle. He places the chair in the shower while I watch and then turns, holding the bottle out to me.

"Drink," he orders. The familiar command pushes me over the edge.

I lunge past him and manage to reach the toilet before throwing up, the memories from earlier today all too fresh to handle a threat like drinking something.

"Sorry," my master says, rubbing my back gently.

I try to shake him off, but he's as stubborn as I am.

"It's a sports drink," he explains calmly. "Electrolytes. Minerals. Sodium. You need it. I promise it will make you feel better."

I tremble, shaking my head. "I'll throw up," I try, an inadequate explanation.

"You're throwing up already," he reminds me. "Trust me, Sascha. Think back to your high school anatomy class and the early effects of water intoxication."

I do as he says, and it does sort of add up. "That's why he gave me salt," I mumble, realizing it now. I thought it was just because he enjoyed the way it burned my throat, raw from screaming.

My master nods. "He wouldn't have let you go too far, but he did enough. Sascha... I'm so sorry."

I accept the drink from him, the salty cherry taste thick on my tongue. He hands me a small pill as well, which I swallow without comment.

"Diuretic," he explains.

I shudder. "He gave me some of those, too." I thought it was just to increase the need to piss, torturing me more.

Cashiel nods, waiting on me to make the next move.

"You knew?" I ask, finally, when I can't handle any more sports drink. "You knew he'd do this?"

"I've known him for a long time. His proclivities haven't changed much, as far as I can tell." He looks ashamed. "I should never have let you do this."

"I wanted to," I recall, wondering what the hell I was thinking. I start shaking, badly, and I can't quite figure out why.

"Let's get you in the shower," my master says, half-lifting me and placing me on the chair he's sat in there.

I think he's going to leave me to clean myself up, to get rid of the evidence of the dirty, disgusting mess I've become, but he starts stripping off his own clothes, and I realize he's going to join me.

"Please, Cash, just leave," I shake my head. "I don't want you to see me like this."

"Don't argue with me," he insists, stepping inside. "It's my goddamn fault you're hurt like this, it's the least I can do to help you clean up. Besides, you aren't so mobile at the moment."

I want to fight him, but there's no fight left in me. I go limp, feeling like a rag doll as he hoses everything off of my body and props me up when my body threatens to fall over, despite the chair and the wall of the shower supporting me. The sight of blood and the smell of piss, real or imagined, has me gagging in seconds, and it's only my master's quick reflexes of pulling a trash can into the shower with us that saves us both from being covered in red sports drink. I can't stop crying after this, not even when my master starts to look disturbed and annoyed.

Finally, he finishes washing me twice, himself once, and I flash back to the day he brought me home, how I wondered if he'd like to delouse me. I look worse now, I'm sure. I feel worse. How did I do it back then? How did I survive months of torture like this?

He's carrying me again, I'm dimly aware. I feel myself being placed on his bed. I start to struggle, panicking. He hates his bed getting dirty, and I'm sure I'm still bleeding, and I smell bad. I should be on the floor or something.

"Calm the fuck down before you hurt yourself!" my master orders, stilling me instantly.

I feel a sharp sting and I jump, relaxing when I realize it's disinfectant spray he's put on me. I'm quiet as he does the rest, applying bandages over the worst ones, the ones that are still bleeding. There are startlingly few, given the pain I'm in, but bruising covers most of my body. I know it will only look worse tomorrow. I catch a glance of my master's face, and he is clearly furious.

I wait, apprehensive, until he's finished everything, checked for broken bones, even fondled my ass and dick in the most clinical way possible to make sure everything is intact. Maybe I should have let him take me to the hospital; they wouldn't have been so fucking thorough.

"You'll heal," he says quietly, as if it's some sort of surprise to him.

He crawls into bed carefully, on the other side, and I hope that he will just go to sleep and leave me to my misery. No such luck. I feel his hand brushing lightly across my back, and the very sense of being touched makes me shudder.

"Please, Cash," I whisper, feeling sick again as I say it.

"I'm sorry, Sascha," he repeats, his voice bitter and quiet. "This… it wasn't worth it."

He's right. I'm spoiled now, ruined. I thought I couldn't be taken any lower, but I was, I am, and now he doesn't want me here, doesn't want me at all, and I've fucked everything up. "I'll go," I mumble, turning to roll out of bed.

Rough hands grab an arm and a leg and pull me back down.

"You'll stay right fucking here," he growls.

I lie there silently, trying to check out again. The things that Toren-ze did, at the end, they were just to my body. I wasn't really there. I could go again, leave my body, take the rest of me somewhere safe.

The sensation of fingers on my back again jerks me into the present and I try to squirm away.

"Sascha." His voice is a warning tone.

"Please, Cash…"

His touch is more demanding; he reaches around to embrace me and trap me. All I can think is how little I've been reduced to, how I don't deserve the soft touches anymore. If he wants to fuck me, he should. He should do it roughly, violently, like I deserve. He shouldn't soil himself by touching me more than he has to.

"Don't touch me." It comes out as a whisper, but it's somewhere between an order and a plea.

I'm jerked up to a sitting position, turned roughly so that I'm facing my master, who keeps a firm grip on my shoulders.

"Do you get to tell me not to touch you?"

His voice sounds so dangerous. I reply automatically, the trembling starting even before I notice it. "No, master." My voice is as dead as I feel.

He shakes me, and I figure it's my punishment for denying him before I hear him speak.

"Wrong."

Another shake. I don't know how to respond, so I just sag in his arms.

"I've told you from the start that you can tell me when you don't want to fuck, haven't I?" he asks, his voice still dangerous, but with a tone of something underneath. I can't figure out what that something is, no matter how hard I try.

"Yes, master." I do recall that conversation, multiple times, actually. "But... but I'm..."

"You're what, Sascha?" his voice is softer now. "Hurt? Scared? Confused? Talk to me, you're worrying me."

"A dirty whore." The words slip out of my mouth without a conscious thought; I've been told that so many times today, and it's true. I've been one for years. But today has made me feel it. I'm not smart or special; just because my master treats me nicely, I'm still a dirty whore to be used and fucked and humiliated. I shouldn't have ever forgotten it.

"You were doing what you had to do," my master tries to convince me. "Making a sacrifice. For me, for the project... for whatever noble reasons you might come up with to do something like this. You're strong, Sascha. Brave."

I shake my head. "I did things... I'm dirty. Don't spoil yourself by touching me."

My master glares at me, and all I can think is how much I want him to take his hands off my shoulders so I can curl up in misery, so he can stop pretending I'm not different. I fucked up, went too far, and I'm not coming back.

"Sascha, if you keep talking like this I'm going to slap the shit out of you, is that clear?"

The threat cuts through in a way that the gentleness doesn't. Cash isn't gentle, and the fact that he tried to be threw me. It registered as a lie, but the threat makes sense. "You wouldn't," I challenge, not entirely sure if he'd really spend the effort or not.

"I promise, I will get out of this bed, grab a belt or a clothes hanger out of my closet, and come back and beat you with it if you don't knock off this attitude."

I've never felt so comforted by a threat, especially not one that I'm pretty sure is real, but it's familiar, it's what I expect. I breathe a small sigh of relief as the part of my brain that has been holding on to terror is convinced that this is actually Cash, not some pale imitation of a white knight that my torture-addled brain has thought up.

"I still feel dirty," I mutter, keeping my head down while glancing up to gauge his reaction.

He doesn't let me down; before I can protest, one hand has dropped from my shoulder and smacked me in the leg. It probably wouldn't hurt, except for the bruises. I yelp, as much in pain as surprise.

"Should I get the belt, then?" his tone is light, conversational. But the look in his eyes says he's serious.

I shake my head. "No, master. I just thought..." I stop myself before earning another smack.

He sighs. "You just thought that some of the awful things Torenze did to you would put me off from you? That I would knowingly send you into a situation where someone would make you undesirable, even though that's not possible?"

I shrug. It does sound silly, looking at it that way. "I didn't think it would affect me this much."

My master raises an eyebrow. "You think that after all you've been through, being dropped off for a day of nonstop torture and humiliation wouldn't affect you?"

I glare at him. He always goes for the logic.

"You're not stupid and neither am I. Between what that woman allowed to be done to you at the brothel and what I allowed Torenze to do to you today, it's fortunate you're not a shriveled mess right now."

I wonder if I'm so far from it. I struggle between wanting to push off my master's touch and wanting to collapse into his arms, never to surface. Shriveled mess does sound about right.

"So, for the record, in case it isn't crystal clear, I do not think that you're dirty, or worthless, or trashy, or a whore, or any of the other things you might have been called today," Cash says firmly. "What you are is a very brave, reckless young man who just spent twelve hours in the home of a well-known torturer and slave-breaker."

I glance up at him at the last few words.

"Yes. When he started out at my mother's company, that was his role. He rose in ranks quickly, due to his skills."

"You don't think any of what he said is true?" I ask him, uncertain. He might not, but I sure as hell do. "I couldn't fight it. Not even for a few hours."

He shakes his head. "We needed him, and you were the bait to bring him in. It worked without complication."

I've noticed how ruthless my master can be before, but damn, do I forget it easily.

"You need to know that nothing he did to you or made you do could make me think any less of you," Cashiel says, his voice carrying a promise. "If anything, it makes me think that much more of you."

I let the words sink in for a minute, reminding myself that this man has no reason to lie to me, he never has. Finally, I relax a little, letting myself sink into his grip. "It was really bad," I manage, unable to put it all into words. "I didn't think he'd be able to break me so quickly."

Cash nods. "I didn't know how to warn you. So I just didn't."

"Wouldn't have believed you anyway," I point out, finally starting to relax and appreciate the way he's holding me.

He studies me for a few moments before speaking again. "Are you still set on not touching? Because I think a little something to chase out the bad memories might be in order."

I smile at him weakly.

"Of course, if you're really not up to it, you can have your space; I won't force you. I just wasn't about to let you keep thinking that I didn't want you."

I reach out, daring to grip his forearms even as he's still holding me tight by my shoulders. I understand. He's not going to let me wallow in misery without making it perfectly clear that he doesn't care about any of the lies Torenze told me. I've rarely felt more attracted to anyone. "Fuck me, Cash," I whisper, begging him with my tone as much as with my eyes.

He smiles, bitterly. "Sorry, but no can do."

I'm thrown for a second, pulling back, and the look on my face must give it away, because my master rushes to correct himself.

"I know you like pain, but I am not adding to the mess that monster made of you," he points out, reminding me of the brutal fuckings

I endured today. "You're barely past bleeding as it is, and I want you healed up so you can enjoy me fucking you."

I know he's being kind, but the tears jump to my eyes anyway. I try to tell myself he really does have my best interests at heart, that he isn't just disgusted to fuck me after another man has used me all day and let his slave use me. I'm not very convincing. "Please?" I whimper, half from sexual need and half from a need to be validated. "You always told me I got to choose!"

I'm suddenly grabbed by the hair and jerked close. I gasp as I feel my master kissing me roughly and violently, abrading the spot where my lip was split open earlier. I'm breathless by the time he pushes me back.

"You *do* get to choose, but so do I," Cash reminds me. "I'm not going to take part in hurting you like that. We can play tonight, but there's no way I'm fucking you until you're healed up, is that clear?"

Jesus Christ, he's hot when he's forceful. "Yes, master," the words come out of my mouth without a thought.

He pins me down suddenly, carefully, avoiding hurting me more than necessary.

"What did I tell you about calling me 'master' when we're in bed?" he demands, but the slight smirk indicates that he's teasing.

"Yes, Cash," I amend, smiling back at him.

"Smartass," he replies, kissing me gentler this time.

I don't say anything. I'm busy enjoying the feeling of his hands as they move across my body, taking possession of what Torenze tried so hard to destroy. Cash's touch is strong and sure, and it reminds me that I belong to him. My body is his to use, but not in the awful way that Torenze made me feel. With Torenze, I felt like an object, a useless, second-hand animal with scars and trauma and a bad attitude. With Cash, I feel like the most valuable, wonderful thing ever, the most valuable, wonderful *person* ever. I can't help but lean into his touch.

"Do you know why you're not worthless, Sascha?" he asks, his mouth pausing from the reveling it's doing on my body.

I could guess, but I know it's not what he wants. "Why?" I play along.

"Because you're mine."

His words are simple, hitting me hard in a way that makes me ache for him. I reach up to pull him close, ignoring the burn of the various welts on my skin as he presses down onto me. He could have used any of a hundred logical arguments to convince me that I wasn't worthless, but instead he went straight for the thing that I was most likely to believe in this state. I'm certain he did it intentionally. I melt into him as he fucks me without ever entering me, taking me into his mouth, his hands, and his possession completely.

I'm spent quickly, too exhausted to even consider reciprocating, and he doesn't demand it. He lies next to me, stroking gently across my skin, standing guard over me as I sleep, as nightmares jerk me awake again and again.

They don't all make sense, especially not the one where I hear him say he loves me, and I think I ask him what he said, and he just shakes his head and kisses me. But that dream was better than a nightmare, and after that one, I sleep dreamlessly.

Chapter 20

Promises

I wake the next morning, eager to find out if Sascha is all right. I'm prepared to take him to the hospital if need be, but he doesn't want to go.

"Please, Cash, I'm fine," he mumbles. "I'm just sore. You checked me out well enough last night that there's nothing left for a doctor to find."

I frown at him. I should demand that he go; he is my property. But the begging wins me over, and I rest beside him in bed. "All right," I concede. "But let me bring you something to eat and drink. You need the nutrients."

Sascha nods, drooping back down into bed. I go to the kitchen and attempt to put together a sort of breakfast, some tea and toast and the chocolate spread I know he likes. A voice in my head berates me for coddling a slave, but the voice sounds like my mother, so I ignore it.

I'm on the way to bring it back to the room when I hear loud knocking at my door, and the sound of one of my security alarms being activated.

I set the food down on an end table and glance at my wristband, which is alerting me of the presence of someone at my house. It also informs me that there has been a formal complaint lodged against me, although I don't bother to read it before making my way to the door. My mother told me just last week that Lisa had called to complain about my ability to manage my slave, and I'm fully prepared to destroy Lisa and her whole family, no matter how much it will hurt Sascha to see his brother go down with her.

What I'm not prepared for is the appearance of my mother along with an armed officer in uniform.

"What the hell are you doing here?" I demand, taking the officer by surprise. He looks from me to my mother, waiting for either of us to explain my outburst.

"Following up on the quality of my services," she replies, a dangerous smile on her face. "Ms. Dover-Gabbamonte filed a complaint against you, but her complaint reflected poorly on my re-education centers. I discussed it with the district judge, and he was more than happy to accept my services in this investigation. After all, I may be nothing but the face of a corporation to you, Mr. Michaud, but to those who matter, I'm a valuable asset. It's a pity we aren't working toward the same goals."

I hear her throwing my own words back at me and I want to reach out and slap her like she used to slap me as a child. Only the thought of leaving Sascha alone while I am inevitably taken to jail makes me hold my temper.

"My services will ensure that my re-education centers are providing top-notch training, but will also represent the Miller System's ongoing commitment to civic responsibility," she explains. "And, of course, if there are any problems, Officer Eisen will be more than happy to assist. I'm sure you'll be willing to cooperate, won't you, Mr. Michaud?"

She's pretending she doesn't know me, that we don't have history. The officer is clueless, and looking down at me like I'm some sort of scum. His hand is grazing over his gun and I can only imagine what he'll do if I don't cooperate. My mother shouldn't have any legal authority, but with the legal system wrapped around her evil little finger she has plenty. She wields the officer like a trained dog.

"Of course I'll cooperate," I answer, forcing my voice to be calm. "As the saying goes, my house is your house."

My mother almost snarls at me before remembering we aren't supposed to have history.

"Officer, please accompany this man to retrieve his slave," she orders, and the officer glues himself to my side.

I make my way to the bedroom, where I find Sascha sitting up in bed, clearly listening to the conversation from down the hall. Good, it means he knows what we're up against. I don't mind that he still displays lingering bruises from his time with Oliver. If anything, it makes our case stronger. Good masters discipline their slaves. I trust him to behave; he knows the stakes, and he's as invested in the success as I am.

"This officer is here with Kristine Miller, of the Miller System, to investigate my house," I tell him. "You will cooperate with any and all requests."

"Yes, master," he replies instantly, getting out of bed and trying to hide the look on his face.

I hand him a robe, because we had been sleeping naked, and he doesn't need to be any more exposed. He puts it on and takes his place by my side as the officer escorts us back out to the living room, where my mother is already peeking around.

If my mother is surprised at the state Sascha is in, she doesn't show it. I wonder if Oliver has betrayed us, if my mother knew about our agreement, but she gives me no signs either way. She begins with a tour of my house, inspecting it for any signs of "noncompliance." She takes notes on every part of my home; my bedroom, Sascha's bedroom, the offices, everything. She rifles off a series of questions about what I do, what I use Sascha for, if there have ever been any problems or prior investigations. She demands to see what sort of "correction" tools I own, and I show her the ball gag in addition to a small set of sex toys that I've never even used on Sascha. Such tools aren't required, but I know they make us look better, make me look like more of a compliant slave-owner. Sascha stays huddled close to my side, and I can see from the slight limp he has just how much pain he is in.

Once again, my mother requests our tablets. They are far cleaner than they were last time; the one that Sascha hid my secrets on was cleared when Abriel took him home again, and the rest have been repopulated with trivial data. I'm not stupid enough to get caught the same way again, and Oliver allowed us to store anything we needed for the project on his servers. Our tablets are filled with financial information from Dean & Chanu, popular videos, and fiction books. The slave training manuals stayed on there as well, strengthening our case. My mother looks furious as she jabs at the screen, searching for incriminating evidence that simply doesn't exist, not there.

We might be safe with our data, but I've suffered with my mother for enough years to know she won't stop there. No matter how many times I've safeguarded my interest in the past, she's always been a step ahead of me, finding my blind spots and exploiting them. I am suddenly so grateful for Sascha's involvement. I just hope it's enough.

"Mr. Michaud, why do you think Ms. Dover-Gabbamonte filed a complaint against you and your slave?" my mother asks, still pretending to uphold her civic duties.

"There was a dispute regarding our transaction," I mutter.

My mother pulls out her tablet, seeking some sort of data to justify her invasion of my home. "In her complaint, she describes your slave as 'defiant,' 'disrespectful,' 'corrupted,' and 'spoiled.' She says that he threatened her, stole from her, left his master's residence without permission, and committed numerous offenses against herself, her toddler, and her husband. She even says that he violated their network and posed fraudulently as Mr. Gabbamonte in order to commit these offenses."

I've read the complaint already, and while the accusations are damning, there is no proof. "Mr. Gabbamonte purchased this slave from me for personal reasons. When he brought Sascha home, it created a rift between him and his wife. My slave committed no fraud; he was caught in the middle of a domestic dispute, the same dispute that I believe fueled Ms. Dover-Gabbamonte's filing of this complaint. She was not the owner of the boy; her husband was. If you have any more evidence than hearsay of a jealous wife, I'd love to see it."

She throws the tablets aside, clearly realizing that she's getting nowhere.

"Maybe we should keep the focus of the investigation to the slave, then," she suggests, giving me a challenging glare.

"Go right ahead," I reply, completely confident in Sascha's abilities. "I'm sure he'll do fine. After all, I'm a big fan of your method. It produces very high quality slaves."

My mother doesn't respond, and the officer casts a sideways glance at her. To anyone else, it would seem that I'm complimenting her.

"Officer Eisen," my mother says, staring directly at me with a smug look on her face. "I'd like to strip search the boy. Since he's been accused of being violent, restrain him and keep your gun on him."

I look at Sascha, trying not to be too apologetic. He's pleading with his eyes, begging me to save him. But our long-term safety and the integrity of the project are far more important than a little humiliation. "Do as they say," I give my consent, and Sascha stares from me to the officer, shaking.

The officer is cordial and professional, explaining that he's going to pat Sascha down, and describing each step as he goes along. He runs his hands through Sascha's hair, detached and efficient, before ordering Sascha to remove the robe. He complies, revealing the battered mess he's been reduced to. The officer walks around to his back, inspecting him.

"Put your arms behind your back," he orders, and the moment Sascha complies, his hands are cuffed. Sascha winces and looks at me for help.

"I'll take over from here," my mother announces, shooing the officer away like a fly.

I am more nervous seeing her with Sascha than when I left him with Oliver. At least I knew that Oliver wouldn't do anything to permanently damage him.

"Spread your legs," my mother orders, kicking his ankles apart. "I want to see what you're hiding in there. Make one move and that officer over there will put a bullet through you."

I watch as Sascha freezes, allowing her to violate his flesh. She molests him, glancing back at me now and then with a triumphant smile on her face, especially when she draws a few pained whimpers. She realizes the extent of the damage that's been done to him, and she takes advantage of it, poking and prodding until tears fall from his eyes, which he has clenched tightly shut. Even the officer is looking uncomfortable.

"Don't you think that's enough?" I snap, unable to tolerate the sight of her touching Sascha anymore.

"I believe in being thorough," she remarks, finding a bruised patch of skin and squeezing it between her fingers until he cries out. "Although, it looks like he's already paid for some transgressions."

"Yes," I reply, not supplying any further details.

"Tell me, Mr. Michaud, what was this for?" she motions at Sascha's beaten body. "Was he defiant? Uncooperative? Violent, perhaps? You know, the state does have a vested interest in getting violent slaves off the street. Why did you need to punish him so severely?"

I keep a straight face. "It wasn't really punishment," I reply, trying to sound casual. "It was for entertainment. Fun. A sexual perversion."

My mother's eyes narrow. "For yourself, or for someone else?" she demands. If she didn't expect that Oliver and I have partnered, she will now. Oliver all but signed his name on Sascha's body.

"I find it difficult to see how that connects to the current investigation," I reply, hoping her sense of propriety will rein her in for now.

It does, although she orders the officer to keep his gun trained on Sascha as she searches the house further.

She paws between cracks in the furniture, looks under the trash can, lifts up pieces of furniture, and does everything she can to turn up something. She is desperate, and it shows. It tells me that she has no reason to press further charges. She bumps a floor lamp, and when she does, the tiniest bit of white flashes out from underneath of it. I tear my gaze away immediately, pretending I didn't notice it, but she catches it. She's been watching my reactions more closely than where she's going the whole time. She picks the piece of paper up, smiling for real for the first time since she entered our home.

"Look at this, a list of re-education centers," she says, brushing the dust off of it and scrutinizing it. "What is this doing here?"

My heart drops as I try to figure out a way to explain it. Before I have a chance to say anything, Sascha interrupts

"It's mine, ma'am," he says.

I want to gag him so he can't say another word.

"You did this?" my mother demands. "What does a slave need with a list of re-education centers?"

"I…" Sascha is at a loss. He's shaking, worse than before. I have to do something to help him.

"Answer her, Sascha," I order, trying to make my tone as demeaning and threatening as possible and hoping he will understand it as a bid for more time. "You better explain right now what you have that list for, before I beat it out of you. Remember last time you disobeyed? You want more bruises to add to your collection?"

I draw out my angry censure, enough that even my mother looks impressed. Sascha glances up at me briefly, letting me know he's ready.

"I was looking for a friend of mine," Sascha mumbles. "A boy I went to school with. I had a crush on him. I thought... I just wanted to see if he was okay. I looked up all the re-education centers in the area, and I thought, maybe if I was good, my master would let me call and check."

"You're lying!" My mother snaps. "You probably don't know the first thing about the boys you went to school with! You're helping him, aren't you? You're helping my—"

She came so close to outing herself.

"If it's true, tell me the name of the boy you were looking for. Maybe I can answer your question for you."

Despite his terror, Sascha doesn't hesitate. "Devon Padron," he answers, not even blinking. "We have the same birthday. I always thought it meant we were supposed to be together."

I watch as my mother jabs at her communication device, snapping at a few people before reaching her answer. When she hangs up, she glares at Sascha. "You're little friend is dead," she announces. "Now your master can punish you for sneaking around."

"I will most certainly deal with this once the investigation is over," I announce. "I wouldn't want to waste your time."

My mother waves the paper at me. "The boy is sneaking around behind your back! Doesn't this warrant immediate punishment, given what he's done?"

I pause, considering it. I know what she's demanding, and I know what she wants to see. Sascha defended me, once again, and he will pay the price. "I just didn't want to inconvenience you, Ms. Miller. I assumed you had more important matters to attend to."

"Nothing is more important than protecting my investments," she says coldly. "I'd like to bring the boy into our evaluation center for further questioning, but perhaps if you cooperate, I'll reconsider."

Her threat is clear. I bend, hurt Sascha, and she'll back down. We have so much to lose... I just hope he'll understand.

"There's a whip in the cabinet in the bedroom," I say quietly, unable to so much as look at Sascha. "Go retrieve it, and make it quick."

"Yes, master," he replies.

Naked, beaten, and handcuffed, I can't help but think that Sascha is the bravest person I have ever seen. He makes his way to the bedroom, retrieves the short whip, and carries it, hands cuffed behind him, back to me. I take it and put a hand on his shoulder, leading him into the living room where I position him against the back of the couch. The officer uncuffs him only to cuff him again in front of his body. I can see the tears on his face, but I can't see another way out of this.

"Do you know what you're being punished for, boy?" I ask, reciting the same stock lines my mother's training system demands.

"For sneaking around and stealing things and wasting time that I should have spent serving you, master," Sascha replies, playing his part perfectly. He's sobbing. I can't tell if it's real or if he's acting.

"What punishment do you think you deserve, slave?"

"Whatever you see fit to give me, master."

It's like a careful dance; the next part of the act is the beating itself. I want to make it quick, but I don't. I'm trying to prove something. Not to Sascha, but to my mother. I can be her loyal child, I can follow her dictates, if only long enough to retaliate. I beat him hard, drawing blood to the skin but never breaking it. He dissociates quickly, his sobs quieting as he goes still, the lash moving his body of its own accord. I beat him until my arm tires and he starts to slide down to the floor, and then I stop. I place a hand on his shoulder, bringing him back.

"You may thank me for your punishment."

The look on his face speaks briefly of revulsion, but I'm not sure if it's his expression or my own mirrored in his eyes.

He turns, drops to his knees, and presses his head to my feet. "Thank you, master, for reminding me of my place. I won't disobey you again, or do things behind your back. I'm grateful for your punishment and guidance."

I want to be sick, but I turn to my mother instead. "Are you done questioning the slave?" I ask, as if none of this means anything to me. When she nods, I place my hand on Sascha's head. "Go to your room and stay there," I order, feeling my stomach churn as he flees down the hall without another word.

"Impressive show," my mother comments. "Perhaps if you had implemented a little more of that discipline, Ms. Dover-Gabbamonte wouldn't have lodged a complaint against you."

"Perhaps she's the one who's not fit to own slaves," I suggest.

I notice the officer returning to the room, and I'm surprised that I didn't see him leave. I was so caught up in Sascha and my mother's power play that I forgot about his presence. My mother glances at him, a hopeful look on her face, but he shakes his head. I am desperate to find out what they're communicating about, but I don't ask.

"I believe we've gathered enough information for our investigation," my mother tells me. "Although it's too bad we can't get him into our evaluation center."

"I'm sure the judge will be satisfied with this data," I snap, certain she doesn't have enough evidence to request a warrant. After all, owning slaves is a right, just like owning guns used to be. There's little she can do without due cause.

"Well, I'm sure we'll see each other again," she promises, smiling at me. "Have a lovely day, and remember, the Miller System produces the best slaves in the world!"

I just glare at her. When she leaves, I don't hesitate to go to Sascha.

He's lying in his bed, facedown, and it's hard to pick out the damage I did from what Oliver did. He startles when he hears the door open, and cowers away.

"It's just me," I tell him quickly. "My mother's gone, you—"

Before I can finish, he launches himself at me, pressing himself into my arms and clinging to me. I want to hold him tightly, but I don't want to hurt him, so I settle for stroking his head, instead.

"Sascha, I'm so sorry," I whisper. He must hate me, but I'm all he has. "I should never have done this to you. I'll do anything I can to make it up to you."

He doesn't say anything for a while, just continues to cling to me. After a few moments, he looks up, hatred in his eyes. I know I deserve it. I deserve him to be furious at me. If he wants to hit me back, I'm ready to let him.

"We have to win," he announces. "I don't care what happens, we have to destroy her."

"We will," I promise. She hoped to scare me, but she made me even more motivated.

Chapter 21
Dine 'n' Shine

Despite Cash's requests, I decline to see a doctor. I also decline to hit him in retaliation, although he did give me the option. The offer is a little tempting. The beating he gave me wasn't just for show; it hurt a lot. On top of what Torenze did to me, I feel like my whole body is on fire. I insist that I'm fine; although I do let him lead me back to bed and try again at bringing me breakfast. He follows it up with a healthy dose of painkillers, and I devour them greedily. It eases the pain and makes it a little easier to assess the damage that's been done.

I don't remember Torenze beating me about the head, but apparently he did, and he did a damn awful lot of it. He's mostly avoided my eyes; he must have been making sure he didn't damage the delicate tissue there too badly. But he's more than made up for it in other places, covering my cheeks and nose and forehead with bruises.

It matches the rest of my body. I'm surprised to see the lack of bruising on my stomach and lower back. I remember that Torenze hit me there plenty, but not hard enough to leave the deep, scary bruises like he did almost everywhere else and not enough to damage any internal organs. The other areas are crisscrossed with whip marks from him. And from Cash.

Cash stays with me all that day, allowing me the space and quiet I need to recover. It's great for the first day, but by the next, the painkillers are making the nightmares worse. When I can't sleep, I start thinking about the project, and his mother, and where we stand.

"The project, the research… it's okay, right?"

Cash frowns. "Don't worry about it," he orders, giving me more painkillers.

I appreciate them, but I'd appreciate the truth as well. Hell, I used to get beaten like this all the time and still function. I didn't think I'd turn into such a goddamned baby after just one day.

"Talk to me about Torenze," I say, half-order, half-statement.

"He held up his end of the bargain." Cash is short. If he could have said it in any fewer words, I'm sure he would have.

"How do you know?" I challenge.

"The night I picked you up." He doesn't meet my eyes as he speaks. "I left the paperwork with him. It was signed when I got you. He's done everything he promised. Our data is stored on his servers, now; the funding is sheltered in his accounts."

"Have you spoken with him?"

"You don't need to worry about him anymore."

I frown. "What about your mother?"

"Don't worry about her, either."

It's a lie. As long as either of them are alive, I have to worry about them. If Torenze is involved in our business, I have to worry about him for even more reasons. Worse, though, is the condescension, the dismissal. He's treating me like I'm too fucking stupid or frail or weak to even deserve to hear about this.

"Funny, because it was okay for me to get the shit beaten out of me."

It's a low blow, and Cash gets the message exactly as I intend him to. He finally looks up at me, and beneath the typical anger there's a good deal of shame.

"Do you *want* to hear about this?" my master asks, uncertain. "You don't have to. If you want... you can stay out of it. I won't put you at risk anymore. They're using you to get to me."

"I asked because I wanted to know," I point out, unwilling to back down at all. "I thought we were in on this together?"

Cash sighs. "Fine. Yes, I have spoken to Oliver. I called him yesterday, while you were sleeping, and I called him a monster. And then he laughed at me and asked me about the business, like it was no big deal. Like he hadn't done any of those things to you. Like we just made a nice business arrangement."

I nod. Maybe Cash had expected something different from Torenze, but I didn't. "And your mother? I thought he was supposed to shield us from her."

"He didn't move quickly enough," Cash admitted. "He didn't think she'd be so aggressive, and as he put it, he's going to protect our 'business' interests, not our 'personal' interests."

"I would think that having your house searched would be a 'business' interest," I point out, bitter.

Cash shakes his head. "We need to handle the issue with Lisa and my mother on our own. He'll protect the business data, but he won't protect you."

"So he's in, then, completely in for the project?" I clarify. Reluctance is not something I want to deal with. "He's not going to turn on us, or leave or anything?"

"He's not going to help protect you. He just wants to fuck you and hurt you and make money," Cash says, not answering my question. "I want to be done with him."

"We need him," I point out, keeping my tone and my head level. "Like you've said, we need to make sure he's supporting it so it can't get blown up and exposed before its time. There's a lot of time left, Cash, it'll be a good few weeks before any of this can even possibly go public. Is he really on our side?"

Cash stares at me like I've grown a second bruised and battered head.

"I didn't get this done to me to make a fashion statement," I point out.

"Yes, he's on our side," Cash admits. "I'm not really sure how I feel about that, but he is."

"Feel happy about it," I decide. "We need him, we've got him. Perfect."

"It wasn't perfect," Cash scowls. "It's not perfect. What he did to you, what I did to you —"

"I'm fine, Cash," I point out. "It will heal!"

He glares at me a moment, until I start to cower. He stands up suddenly, towering over me.

I duck, covering my head reflexively with my hands. I wait for the blow, and when it doesn't come, I lower my hands, remembering to breathe. It's a while before I dare to look up at him.

"It wasn't perfect," he points out, placing a soft hand on my shoulder before walking away from the table.

I sit there and tremble for a few more minutes before I can convince myself that I'm being stupid and that I'm safe.

He avoids me for a good portion of the evening, sulking in his office. I hear him coming with some people, yelling at them. I can't make out the words, but he sounds angry, and the look on his face when he joins me in bed that night confirms it.

"What's wrong?" I ask, only somewhat out of self-preservation. I don't think he's angry at me, but anything that can get him this upset is most probably worth my concern.

"My mother," he says, fuming.

I curl up to him, a little nervous. "Tell me what's going on?" I request. "Is this about the project? We're supposed to be in on that together, Cash. Please, let me in?"

He reaches down to put his arm around me, comforting himself as much as me. It feels good.

"I have to tell you something, Sascha," he says quietly. "Something I purposely avoided telling you the other day, because you had enough to deal with."

"Okay," I encourage him.

"My mother and Lisa have been working together to make our lives miserable."

I nod. I knew this; that's what the whole investigation was about. I wait, looking curiously up at Cash.

"It's more than just the complaint," he admits. "At first, that's all it was. Lisa was throwing a fit because your brother didn't bring you home to be punished. But once my mother caught wind of it... she took it further."

The news catches me by surprise, and as it registers, I realize the extent of the potential complications. I had assumed Lisa would be thrilled enough to have me out of her life that she wouldn't have pursued me or Cash, but apparently we wounded her pride.

"What are they doing?" I ask.

"Whatever they can. Not just that first complaint, but others. They've scrutinized the tablet you left at Abriel's, and even though they found nothing on it, they questioned the level of security that was built into it. My mother provided them with a new one, of course.

It seems she's Lisa's new best friend. My mother is helping Lisa lodge complaints about things you supposedly did while you were in her home, saying you harmed the child, that you stole things—there's no proof, but so many allegations raise questions and draw attention to us."

"She doesn't really have any proof, though, does she?" I press. We've covered our trail so well.

"It's a free woman's word against that of a slave," Cash reminds me. "That's proof enough to warrant more investigation, into you, into me, into your brother."

I nod, understanding the implications. Problem slaves are euthanized if there is even a hint of a good reason to do so. A vicious dog would have a better chance at surviving such a case. "Why haven't you told me this before?"

"We need to remove at least one of them from this conflict. Kristine Miller's only dirty secret is me, and we can't survive a public attack or attempt to blackmail her. She's too big. But Lisa isn't. We need to discredit her," he tells me, avoiding my eyes.

I look to Cash, scared.

"Cash, she's Abriel's wife," I protest. "Can't we do something else? Something that won't hurt him? Or Bella?" My niece is a little brat, but it's not her doing. "What do you have on Lisa, anyway?"

Cash is silent for a moment. "Nothing. But her husband should have been Demoted."

I jerk away, horrified. I would rather take a week-long vacation at Torenze's house than even consider outing my brother like that.

Cash looks at me, and instead of his usual ruthless glare, he looks sympathetic. "With any luck, Lisa will back down when she finds out," he tells me, indicating that he's already thought this through. "Maybe nobody will have to know. Just the risk will be enough."

"Cash, no!" I protest. "We can't do this. It's not worth it. The project, the research—"

"I'm sorry, Sascha, but we have to," he says firmly. The ruthless glare returns. "I get it. He's your brother. But he's also married to her. He's the one who didn't make things work out. I know you might hate me for it, but I will do this. I'll try to keep it as minimal as possible, but I've already thought it over."

I feel the tears coming into my eyes, and I try to blink them back. "Cash, please," I say, quiet. "I didn't tell you what happened so you could use it against Abriel. We have to think of something else."

"There is nothing else, Sascha," he tells me. His tone is cold, but his face shows the regret. "It's not even about the project, anymore. I will not risk you."

"I won't let you!" I snap, enraged.

He's surprisingly gentle as he threatens me. "I'll lock you in your room until it's over if I need to. I won't risk you or me being taken away. Not for someone who you've sacrificed too much for already."

I break down, sobbing. He pulls me into his arms and I let him, because I can see how much this anguishes him as well. I want to hate him for it but I can't, just like I couldn't hate him when his mother forced him to whip me. I hear his words replaying over and over again in my head, searching for loopholes, trying to find exceptions. I beat the Assessment when I was just a teenager; surely I can figure something out, now?

It finally comes to me. "What if Abriel vouches for me? He was the one who actually owned me, he would actually have the legal say… what if I can get him to say it was like you said, it was a domestic dispute?"

Cash considers it. "You think Abriel would speak out against his wife?"

"I don't know," I admit. "Not in general, but this… I think I could convince him. I just need to see him again."

Cash shakes his head immediately. "Too risky."

"Cash, I need to see him," I insist, looking up at him, resolute. "If he helps, if he doesn't. I need to talk to him before it happens. You can either help me, or I can wait until you're at work and go on my own."

He frowns at me for a moment, and I almost expect him to make some sort of threat, maybe to lock me up again. But he's not angry at me, he's scared.

"What do you propose?" he asks. "You'll need a place where nobody will notice you, nobody will care if you're there. And you'll need to communicate with him without his wife knowing."

I'm quiet for a moment, thinking it over, and then I smile. "I have the perfect place."

I spend the rest of the day crafting an advertisement for a buy one, get one free "Artery-Clogger Deluxe" at the Dine 'n' Shine Café. Abriel was always privy to my excursions to the dive restaurant when we were kids, and while our hometown is a half-day's commute from where either of us lives, I have a hunch that he will get the message. I email it to him from a disposable email address, along with the words "fifth period," a reference to the time of the school day when I used to frequent my favorite illegitimate dining establishment.

Cash is skeptical when I first propose the plan, but he listens to it, and he defers to me. He explains what kind of statement we will need from Abriel to counteract Lisa's accusations, and he cautions me repeatedly to be careful.

A few days later, he drives me to my old hometown.

It looks the same, but still so different. New businesses, different landscaping. I want to drive by my parents' house, but I know better. We head straight to the Dine 'n' Shine, the rental hov-car we picked up this morning fitting in well in the parking lot. We wait in silence, too anxious to speak, until we see Abriel enter the establishment.

"Do you want me to come in with you?" Cash offers.

I shake my head, leaning over to kiss him. I need to do this on my own.

The Dine 'n' Shine is exactly how I remember it, from the skeevy customers, to the barely functional robo-clerks, to the invasive smell of greasy food being cooked in the back. At this time of day, just like when I was a student, most of the clientele are visiting the back of the restaurant, and they do so with lowered eyes. Few places are more anonymous than a whorehouse.

I slide into a seat across from Abriel. "Thank you for meeting me," I say quietly. "Does anyone else know you're here?"

He looks at me in confusion. "No. Sascha, what's wrong? Are you in danger? Are those bruises on your face? I got this weird message, and I knew it had to be from you. I thought that rich guy said you could talk to me? Is he hurting you?"

I shake my head. His concern is touching, if misplaced. "We need to talk about Lisa," I announce, and I tell him in hushed tones what she's been doing, what she's threatening me and Cash with.

"My master wants her silenced, and he's willing to blackmail you to do it."

The look on my brother's face kills me. "The Assessment thing?" he asks, going pale.

I nod. "I told him about it. I trusted him."

"And this is how he repays you?" Abriel says, still looking hurt.

"He cares about me, Abriel," I remind him. "He wants me safe. He'd do anything for me, even if it means destroying your family."

"Why are you telling me this?" he asks, after a moment. "Did you just ask me here to warn me? To see how much you could hurt me?"

"Abriel, I've tried to keep you safe our entire life!" I remind him. "I'm still trying to do it. I convinced Cash to let me talk to you. I need you to vouch for me, sign a statement contradicting Lisa, agree to testify for us if you're asked. She may be your wife, but you were the one who actually owned me. Say it was a domestic dispute, that you got rid of me because she didn't like me, that she's angry at our relationship. Help me make this go away, and I can make sure that the stuff about the Assessment doesn't come out."

Abriel shakes his head. "She'll be furious at me."

I sigh. "If this comes out, do you think she'll still want you? Do you think she'll want to stay married to someone who's a public example of fraud? And what about Bella? She'll grow up without her daddy, or worse, she'll grow up knowing that she never should have existed. You'll likely be put in prison — do you know the statistics for children who grow up with a parent in prison? How much more likely they are to be Demoted?"

Abriel stares at me like I'm a stranger. "How dare you."

I flinch. "I'm not trying to threaten you," I explain. "But my master is. I don't want that for you, or Bella. Help me, help yourself. It's for the best, Abriel."

He considers it for a moment. "I don't have much of a choice, do I?"

I just wait. It's true. "Lisa was the one who pushed this issue," I remind him. "I just want to minimize the damage. I can't sacrifice myself for you again, Abriel; I can't go any lower. If the authorities want to make a case out of this, you're the one with something to lose."

"What do I tell Lisa?" he asks, looking at me desperately.

"That you want to put the whole mess with me behind you and focus on her and Bella," I tell him. "That you're sick of hunting for problems when you should be getting your little girl better prepared. That you regret ever looking for me, or buying me, or seeing me again, and she was right, and it was a waste of time. That's what she wants, Abriel. She wants me out of her life. Give it to her, and if that doesn't work, tell her the truth. She wouldn't expose you, it's too risky for her. For Bella."

Abriel just gapes at me. He's never been capable of cruelty, or the sort of callous planning that Cash and I engage in. But he was right when he said that he had been following me his whole life, and it's easy for him to do it, now.

I slide over a paper with a statement I've drawn up, written from his perspective, counteracting Lisa's complaints. He reads it without a word, then goes back to the top and reads it again.

"It sounds like I wrote this," he mutters.

"I used to know you pretty well," I remind him, trying not to choke up at the memory.

"I won't ever see you again, will I?" he asks, his voice raw.

We both know it's true. Just like we both knew that he would be Demoted one day after failing the Assessment. I changed that; I doubt I can fix this. "Maybe someday," I lie to him, just like I did back then.

We sit in silence a while longer.

"Will this make up for it?" he asks. "For getting you Demoted, for giving your life up for me, for letting Lisa treat you the way I did, for all that? Will this fix things?"

I don't tell him that he never needed to fix anything. "Yes," I say, instead. "This would be the best favor you could ever do for me."

He nods. "I love you, Sascha," he says, the words coming out anguished. "I never meant for any of this to happen."

"I didn't either." I wait for him to sign the statement. I dread it, knowing it will be the last time I see or hear from him, but I know it needs to be done.

Slowly, he reads it over again, and then he signs it. We sit there a moment longer.

"I guess this is goodbye."

I nod.

"I'll see what I can tell Lisa," he muses. "I guess she's always known something wasn't quite right. And if anyone coms me or anything, I'll vouch for you."

"Thank you," I say quietly. I can't say anything else.

"Bye, Cha-Cha," he says as he stands. He squeezes my shoulder for just a moment, and then he's gone.

I sit at the dingy table for a moment after he leaves, willing my body to work again. Finally, I force myself to stand and head out to the car, the chirps of the robo-clerks sounding far too happy as I leave. I drop into the passenger seat, hand the statement to Cash and start to sob.

Chapter 22

Meant It

Sascha seems more shaken by blackmailing his brother than he did by being tortured by Oliver. It's alarming, because he was extremely shaken by the torture.

He doesn't speak a word for days. He sleeps in my bed, but he shrugs off my touch. I don't press the issue, because I can't blame him for resenting me. I held his brother's life to the fire; no matter how well-intentioned I was toward Sascha, I know I hurt him.

While he's ignoring me, I'm stuck dealing with the rest of the threats. My mother leaves me alone, surprisingly, but word spreads through the industry that she's beginning to take a more active role in enforcement and quality control. For everyone else, this is just a new move in her business; for me and Sascha, this is a threat. A threat we can't even move on. She makes public statements about the importance of helping the national effort to maintain a quality pool of Demoted people, and the equal importance of every slave owner to take care not to disrupt the system. She even proposes "booster sessions," similar to vaccinations, that will ensure that the Demoted remain subjugated and compliant. Her plans are a long way from being developed, much less implemented, but she's still a threat.

Oliver is holding up his end of our bargain quite nicely, facilitating the hiding of our data. I almost think that he's too happy to go along, but either he was that enamored with Sascha, or he really does want to see my mother fail. Either one is equally likely.

I find Sascha in the bathroom, meticulously caring for the tiny scabs that have startled to appear from his time with Oliver. At the rate he's going, he'll be healed before our project is ready.

I come up behind him, placing my hands on his waist and pulling him close. "I'm sorry that I threatened to blackmail your brother without consulting you first."

He glances at me in the mirror, then back down to the cream he's applying. "It's your right," he replies.

I sigh. He can cry on my shoulder when he cuts ties with Abriel, but he can't so much as talk to me. "Yes, but I still shouldn't have done it," I insist. "And not because I give a shit about him, or rights, or any of that. I care about you, Sascha. I shouldn't have risked hurting you like that."

Finally, he turns to look at me. "Are you going to apologize for threatening to lock me in my room, too?"

I sigh. "We were at risk. I thought I was doing the right thing for both of us."

"You didn't consult me before your mother made you beat me," he reminds me. "Besides, we're at risk every day."

It's true, but his blunt dismissal isn't very kind. He's trying to bait me, but I won't fall for it. "Thank you for covering for me," I tell him. "The lie, about the re-education centers, the whipping, the plan with Abriel…. Sascha, you're brilliant. I couldn't have done any of this without you."

He shrugs. "I got lucky."

I don't want to argue with me, but I do want to do something. I grab him, turn him the rest of the way around, forcing him to face me. I kiss him, deep, demanding his mouth as I crush our lips together. It's so nice to feel his tongue against mine that I forget for a moment that we were ever in danger. He's stiff at first, like he has been when we lie together in bed at night, but in just moments, he relaxes against me, holding onto my arms for support as the rest of his body almost collapses.

"No. Not lucky. You were brilliant," I insist, once I finally let us separate. "Every idea you had, it was genius."

He shakes his head. "I just did what I had to do."

I smile at him, amazed at how smart he can be, and yet, so humble. "Do you know how many times I've beat her at her game? Never. She taught me everything I know about manipulation, but she's always been better, smarter, faster on her feet. I've never won against her before."

"Did we beat her?" Sascha asks, guarded.

"For now," I tell him. "She's never been much of one to draw things out. She likes immediate consequences, and she likes to prove her point before anyone has the chance to shoot her down. She hasn't moved on the thing with Lisa, she hasn't followed up on this investigation... I'm sure it's going to be okay."

"And Torenze is still helping us?" Sascha confirms.

"Yes," I tell him, smiling. "But that's not what matters. I could never have done any of this without you."

Sascha considers it, grinning at me for a moment. "Maybe you just needed a better partner," he says, teasing.

"I found one," I reply quietly. I can't seem to take my hands off of him. I'm afraid he'll disappear.

"Should we celebrate our victory?" Sascha suggests, putting his arms around his neck and looking into my eyes. "I've been so angry, at you, at everything. But I miss feeling you touch me. After Torenze... we never really had a chance to come back together. I want to feel you inside of me."

He leans up as he says the last words, trailing his teeth over my neck, nibbling gently. I take a sharp breath, amazed by what he can do to me with just a little touch, and I feel myself growing hard. We can finally relax together.

"Are you sure you're ready?" I ask, touching him gently. "I don't want to hurt you."

"I've been ready," Sascha insists.

It's not that we've been celibate. We haven't been, but it's been different than it used to before everything happened. I don't want to be rough with him, to risk hurting him, and he's so often not in the mood. He pouts, he looks away, and when I try to do more than kiss him gently or give him a blowjob, he turns pale and shaky. I can't tell if it's because of what Oliver did to him, or what I threatened to do to Abriel.

"I'll be careful," I promise. I don't just mean in bed, I mean with all of him. The threat of losing him to my mother for evaluation was terrifying, but the threat of losing him to my own greed is worse.

"I don't want you to treat me like I'm broken," he insists. "I'm still a little bruised, but I'll be fine. I've been through worse. I need you."

He leads me to the bedroom as he speaks, pulling me down onto the bed with him. "You can't treat me like I'm damaged unless you really believe I am. And if I'm so damaged, how could I stand up to your mother? I want to help you, and I want to feel you fucking me. You can trust me."

I contemplate it, the idea of trusting him. I value him, I trust his opinion, but I don't trust him to care for himself. But he had been taking care of himself for so long before I came around. He is more than capable. I strip my shirt off, and my pants as well, and I sit next to Sascha on the bed, my hand coming behind his neck to pull him into a possessive kiss. I half expect him to pull away, but he doesn't. He leans in closer, letting me touch and kiss him until he's shuddering and melting into my touch. I have missed him so much.

"Not damaged," I admit, breaking away and trailing a line of kisses and soft bites down his neck. "You're perfect. Stronger than I ever thought possible."

Sascha leans into my touch and my words. "Then fuck me," he whispers, and somehow it doesn't seem vulgar, or base, it just seems honest. "I want to be yours again."

I lift him and place him against the pillows, moving him easily and taking his cock into my hand like I own it. I suppose I do.

"You never stopped being mine," I tell him, leaving no room for argument as my hands work his cock and his ass. "I just didn't want to be responsible for hurting you anymore."

"I chose to go along with the plan with Torenze," he mumbles, in between gasps as I add lube and my tongue to the mix, working his body carefully. "I suggested it, if you recall, and I took the blame when your mother was here. I never blamed you. I need you to stop blaming yourself, because it's taking time away from us, and I need you with me. I need you to consult me on things. This project isn't just yours, it's mine, too, and I get to do things to make it better. If that means letting Torenze beat me, fine. If it means outsmarting your mother, I'm up for it. If it means talking to my brother.... I just need you to work with me."

"It will never happen again," I decide, stretching him seductively and letting the words vibrate off his cock. "None of those things. I'll keep you safe."

"We both know that might not be true," Sascha insists, clutching at the covers and attempting to speak rationally, despite the way I'm touching him. "And I don't care. Let me choose. Support me. And for the love of god, keep fucking me."

I smile, and I do just that. I prepare him forever, getting him ready, stretching his ass, and working even more lube into him. I know it shouldn't hurt anymore, but I still want to be careful with him. He's mine, and I want to make him feel good again. I missed touching him, and if the way he thrusts himself against me is any sign, he misses being touched. I tease him, working his body to relax and open for me, flicking my tongue out and over his cock, biting gently at the insides of his legs. Everything is calm for once, and I want to take my time with him.

Sascha tries to keep speaking, but he quickly loses the ability. I keep touching him, feeling him yield to me. For once, there are no immediate threats hanging over either of our heads, and I let myself relax, feeling myself grow hard and excited as I do. I slide up, kissing Sascha deeply, pressing against his body with mine. After I've taken all I can handle, I slide him down the pillows, arranging him on the mattress exactly where I want him. He looks up at me with excitement and a little fear, and I love that I inspire that in him. He leans up to kiss me and I push him back down, holding him there. I like his input, but I have my own ideas of what I want to do with him tonight. When he acquiesces, lying still for me, I climb on top of him, framing his body with my own, lining my cock up, ready to take him. I pause, admiring him below me.

He shudders, just slightly, and he smiles up at me. I keep pinning him there, even as he tries to move. He wiggles his ass against my cock a tiny bit until I push a little harder, forcing him to stay still.

"You're mine," I remind him, pressing him hard into the mattress with my hands and my hips.

Sascha nods, and I can feel his cock growing harder between us. "Prove it," he challenges me, although his tone is barely different from begging.

I don't deny him. I prove just how much he is mine, and I do so slowly, holding him down when he even tries to move. He tries to take me into him faster, meeting my thrusts, but I won't have it. I force him to wait, to feel me sliding in and out of him slowly, sensually. I feel his arms twitch; he's trying to grab me and pull me closer, but I trap him and keep him pinned to the bed. I make my way inside of him as slowly as I can tolerate, and when I finish, I continue to hold him in place. I smile at him feeling like I've won the challenge.

"Please?" Sascha caves, begging.

He tightens and loosens his muscles around me, trying to pull me in deeper or make me move, but it is to no avail. I am hard inside of him, and I can feel him, desperate for me. I want to move, to plunge into him, to slide out, and to do it again. But the waiting is even more divine.

"Come on, Cash, it's been too long! Just fuck me?"

It's nearly impossible to turn him down, but I continue to tease him. I fuck him, slowly at first, so slowly that he doesn't even seem to notice it. I build up speed gradually, stroking his cock and his face as I do, and I feel something slipping back into place between us. He is mine, not because I own him, or because I demand him, but because he's given himself to me. He trusts me, just as much as I trust him, if not more. He begs me to fuck him, and I comply with his requests. Over and over, I slide into him, until he's screaming and moaning, begging me to go faster. I follow his lead, and I feel like I am as much at his command as he is at mine.

As resolute as I was about fucking him slowly, once I build up speed, I maintain it. I drive into him, hard and fast, and I smile as Sascha struggles to keep up. It's unnecessary. Regardless of what he does, whether he tenses or relaxes, whether he struggles to meet me with his hips or not, I keep fucking him at the same pace, the same desperate need driving me into him again and again.

I change position, bracing my hand just inches from his face to hold myself up. He jumps in fear and excitement, but before I have a chance to reconsider, I realize how much he likes it. I drive my cock into him, changing angles, and I hear him moan as I hit the perfect spot. I do it again and again, stroking his cock as he gasps for air.

I lean forward to kiss him, tasting his lips, and after a few moments, I order him to come. I pump his cock with one hand while the other is stretched out next to his head where I slammed it down just moments before. I give the order and I drag my teeth across his lower lip, catching it and biting down while he smiles up at me. He comes just seconds before I do, the timing perfect enough to draw delicious sounds from Sascha's mouth. He reaches up to clutch at my back with his hands, only increasing my excitement. I finish and ease out of him carefully, coming to lie next to him.

"Perfect," I whispers, pulling him close. Sascha nods his agreement and curls into my arms.

We lie there in silence, some sort of balance restored. It doesn't matter what Torenze did, or any of the others. It doesn't matter what sorts of threats face us, or what my mother and Lisa are trying to do to destroy our project. We can beat them all, and we can deal with anyone else that gets in our way. I've always yearned for an equal, and I've found one in Sascha. For the first time in years, I feel like nothing can get in our way.

I lie quietly with Sascha in my arms, considering our perfect fit with one another, our strategic partnership. Somehow, this little brothel whore wormed his way into my home, and my heart. I would do anything to make sure he is safe, but he would do anything to make sure our project moves forward. It's a tough line, and I just hope we don't have to pick and choose between the two again.

Sascha looks up at me, a nervous expression on his face.

"Cash... the other night," he fumbles, looking scared and embarrassed. "When you brought me back from Torenze's, and I kept waking up with nightmares. Did you say, I mean... did you really mean...."

I know what I said, and so does he, but neither one of us is strong enough to repeat it right now. I tell myself that I'm being chivalrous by not making him say it, not that I'm being a coward by avoiding the words.

"Yes," I whisper, pulling him close. "And I meant it."

Chapter 23
Fade to Black

The next few weeks are amazing. Cash works hard to keep me updated on everything that's happening, even things that scare me, like when he tells me that Torenze was "highly pleased" by our night together, and that he would "just love" to see me again.

It turns my stomach, but I would do it if I had to. Cash assures me that I never will, and I try to believe him. Even better, when I tell him that I'll damn well do it if I want, Cash just nods and agrees with me. Clearly, he doesn't like the idea any more than I do, but he's willing to let me take my own risks. It fills me with a strange happiness that I've never felt before.

We hear word that the statement Abriel signed was submitted, and we don't hear back from Kristine or Lisa. Having them out of our lives is a huge relief, and it allows us to concentrate on what's important: the research, and each other.

The research is amazing. Without the roadblocks of paranoia and a lack of funds, we move through it quickly. We see the preliminary data, and I am thrilled and excited to look it over, to make sense of it, to confirm the hypotheses that my master had come so close to confirming years ago. He explains why we need an outside person, one who isn't Demoted, to do the data analysis, and I fully agree. Still, I want to review it for my own satisfaction and enjoyment. The results aren't surprising; it's exactly what Cash predicted, what he almost discovered last time, except this time, his research is flawless, perfect, incriminating. As each bruise fades from my skin, I keep thinking that it's Kristine Miller's hold on the slave industry fading away, only to be replaced by something new.

Cash sets me to arranging for the release of the data, explaining how we are going to target every media outlet in the country, and a few international ones as well.

"The second we stop worrying about being discovered, our biggest threat is being silenced," he warns. "So we need to make sure our message gets out everywhere."

I take his word seriously, accumulating a massive database of contact information and places to submit to, and I tailor each message carefully to ensure it won't be overlooked. It's all I work on for weeks, while my master puts in his time at his day job, arranges for the research to be published and verified, and meets regularly with Torenze. As more data becomes available, I add it to the messages, one by one, making sure that they will be ready to go when the time comes.

Aside from that, things are calm. Cash and I spend a lot of time together, debating, sharing stories, and having amazing sex. He treats me better than a slave, better than most would treat a boyfriend, really. Even when he takes me out in public with him, to peek in on the lives of others, he asks me first, makes sure I want to go.

Afterward, he rewards me with some of the most amazing sex I've ever had.

He comes home from work one day with a big box of takeout food and a bouquet of flowers. I smile at him, because it's just too romantic to be his style.

He comes in the door, sets the food and flowers down on the table, and pulls me close for a kiss, ignoring the smile on my face until he's thoroughly ravished my mouth.

"The secretary at work said it was the nice thing to do to celebrate," he mutters, blushing a little.

"And what are we celebrating?" I ask, curious. He has yet to inform me of anything celebration-worthy.

He grins. "I told her that I was celebrating my partner's promotion," he admits. "I couldn't very well tell her that our research project has come to a conclusion, and should be ready to be released in a few weeks."

"Really?" I ask, excited. I can't believe it. It happened so fast.

Cash nods. "The final data was collected today and sent over to our data analyst. He said it will be a couple of weeks before it's ready, but if it matches what we've gathered so far, we're set to go."

"I should go update it!" I announce, thrilled at the prospect.

"You'll do no such thing," Cash warns, trying to give me a stern look and failing miserably. "I brought dinner, and flowers, and wine, and I plan to have a lovely dinner."

"And then I can update it?" I ask, hopeful, and trying to antagonize my master a bit.

He gives me a light slap on the ass, just enough to make me long for more. "And then I'm going to take you to bed and fuck you until you don't even want to think about updating your damn database."

I smile, leaning in to kiss him again, pleased when he indulges me. When we finally separate, I raise an eyebrow at him hopefully. "Can we at least talk about the results over dinner?" I suggest.

"Of course," he agrees.

He's just as excited to talk about his plans as I am. We take turns gushing about the turn of events, and the possibilities of what will happen once it's released, and how we plan to reinvent the re-education centers. I feel a little strange, discussing how to turn the next generation of humans into slaves, but I know it could have been better. My life didn't have to be as terrible as it was during the first few years, and if the process hadn't been so horrible, maybe I wouldn't have taken my brother's place in the Demoted system at all. The system can't be just thrown away, it needs to be made better, first, and I'm proud to be a part of it.

We finish dinner and a bottle of wine, and Cash comes to me, holding out a hand to escort me to bed. It's silly, but I appreciate it. I never thought that we would get this far.

He leads me to bed and lies beside me, placing light, tender kisses across my body. I ache for him, and I want to feel him inside of me, but he reminds me that we don't have to rush. It's still early, not even dark, yet, and if he wants to take his time with me, I'm more than happy to let him.

He's just started to slide his hands under my clothes to feel my skin when we hear a knock at the door.

"Let's just pretend we aren't home," I suggest, pulling him down for another kiss. I can feel him getting tense, and I reluctantly let him get up.

As I do, the alarm on his wristband goes off, the one that went off last time when his mother intruded on us. I clutch at his arms, my eyes going wide.

"Cash, what is it?" I whisper, irrationally afraid that someone will hear me.

He glances at the message, but doesn't reply.

He gets up out of bed abruptly, making his way to the front door. "Stay here," he orders, slamming the bedroom door behind him.

I've never been very good at following orders, so the second I hear his footsteps retreating away from the door, I follow him.

His body, so relaxed just moments ago, gives away how nervous his is, even though I can't see who's at the door from where I'm hiding. I can hear, though, and I hear a very official voice announcing that the state has a warrant for the seizure and examination of the slave residing at the address… which is me.

I feel myself growing dizzy, and I try not to panic. They discuss the "temporary" evaluation, the complaint lodged well over a month ago, the "concern" of the founder of the Miller System. Kristine Miller is nowhere to be seen; she's letting someone else do her dirty work. Cash tries to fight it, tries to argue that there's no case, that there was a counter claim submitted, that he'll have everyone arrested and fired and worse. They respond by reminding him that interfering with a state evaluation of a Demoted case is a crime, maybe even a federal crime.

My master has always seemed so powerful, it frightens me to see this power stripped from him.

I do the only thing that makes sense. I find the database, I run a few scripts, and I initiate it to send the preliminary research to everywhere it can possibly go. In my experience, when I am taken from a place, I don't usually return, and I am determined to complete this job before I am taken away. I finish before the officers push my master away from the door, and I'm standing in the middle of the hallway when they come for me. My master's face is stricken, he is more scared than he ever looked before.

"Sascha… you have to go with them," he says, his tone flat. "You have to do what they say."

"I know," I admit. I go to him and feel his arms around me one more time. I know he'll try to come for me, I just don't know if there will be anything left of me to come for.

The officers aren't particularly gentle, but they aren't cruel, either. They load me into the back of a hov-van after cuffing my hands together, and I don't even have a window to look out of. I wonder if they're really taking me to an evaluation center, or if they're taking me somewhere worse. I try not to cry, because I don't want them to see weakness.

When the doors open, I'm not surprised to see my master's mother standing there, proud as can be. She drags me out by my hands, but she doesn't hurt me. I don't speak, and neither does she, but from what I can see, we really are in an official building. It looks like the re-education centers, but also looks suspiciously like an old licensing office for hov-cars. Maybe this is what they do with them when they become outdated.

She drags me into a small, bare room, shoves me inside, and locks the door when she leaves. It's rather anticlimactic, but I can't do anything about it. I sit with my hands bound and waiting, worrying about my master.

It feels like hours before she returns, but there is no way of marking time in the small, dark room. Still, it's been long enough that my tongue has loosened; the fact that I wasn't immediately tortured gave me courage.

She walks in the door and glares at me, and I roll my eyes. "So, this is evaluation?" I ask.

She walks over, a tablet in her hands, and smacks me in the head with it. "Cut your attitude or you'll lose points for real," she snaps, and immediately orders me to follow a variety of orders.

The evaluation is something like what we did at the re-education centers, practicing poses, positions, stock phrases. Kristine is about as interested in it as I am, which makes me wonder why she insisted on it, anyway. More than anything, she seems to be going through the motions, and every once in a while, she'll pause, flicking over to something else on her tablet. I don't ask, I just keep performing when she asks me to. Finally, she finishes, and she takes me to another room and seats me at a table. I assume she's going to interrogate me, and

I'm right.

"What do you know about the re-education centers?" she demands.

"They teach high school students how to be slaves, ma'am," I reply, glaring up at her. "The Miller System, which you developed, is the most popular training method, but may or may not be the most effective."

She slaps me, but it was worth it to see the look on her face.

"Don't lie to me," she hisses. "What else do you know?"

"I know a slave can't legally be compelled to testify against its master," I supply.

"Your master," she hisses. "Do you know what he's doing right now?"

I hope he's safe. I hope she hasn't mobilized forces against him as well.

"Take a look," she orders, shoving her tablet at me. I see a video feed of my master at home, the time stamp from a few hours ago, and I see him later visiting Torenze, and I see him now, walking into a courthouse, a furious look on his face.

"He's getting me out," I realize, relieved. I really can count on him to save me.

"He's trying," Kristine corrects, smiling. She pokes at the tablet a few times, and reveals a team of armed officers at the house, rifling through everything in there. In addition to the officers, there are uniformed agents with the words "Miller System," emblazoned on their backs. Everyone is taking things, touching things, destroying things.

"You can't do this!" I protest. "My brother, he submitted the statement, he fixed things, he —"

"Shut up," Kristine orders. "Yes, your dear brother did make it difficult. He submitted his statement, and his wife even retracted hers. I must say, your family has quite the charisma."

"Then, why...."

"Oh, the warrant?" she laughs. "Seems a little birdie placed a recording device in the dining room while your master was whipping you. Nobody knows who might have done such a thing, but the records came to my office, and I just had to let the district judge know that someone was planning to destroy me, and maybe the whole re-education center! It would have been a lot faster, but it seems my son has forgotten his manners, and rarely does anything more than chew with his mouth open and talk about doing lewd things to you in the dining room."

I sit silently, thinking of the conversation we had last night. All our secrets, all our plans... everything was exposed.

"Where do you think you'll end up, Sascha?" Kristine asks, her smile widening. "Do you think anyone will buy the slave of a convicted felon?"

"He's not a felon!" I snap, but even as I watch in horror, the video feed shows him being accosted by more officers, handcuffed, dragged into a police hov-car. "His research... it will show what he's doing! It will show all of it; you'll be the felon for trying to cover it up!"

She comes over, grabs a small handful of hair, and twists it until I scream. "Why do you think my company is involved?" she asks. "We'll make sure that the public only sees what they need to see to prove Cashiel is a corrupt man who deserves no less than a few life sentences in prison. Oliver Torenze will take my offer and wash his hands of the whole thing in order to rejoin my company, and you... well, you'll go someplace nobody will ever find you. I've been trying to find a way to get Cashiel out of his house and away from his security system long enough to raid it for months, but I never realized just how attached he was to you until last time I was there. Can you believe it? Everything he's done, destroyed, just because he fell for a stupid little whore."

I think back to weeks ago, when Cash first told me about the project.

Once the data is out, it can't be erased. Not from public record, not from people's minds. They stopped me before that happened last time; this time, it can't happen again. You're a part of that.

I smile up at her. "You're too late," I inform her, starting to laugh. This whole, grand plan, and she forgot the simple input of a slave.

"What are you talking about?" she demands. "I arrived just in time! You saw the video feed. Everything is being destroyed. With any luck, that will include you."

"Bring up a tabloid," I suggest. "Or a major news venue. From here, international... it will start with the tabloids, but it will spread.

They all got the same information."

She glares at me, but she does as I suggest. I see her face growing more and more red as she searches, finding the preliminary report all over the internet. It's spreading like fire, more and more people are boosting the signal to other sites, questioning the validity, wondering how this massive information bomb had been sent, and why. The news site she pulled up has two images, one, a compilation of the data, the other, an image of my master being placed in the police hovcar and driven away.

"Everyone will see," I remind her, just as the doors to the evaluation room burst open.

"Ms. Miller, we're going to have to ask that you hand the slave over to state custody," they inform her. "His master's being sent to prison, and he's scheduled to go to the slave Detention Center immediately, for his safety and ours. They're predicting riots."

I see Kristine Miller draw back her hand, and I feel a sharp pain in my head before everything fades to black. The last thought I have is how it's up to me to save Cashiel — again.

If you enjoyed this story, you can sign up for a free membership at
ForbiddenFiction and discuss it with other readers
and the author at the *Demoted 2: Sedition* story page
at http://forbiddenfiction.com/story/AC2-1.000220.

We do our best to proof all our work, but if you spot a text error we missed,
please let us know via our website
Contact Form at http://forbiddenfiction.com/contact.

Author's Notes

The earliest form of *Demoted* was just one book... one very, very long book, without much of a plot. Thankfully, with the help of FFP editor James L. Wolf, it evolved into two books, both with plots! Behold the amazement! Tearing the original book apart and rebuilding it into two books was a challenge, but I love the way they both turned out. The boys get a chance to love each other even more, and the villains get a chance to dig their claws in.

Speaking of villains, probably my favorite addition to *Demoted* is Cash's mother. While she has always been a part of the story, her particular evilness really got developed in the editing stage of *Sedition*. I just don't think there are enough truly evil mothers in fiction. There are plenty of evil stepmothers, evil fathers, and even evil children, but I think mother really knows evil best! I was even fortunate enough to have a real-life inspiration source while I was editing, although that source shall never be revealed.

You may have noticed that I left you with a little cliffhanger. Okay, maybe not so little! Never fear, you'll have a chance to find out what happens with Cash and Sascha in the third and final book in the series. *Succession* wraps up the trilogy, and all your beloved (and hated) characters are back in action — as well as a few new friends. *Succession* is in the works right now, and I can guarantee that it is just as sexy and exciting as the first two, if not more.

— Alicia Cameron

About the Author

Alicia Cameron has been making up stories since before she can remember. After discovering erotica during a high school banned books project, she never really turned back. She lives in Denver, Colorado with two tiny dogs and a rabbit who conspire regularly to distract her from doing anything productive. By day she works in the mental health field and is passionate about youth rights and welfare. In her spare time, she enjoys traveling, glitter, and punk rock concerts.

ForbiddenFiction works by Alicia Cameron

Inherent Gifts Series
Inherent Gifts

Inherent Risk

Inherent Cost

Short Stories
Cuts so Deep

Dangerous Steps

In Other Hands

Jingle Boy

Twisted Gifts

Party Favors

Hot Rain

Lessons Learned

Demoted Series
Subjection

Sedition

Succession

DEMOTED

The superior lead. The inferior are DEMOTED.

Cashiel and Sascha aren't revolutionaries. Cashiel just wants to use his privilege to make the world a better place. Sacha just wants to save his brother from being Demoted. Unfortunately, they're both trapped within the system.

In the past, lesser people rose above their natural station, and greater persons found themselves stifled under the incompetent leadership of their inferiors. Today, the Miller System conditions the Demoted to serve; persons otherwise lost are given purpose, and placed under the ownership and guidance of responsible citizens.

Cashiel's mother invented the Miller System, and trying to prove that the Demoted should be treated humanely sets him against his mother and all her political power. Sascha succeeded in saving his brother from the system, but only by taking his place and being made into a brothel slave.

It isn't exactly love at first sight when Cashiel buys Sascha. If they can work together, though, they might be able to bring down a system of institutionalized abuse, and find some happiness for themselves.

About the Publisher

 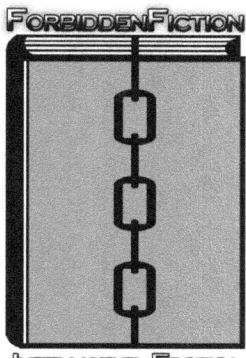

ForbiddenFiction.com is a publisher devoted to writing that breaks the boundaries of original erotic fiction. Our stories combine intense sexuality with quality writing. Stories at Forbidden Fiction.com not only arouse readers through sensations, but also engage them emotionally and mentally through storytelling as well-crafted as the sex is hot.

ForbiddenFiction.com is also designed to be a social reading environment. You'll have fun even if just reading the latest post each day, yet you will have the chance for so much more. Readers and authors can be part of ongoing discussions of specific works and individual authors as well as more general topics.

Sign up for a FREE Membership today at ForbiddenFiction.com.